# Whimsical Wanderings

# Whimsical Wanderings

Lighthearted stories and observations from a country boy

Kent Kloepping

*Whimsical Wanderings: Lighthearted stories and observations from a country boy*

Published by Wheatmark®
1760 East River Road, Suite 145
Tucson, Arizona 85718 U.S.A.
www.wheatmark.com

ISBN: 978-1-60494-796-0
LCCN: 2012939831

*For my father and the vanishing*
*breed of storytellers who practiced and*
*preserved the rural oral anecdotal*
*traditions*

# Contents

# *Foreword*

MY MOTHER WAS A prolific letter writer. She carried on regular correspondence with former high-school classmates, relatives, family friends, and likely others I didn't know about. Her style of writing was very personal, as if she were sitting across a table from you, maybe over a cup of tea. The tone of her letters was uncomplicated, upbeat, and punctuated with queries, which of course elicited responses that she would be obliged to answer.

She wrote letters of condolence, appreciation, encouragement, and congratulations; but some of her best work spoke to daily mundane happenings such as canning produce from her garden, friends who stopped in to visit, or some local gossip or rumor. She often, in the middle of the dialogue, would throw in a bit of her religious or political philosophy, I think just to make sure the reader was paying attention. Mom loved words and language, and as a child and young adult, at her behest, I frequently consulted our dictionary to discover a new meaning.

My father, who relished humor and all manner of anecdotes, was himself a masterful teller of tales. I recall, particularly on cold, wintry evenings, Dad, a dairy farmer, then free of the heavy labors of spring and summer, making popcorn and entertaining us with not only stories of family history, but also humorous anecdotes, riddles, and conundrums to solve.

Mom must have written ten thousand letters in her lifetime, maybe more. Dad also appeared to have an endless reservoir of stories encompassing a broad range of subjects. Many of his tales, while couched in humor or seemingly innocuous tales of everyday living, were in fact lessons for life and carried subliminal or very apparent messages of right and wrong. He always seemed able to deliver a timely anecdote when the occasion demanded a dash of his rural, homespun wisdom. Several anecdotes that he related to me, some on more than one occasion, appear in this effort.

While I did take a few writing classes, my best instructors were my parents. I don't think I write as well as my mother did, and although I enjoy humor as much as my father, he was the superior storyteller.

In quiet moments, if I begin to reminisce about her writing and his stories, invariably I have to smile, for the joy and self-satisfaction I derive from my writing endeavors is a legacy from them.

As I am the sole author of what follows, with the exception of anecdotes that precede many of the short stories, initially I thought a listing of acknowledgments and thank-yous was not warranted. Then I reasoned that there probably isn't any endeavor in life, great or small, that represents a completely solitary effort. For that to be true, one would have to live in a vacuum.

Thus, briefly, a thank-you to my sister, Carol, who several years ago encouraged me to compile some of my poems and stories into book form. She also provided some helpful organizational ideas and corrected factual data related to stories of family. To my wife, Marlys, who allowed me the space to write and type uninterrupted on my own schedule, thanks, dear; I am a "techno-peasant," that is barely computer literate. My son, Matthew, rescued me on numerous occasions (more like innumerable) from a continuing series of faux pas using that infernal piece of technology. Most gratifying was his retrieval of an entire story, almost intact, from the bowels of the machine where I had painstakingly typed it, one finger stroke at a time, and then inadvertently deleted it. What a guy!

And it seems I also owe a large debt of gratitude to all the folks whose names appear in this work. Each one of them, in their unique humanness, struggles, and triumphs, has in some measure impacted and enriched my life. For that matter, I should also acknowledge Mother Nature for the gifts of all her critters. Wouldn't life be dull without them? It is because of our journey together, even if only for a moment, that I can offer what follows.

# I

*Illinois: Memories of Youth*

# Dusty Lane

Do you remember a place called Dusty Lane? The time of our
   childhood, honest and plain.
Family and friends with abundant love, a community of caring and
   goodness from above.

But images fade and memories dim, and the chance for
   remembering is a passing whim.
What then is it that we might recall, those days and things that were
   special to all?

The melodies of cowbells on a wet June morn, a lullaby of cattle,
   serene yet forlorn.
A call to toil at the break of day, knowledge of purpose for which
   many pray.

Innocent youth, the children of farms, the perfume of sweat on our
   father's arms.
A mother and father and a quality of life, a sense of order, free from
   strife.

The old swimming hole on a hot summer day, a neighborhood
   gathering for carefree play.
Kids and dogs and snakes for a scare, laughter and frogs and mud in
   your hair.

Spark and Rusty and old Butch too, and hiding those jars of root
   beer brew.
Ponies and bikes and sailing crafts, the pride of the neighborhood,
   those Rock Run rafts.

Green apple belly aches and "road apple" fights, not for the sissies
   from the city lights.
Two longs, two shorts, the Kloepping family telephone code, haze
   in the morning from a choking dusty road.

Bright winter nights and the crunch of snow, popcorn and fudge
   and cheeks with a glow.
Bob and his horses, sleigh rides for all, gee Dad, a ten foot tree may
   be too tall!

Morels and watercress, fruits of spring, the first signs of plenty warm
   rains bring.
Dig out those cane poles and head for the creek, chubs and suckers
   fat and sleek.

Saturday night at the old Chalet, then Sunday, the Sabbath, a
   special day.
Church in the morning, Grandma's about noon, a melody of life in
   harmony and tune.

A home for growing, safe and secure, and for that gift we thank you
   on your sixtieth year.
They taught higher values than fortune or fame, to praise the Father
   and honor one's name.

A cry is for birth, tears for death, life is a whisper, a single breath.
   What then was our time at
Dusty Lane? Fleeting moments, idyllic times, never again can we
   reclaim.

The Lord in his goodness has blessed mankind, humility in life, His path we must find.

The yoke of our burdens will know true release, in submission to God we shall have lasting peace.

*The sins of the Midwest: flatness, emptiness, a necessary acceptance of the familiar. Where is the romance in being buried alive? In growing old?*[1]

# Mattie

HER GIVEN NAME WAS Mary Martha Eulah Pyle. I never knew the origin of the somewhat unusual name Eulah, but then again she had a brother named Cortez, and two other brothers carried the middle names Cavanaugh and Omega. Maybe the most nontraditional name I found related to her was Onicypherous. He was an ancestor of Mary Martha, and in the family genealogy his mother was listed simply as "a Cherokee Indian." If I had been a biblical scholar, I might have known that the name Onicypherous (sic) came from the book of Timothy. He was a friend of the apostle Paul, and a translation of the name is "bringing profit." I was aware from early childhood that, according to family lore, we supposedly had Cherokee blood in our veins—though not enough to get free land, as one ancestor attempted.

Mary Martha was born on April 4, 1894, in Missouri. She came to Wisconsin at the age of fifteen or sixteen and married Luther Roden-bough at age eighteen in 1912. Luther was the son of a Pennsylvania Dutchman who had migrated to Green County, Wisconsin, around 1878. Her birthplace and subsequent young life was in the Ozark hill country of Missouri that the locals called "mountains." When I was maybe ten or twelve years old, I became aware of the slang term "hillbilly." Ah, it occurred to me, that is a descriptor that would apply to Mary Martha's roots. Also I had learned that her husband,

Luther, as well as her more intimate friends, called her Mattie. One day, armed with my newly acquired understanding of the term "hillbilly," I casually, and somewhat proudly, informed Mary Martha that I realized that she and her family were in fact hillbillies. She took great exception to my precociousness and made it abundantly clear that the slur did not apply to her family. I recall that her stern and unforgettable rebuke included a concomitant lecture on the topic of "white trash," who was, and who wasn't. That encounter had such a profound impact on me that never again did I make reference to the matter of hillbillies to Mary Martha Eulah (Pyle) Rodenbough, whom I fondly remember as my grandmother, Mattie Rodenbough.

She passed away in 1988 at age ninety-four, and after her death I began to think more about her as an individual—the kind of person she was—and not simply as my grandma. As I reflected back on my time with her and recalled the many experiences and anecdotes (both shared by her and by other family members), it began to dawn on me that I had known a very special person. This small woman, born to humble circumstances in Seybert, near the "populated place" of Cane Hill, in Cedar County, Missouri, was in many respects a very unique individual. On more than one occasion, my mother remarked that her mother (my grandmother) had been "born fifty years ahead of her time." Although Mom seemed reluctant to fully explain what she meant, I came to think she was reflecting on her mother's apparent frequent struggles living in a tradition-bound Midwestern environment where gender roles and expectations were clearly defined and firmly rooted in a male-dominated culture. It seems to me that the more narrow, often restrictive roles expected, even required of women in early twentieth-century America—deferential wife, good mother, homemaker, being a "lady," and submissive, especially in matters important to men—were at times suffocating and stifling for her. I

8

also believe my mother saw her mother as a progressive and modern woman, terms difficult to explain, but to me it meant Grandmother envisioned and accurately understood new and emerging roles for women long before almost everyone thought about such ideas.

As a child, visiting Grandmother and Grandfather Rodenbough was always a treat. Grandma was lively and witty; we described her as being a "bundle of energy," and invariably she seemed to have a unique project under way to entertain us. She was an astute observer of human behavior, and she had easily surmised that we grandchildren made and smoked corncob pipes, using a variety of tobacco-like fillings. She didn't approve, but her method of conveying her feelings was to introduce us to smoking wild grapevine. One sunny afternoon, probably a Sunday, at a family picnic along the Sugar River, she pointed out that the dried grapevines were a ready and almost endless supply of a pretty good alternative to cob pipes or illicit, store-bought cigarettes. As a poor child, she and her family had learned to live off the land. People in poverty didn't buy cigars and cigarettes; they found alternatives. We all cut four-to-six-inch "cigarettes" and lighted up. As I recall, it was the last time any of us kids ever tried smoking the vines again. One good puff on the smoldering vine was something akin to sucking on the business end of a mini blowtorch. She had dealt us all a rather creative lesson in the downside of smoking.

As I remember, she really didn't care much for gossip or small talk. A favorite story told to me concerned her experience in an agricultural home extension group of local ladies. Apparently having Indian blood had become somewhat fashionable during that particular time. After listening ad nauseam to the claims of a number of ladies, all attempting to one-up each other, Grandmother suddenly interjected, "Well, you know, I have a little Indian in me also. It's probably about the size of a squirrel!" She successfully extinguished the mundane discussion of real or imagined Indian lineage, while communicating to the shocked ladies that she was pregnant.

As I grew into adulthood, I learned that her family and others used the term "restless spirit" in describing her. My mother told me that Grandma would at times inexplicably and abruptly make decisions or engage in behaviors that really "upset the apple cart." She meant, I think, capricious acts that would disrupt the daily harmony and direction of the family and or friends. As a child and young woman growing up in what must have been significant poverty, the deprivations she may have undergone and experienced very likely left an indelible mark on her character and personality. I came to understand that, notwithstanding the circumstances of my Grandmother Rodenbough's younger years, the person who emerged from that environment was a truly remarkable lady. For folks who didn't know her well, I guess she appeared to be a typical Midwestern housewife of the pre- and post-WWII era. For us, her family, who knew her more intimately, she was anything but typical. She was extremely quick and efficient in approaching her daily responsibilities and very accomplished and creative in her leisure-time avocational pursuits.

She had a Guernsey cow that she milked daily, and she made wonderful butter in an old wooden churn. Her vegetable and flower gardens were perfectly maintained and weedless, and she produced an abundance of bounty, much of which she preserved for use during the winter months. Along with the usual variety of plants, she also had peach and cherry trees, a grape arbor, red raspberries, black raspberries, ground cherries, currants, and strawberries. I recall, before I had polio, walking carefully through the garden with her, and even at a young age realizing there was a creative symmetry and organization of the flowers, fruits, and vegetables. I couldn't put into words what I experienced in that place, but I felt and knew it was a special garden.

She was a hunter; she had a small, single-shot .22-caliber rifle, and if she decided to have rabbit or squirrel as a main course, she proceeded to shoot, clean the game, and prepare the meat. Traditionally folks in the rural Midwest engaged in what I thought was a ritual they called "spring housecleaning." Throughout the winter months, people mainly hunkered down against the cold and misery of the season, but with the snow gone, the sun again appearing daily, and new life awakening from the earth, the good God-fearing people began a frenzy of cleaning their homes from attic to basement. Grandmother also cleaned from top to bottom, but she went several steps beyond what was considered an acceptable standard, as she repaired, renovated, and painted, essentially redecorating portions of her home. Not only was she adept with hammer, saw, and nails, but another of her specialties was painting walls, ceilings, and floors. She had a technique for painting floors that she called "stippling." Using a brush or wadded-up old newspaper, she twisted the handle of the brush or the paper as she applied the paint, creating a swirled effect. She would initially apply a single color as a base coat and then use two or more different colors in applying the stippling. The effect was quite dramatic and pleasing; I never saw anyone else use the technique.

She was a wonderful seamstress. She made clothes for herself and her daughters, clothes for my sisters (including formal wear and women's suits), and my first suit. Her designs, particularly for women's clothes, were very fashionable beyond the simple conservative styles of her time. My mother belonged to an organization called Eastern Star, and yearly they had an event that required wearing formal attire. Mom didn't have shoes to match the colors of her gown, and she was reluctant to purchase shoes for a single occasion. Grandmother solved the problem for her. She took a pair of old shoes, mixed her art paints to match the gown, and baked the shoes in the oven! The result was a very nice, expensive-appearing addition to the ensemble.

Her inherent frugal nature, imagination, excellent eye-hand coordination, sense of proportion, and ability to see beyond the ordinary were linked to other creative endeavors. She fashioned elaborate jewelry from old, discarded copper wire. She built, to scale, doll furniture from scrap wood and old leather that included chairs and a sofa with soft, filled cushions. She rescued old burlap feed sacks, on which she painted intricate designs and used for table placemats. All of these finished products were of extremely high-quality workmanship, attractive, and in today's craft mania would command high prices. She was, of course, a good cook, although I believe it was not her favorite pastime; while the quality of what she prepared was always high, it was the speed with which she could prepare a meal, from start to table-ready, that was truly amazing. She literally could get a full meal of potatoes, vegetables, a meat dish, and dessert ready in twenty to thirty minutes, sometimes faster. Everyone had to vacate the kitchen and leave her alone; the pots and pans clanged and banged as she flew about her kitchen. It was remarkable how rapidly she could complete the preparation. Of all the food she must have made for us, one dish, a cherry pie, stands out in my memory. As a reflection of the austerity of her early years, she was very attentive to preparing food with the utmost frugality in mind. While my paternal Grandmother Kloepping spared no expense in her cooking, and her cherry pies had a full quart of cherries, folklore had it that Grandmother Rodenbough could make a similar pie with about a dozen cherries. It had a lot of cornstarch filling, I think, but I recall that the pie was still really quite tasty.

She wrote poetry, which most often spoke to the ebb and flow of living in rural America. I still have a file of her work that I rescued from among old newspapers about to be discarded. She bought a viola and taught herself to play. My mother said that Grandmother had something called "perfect pitch," and she learned and played all of her music by ear. That apparently meant she didn't (maybe couldn't) read music, but when she played a song she knew by the sound, she had the correct tune.

Her creative instincts continued to flourish, and in her forties she took up painting. Initially she did watercolors, but soon she switched to the more demanding medium of oil. After traveling to Washington, D. C., in the early 1940s to see her daughter Esther, who was working there, she had the opportunity to visit the Cocoran School of Art. My Aunt Esther told me that Grandmother's visit to the school was apparently very inspiring for her and was a major impetus in her desire to become an accomplished artist. Grandmother painted landscapes, animals, portraits, flowers, and large religious paintings, which hung in many Midwestern Christian churches.

In a Wisconsin statewide competition, her painting *Oakley Valley* was selected to be housed in the permanent collection of the University of Wisconsin. Sadly, I feel, not only for our family, but for the public as well, it disappeared. In my more conspiratorial states of thinking, I know some SOB likely stole it for his private collection. I realize that now, many years past, there is little hope of her painting ever resurfacing; however, if that dastardly soul or a descendant of the scoundrel should happen to read this piece, *please return the painting!* Slim chance, don't you suppose?

In her later years Grandma began to have rather significant mental health issues. I have to believe that with the passing of her husband, Luther, who was a stabilizing influence, and the difficult legacy of her early years, she struggled to cope with past demons that at times overwhelmed her ability to grasp reality. She experienced significant episodes of paranoia, reporting at times that she was receiving coded messages, usually through her television set, and often from well-known television personalities. While her behavior was often erratic and unpredictable, she often had periods of mental clarity and interacted appropriately with others. Eventually the family placed her in a wonderful local care facility that mostly had residents from the communities where Grandma had lived.

Shortly thereafter we were to learn that her creative abilities had not left her. On an initial visit to see Grandmother, my mother was met by the nursing staff exuding admiration for their new resident, Dr. Mary Martha Rodenbough. She had completely convinced the entire staff of her long career as a physician, apparently in depth and detail. Even with her life struggles, she still maintained a reservoir of mental intellect and clarity.

In retrospect I can recall her speaking with authority about historical happenings, world and current events, and about many well-known persons, some of whom she had met or encountered in her life. Only later were we to learn that some of her stories, particularly of notable individuals, had been fabricated. She wasn't being malicious; rather, I think she was simply practicing and sharpening her creative storytelling skills. She was really very entertaining in her telling of tales, whether true or a product of her imagination.

I remember her today with much fondness. She was an extremely bright, creative, and perceptive individual who not only brought a breath of fresh air, but also at times brought a whirlwind into the sometimes staid and tradition-bound Midwestern environment; and I believe that during her lifetime we may have only glimpsed a small portion of the breadth and depth of her abilities.

# *Wisconsin Summer*

"GATHERING OF THE WATERS," the Ojibwa name for the land called Wisconsin. Trees and forests, bluff and dell, swift waters and green. Sanctuary for all manner of wild things: deer, turkey, badger, and hare. Lake and marsh teeming with fish and fowl. Where early people once roamed free and prospered: the Winnebago, Chippewa, Menominee, and Sac. Marquette, Joliet, Perrot, Prairie Du Chien, Fort Crawford, and Sibley—names and places ushering in change.

Then the sons and daughters of Europe and the British Isles came, the tongues of many nations, to conquer the land. Czech and Finn, Pole and Dane, and descendants of the fierce Norsemen. To a county in the south, called Green; miners from Cornwall, Bohemian cooks, and Italian priests. Germans and Pennsylvania Dutch, named Rodenbough. In great numbers the ancestral blood of Switzerland, Gobeli, Jaeggi, and Kundert, generations now rooted deeply in the limestone hills.

Picturesque hamlets of Monroe and New Glarus nestled among a patchwork of fields in the vibrant countryside, caressed by glacial ice. Rolling hills and verdant valleys. Tall red barns and strong white houses and silos. Silos, gray and blue, sentinels standing alone and side by side. Silver domes gleaming in the bright sunshine. Testimony to the nature and order of this place. Beacons of reassurance, guardians of the land.

Golden grain, corn and an abundance of hay—to fuel the herds that dot the landscape. Holsteins, rangy, black and white; chalky Brown Swiss; and Guernseys, pale orange and white. White liquid gold for cheese. Mild cheddar and potent Limburger. Wheels of pungent old Swiss to bite your tongue. A taste for every palate.

High on a hilltop, a country lane, adorned with wild phlox, blue chicory, flame-orange lily, and delicate Queen Anne's lace. In the solitude the tranquil grandeur stirs the soul, to wonderment, yearning, private dreams, a kaleidoscope of the spirit. And borne on the fragrant summer breeze, whispered murmurs of voices past who have known Wisconsin. Fresh and clean, gentle, and green.

# Grandpa's Orchard

I WAS A CHILD, and I knew an enchanted place, for discovery, to pretend, and to relish the solitude. There was the weathered hulk of an old '27 Essex, no windshield, the passenger door askew, permanently mired axle-deep, rotting, mildewed floorboards and a tattered dusty seat, home to bold noisy bumblebees. The rusting steering wheel and throttle still worked. A faded gray woodpile, a mountain to a child of seven or so, full of the incessant chirp of fat, black crickets, and a powderpuff flash of the cottontail.

Apple trees, the old kind, Winesap, Northern Spy, Duchess, and Greening. Transparent, pale green, first ripe in July, crunchy and juicy. Brown-skinned sweet apples, yellow flesh for preserves, and Snow apples, skin the color of dark blood from the vein and, inside, unblemished whiteness.

A secret hideout in a dense thicket of elderberry bushes. Cool and dark under a fragile canopy heavy with clusters of deep purple fruit. The gentle swaying of the slender branches splashes the bed of late summer grass with flashes of sunlight.

Barnyard cats of all vintages silently glide through the acre of waist-high green and golden grasses, stalking furtive field mice and imaginary bigger game.

A patch of pungent burdock with drooping, dark-green, elephant-eared leaves; a center spike adorned with tight brown balls of nature's Velcro, sticking to every living thing.

A ramshackle hog coop, the doors, windows, and floor gone. Dusty, filled with cobwebs, half a roof, and a niche to hide a water-stained pack of Lucky Strikes and keep the matches dry.

Songbirds, brilliant in colors of blue, yellow, black, and orange; a raucous crow and millions of things dancing in the air, center stage in the shafts of late-afternoon rays of sun.

Carefree hours, a comforting place, and time standing still.

*Two men were walking through the woods and came upon a big, black, deep hole. One man picked up a rock, tossed it into the hole, and stood listening for the rock to hit bottom. Nothing. He turned to the other fellow and said, "That must be a deep hole. Let's throw a bigger rock in there and listen for it to hit bottom." The men found a bigger rock, and both picked it up, lugged it to the hole, and dropped it in. They listened for some time … nothing. Again they agreed that this must be one deep hole and maybe they should throw something even bigger into it. One man spotted a big log nearby. They picked it up, grunting and groaning, and threw it into the hole, listening intently … nothing. All of a sudden a goat came flying out of the woods, running like the wind, flew past the men, and jumped straight into the hole. The men were astounded. They walked on through the woods, and a little later they met an old farmer who asked the men if they had seen a goat. One man told the farmer of the incredible incident they had witnessed: that they had just seen a goat fly out of the woods and leap into the big hole. He asked the farmer if this could have been his goat. The old farmer said, "Naw, that can't be my goat. He was chained to a big log."*[1]

# Billy Goat Henry

IN THE YEAR OF our Lord nineteen hundred and twenty-four, a young boy named Virgil, who lived on a farm close to the Illinois-Wisconsin state line, pleaded with his father to buy him a pet goat. His father, Will, known to the locals as "Willie," finally relented, and Virgil got his very own goat, a male, which is called a billy goat, or billy for short.

Will was not very knowledgeable of goat behavior in general and specifically that of a billy goat. In subsequent months, however, he was to learn firsthand many of the unique characteristics of adult male goats.

This is a true story told to me by my father one evening in the 1990s. My parents were *snowbirds*—winter visitors to warm climes; they owned a cozy twelve-by-fifty-foot mobile home on the east side of Tucson, Arizona, only a mile from where I lived with my wife and son.

I often sat around their kitchen table writing down his anecdotes over a cup of coffee: stories of his youth and the early years of their marriage during the Depression, and his sage commentaries on religion, politics, raising and caring for children and animals, and life and values in rural America. Some of the most hilarious stories (all true) he would tell me only after Mom had gone to bed for the evening. They are classic tales of early twentieth-century rural high jinks, the kind of anecdotes that I will likely never publish, as a number of them might be considered politically incorrect and others involve relatively close ancestors. I'll pass them along to my son one day, and he can then decide to what extent he may wish to sully the reputations of a few of his now long-deceased relatives.

My father's vivid descriptions of the time and place in the story of little Virgil and his goat, although then seventy-five years past, rekindled many memories of my youth in the country in an earlier time.

My grandfather Daniel Kloepping was a shrewd rural entrepreneur; he had a sawmill, his own electric plant, a line of machinery for doing custom farm work, and many beehives for selling honey. His wide array of domestic farm animals included horses, dairy cattle, pigs, chickens, ducks, geese, sheep, goats, and of course, dogs and cats.

Grandpa and his wife, Della, were good friends with a couple named Will and Bertha Meinert. Grandma Della was a member of the national Woman's Christian Temperance Union, whose primary goal (maybe they had others) was to ensure that people (specifically men and husbands) didn't succumb to the "elixir of Satan" (that is, alcohol) and thus turn to a life of debauchery. Bertha was the Wisconsin state president of the WCTU, and the families visited regularly at each other's farmsteads. On each occasion, Will and Bertha's son Virgil seemed to gravitate to the goats on the Kloepping farm, particularly the very young goats, referred to as *kids*.

Baby goats are frisky, playful, and extremely endearing. Virgil, upon arrival at the farm, invariably sought out and frolicked with the little goats while imploring his father to let him have a goat of his own. Grandpa Dan attempted to warn Will that goats were fine animals but they could test one's resolve on account of their high level

21

of intelligence, inquisitiveness, and independence. Notwithstanding, Will finally relented, and Grandpa gave Virgil a young male goat as a gift. So, much to young Virgil's delight, at the conclusion of a Sunday afternoon visit, the Mienert family left for home accompanied by a little billy goat. Virgil named him Henry.

Goats have a long history with mankind, as they are one of the earliest known domesticated animals. Remains in archaeological sites in western Asia date back to between 7000 and 6000 BC. They are amazingly utilitarian animals, producing milk, meat, butter, cheese, wool, and leather. They are used to carry packs, to pull small wagons and carts, and to guard flocks of sheep.

The usefulness of goats in general notwithstanding, billy goats do not compare with most of the positive attributes of adult female goats, called *nanny goats*, or *nannies*. Males can become irascible and overly aggressive (ramming with their heads lowered), and their habit and method of marking their territory has to be one of their most disgusting characteristics. They literally urinate on their face, front legs, and beards and proceed to rub the residue on everything in sight. The odor can become overpowering when this is done over a period of time. Billies were often separated from milking nannies to prevent the smell from permeating the milk. I don't know how much information about billies in particular my grandfather had given to old Will, but no matter—little Virgil had his very own pet goat!

It was a number of months after Virgil had acquired Henry when Grandpa Dan asked Will how things were with the goat.

Will, a mild-mannered man, replied, "Well, Dan, we initially had Henry in our house yard so he couldn't run off, but you know, he really became a problem."

"How's that?" asked Dan.

"While Virgil enjoyed having him in the yard, every time we

opened the front door he would bleat loudly, *baaah, baaah,* and try to sneak into the house. Then he began to eat Bertha's flowers, including the rose bushes. We had a short fence separating the yard from the garden, which he quickly learned to jump, so then he began eating the vegetables. But the final insult was when Bertha caught him eating one of my socks that she had just hung on the clothesline."

"Yes, they can really become pests, can't they?" replied Grandpa Dan.

"Well, that's not all," said a somewhat exasperated Will. "Bertha was also missing a pair of her fine bloomers, and she accused Henry! Much to Virgil's disappointment, we finally locked him out of the house yard and allowed him to roam freely among the farm buildings."

Dan asked, "Didn't he run away since he had access to the road?"

"No," replied Will, "but at times I sort of hoped he would."

Well, the trouble had only begun for the good, God-fearing Meinert family. On a subsequent visit of the two families, likely a Sunday afternoon after church, Grandfather Dan again asked Will how the goat Henry was doing.

With a tone of resignation in his voice, Will offered, "You know, Dan, I have never been around an animal like that billy goat in my entire life."

"How's that, Will?"

"Well, he's constantly getting into mischief. He of course discovered he could jump over the relatively low chicken-yard fence, and I caught him in the henhouse eating chicken feed, so I had to raise the fence. Then he started going in the machine shed, where I had cat and dog food, and he would eat as much as he could. And gosh darn his hide, he would tear open any paper sack in the building, including feed sacks, seed corn, and even cement sacks!"

"Oh, my," Dan chuckled.

"Besides all that, he began to get more aggressive toward people who came on the place. Initially they thought he was cute and friendly, as he boldly approached everyone who arrived, but when they turned their backs to him, he would butt them—and increasingly with more authority."

"Well, that's not too good, Will. What did you do?"

"I finally got so exasperated that I put him in with the dairy herd."

"Did that solve the problem?"

"No, it didn't," Will replied with a heavy sigh. "The darn little bugger was really smart and quickly figured out that when we let the cows in for the evening milking, there was ground feed waiting for each cow in her stanchion. He'd rush in ahead of the cows, pick a spot, and keep the cow at bay while he gobbled her feed. At other times he'd head straight for the feed room and gorge himself before we could get him out of the barn."

"By golly, Will, what did you do?"

"Well, Dan, I threw him in with the hogs, and that solved the matter. Now every time I slop the hogs, he stands up against the fence and bleats at me. He eats the corn I throw in and drinks the swill. I can't imagine he likes it, but he bullies his way to a spot on the trough and fills up. He's filthy and raunchy-looking, but he's fat and sassy too, the top hog in the pen, and appears to be thriving."

Apparently Will had solved the dilemma of Henry the billy goat, and Grandfather Dan forgot about the matter. The two families continued to visit one another, I suppose most often for a meal, rotating whose farmstead would host. Months passed, and into the following year the topic of Henry had never resurfaced.

However, on the occasion of one visit later in the year, Grandfather Dan thought of Henry and asked, "Say, Will, how did that goat ever turn out?"

With a twinkle in his eye, Will smiled pleasantly and replied, "Well, Dan, you know how pushy goats can be, always butting in where they are not wanted or going wherever other animals go?"

"Yes, that's true," said Dan.

"Last fall I shipped a load of hogs by semitrailer to Chicago. The driver backed up the truck, lowered the loading ramp, and began hustling the hogs up into the back."

At this point of the story Will seemed to feign innocence as he remarked, "Now, Dan, I didn't carefully watch the loading, so I couldn't say which hogs got on the truck and which ones didn't. After the semitrailer left I went into the hog lot to make sure the correct number of hogs had been taken. As I was counting the remaining animals, it was then I noticed I didn't see Henry in the yard. I looked all over the place, and he just wasn't there."

Dan only smiled as Will continued.

"Dan, the only thing I could figure was that Henry decided he needed a change of scenery and decided to take a ride to Chicago with the hogs."

Will laughed out loud as he concluded his story of Henry. "I'll bet the boys in Chicago were in for a surprise when that load of hogs arrived and they encountered old Henry. You know, Dan, that goat always seemed to land on his feet. I can't imagine what they did with him, but it wouldn't at all surprise me if today he was a star attraction at the prestigious Brookfield Zoo!"

Ernest "Ernie" Banks signed with the Kansas City Monarchs of the Negro American League in 1950 and broke into the major leagues in 1953 with the Chicago Cubs as their first black player. He played for the Cubs his entire career, starting at shortstop and moving to first base in 1962.

Initially Banks's double-play partner was Gene Baker, the second black player on the Cubs and Banks's roommate on road trips, thus making Banks and Baker the first all-black double-play combination in major league history. When Steve Bilko would play first base, Cubs announcer and hometown rooter Bert Wilson would refer to the Banks-Baker-Bilko double-play combination as "Bingo to Bango to Bilko." This combination would not last quite as long as "Tinker to Evers to Chance," but Banks would become a Cubs institution.[1]

# A Day at Wrigley

IN 1951, MAJOR LEAGUE baseball was no longer the exclusive domain of white men, but just barely; it was only four years past when one of baseball's moguls recognized the huge financial rewards to be reaped by allowing some of the best athletes in the world, African Americans, to play major league baseball. I never believed it was totally a decision of conscience; I'd guess winning and money were equally important issues. It seems the almighty dollar often sends one toward the path of enlightenment.

That year, I attended my first major league baseball game, and neither my family nor I was prepared for what was to transpire that day. As a thirteen-year-old kid, I, like millions of other Americans, religiously followed the fortunes of my favorite major league team. Daily I listened to the radio play-by-play of my heroes, carefully devouring any new statistical data that the announcer slipped in between calling the action. In those days, as fans we were loyal to our teams and ferociously defended our heroes, those "boys of summer." Being loyal to your team if you lived in Illinois in the '50s was an act of courage, for my team was the Cubs, those lovable losers from the north side of Chicago. The '50s were lean years for the Cubs and their fans. They would typically start the year quickly, play well, raise our hopes and expectations, but around the middle of June begin to wilt like early spring flowers in the summer heat. We tried to remain hopeful, privately praying for miracles, publicly maintaining our bravado in the face of yet another season deteriorating with the dog days of summer.

One evening during an impromptu drop-in visit and evening snacks of crackers and cheese, my Uncle Hub casually asked me if I would be interested in seeing the Cubs and Dodgers play baseball on Sunday. I almost fell out of my wheelchair. He did say "see," and I was stunned. I couldn't sleep for days waiting for the day. Aunt Esther had gotten tickets for a late September game, the sixteenth, and my father, Hub, Esther, and I were off to Chicago for a Sunday afternoon game.

Wow, the Dodgers, arguably the most powerful team in all of baseball. Their lineup was sprinkled with future Hall-of-Famers, names like Pee Wee Reese, Duke Snider, Gil Hodges, Roy Campanella, Don Newcombe, and a guy named Robinson—Jackie was his first name. The Cubs, by contrast, were again a struggling last-place team: lots of heart, but also lots of losses. But they were my team, and today they could win. I was awestruck by the sights and sounds of the ballpark. The giant stadium, small by today's standards, was packed. The sounds, colors, beer vendors, smartly dressed Andy Frain ushers, the grass, and the ivy-covered brick outfield walls all combined in a mind-boggling assault on the senses. The crowd was fascinatingly diverse: kids and oldsters, men and women, but notably a large percentage of people in the stadium were not white. There were many African Americans, a different experience for me, born and raised in an almost 100 percent white rural community. The attire of many fans was almost spectacular, again specifically among the black folks. Many of them were extremely well-dressed: men in white shirts, ties, even some with sport coats and sharp Sunday hats. The women wore beautiful, colorful dresses, long stockings, lots of jewelry, high heels, and out-of-this-world summer bonnets.

As game time neared, the excitement and noise levels increased in anticipation. Then suddenly it was quiet for the national anthem. At the final note of the anthem, thirty thousand-plus fans erupted with a mighty roar. As the din subsided, a strange hush fell over the entire stadium. Almost imperceptibly at first, a faint murmuring sound began. The still, heavy air seemed electric … no, more like charged with a building force of energy. It became almost oppressive for me, and I suddenly gasped for air. "Dad, what's happening? Can you feel it?"

"Yes," he replied gently as he looked at me.

I asked, "What is it?"

"It's Robinson, I think. Jackie."

I stared at my father in amazement. "What do you mean, it's Jackie? What's he doing?" What was this silent yet powerful crescendo building and enveloping everyone?

I was jolted by the sudden loud, staccato voice from the PA system. "Attention! Attention, please. Now batting for the Brooklyn Dodgers, playing second base—Jackie Robinson."

The crowd rose as one, and another mighty roar came from thousands of throats, but unlike the enthusiastic cheering at the conclusion of the anthem, there was a strange dissonance of sounds: shrieks of joy, but also mournful sounds, his name spoken repeatedly, chords of adulation, as if in supplication to a master or even a messiah. It was like a symphony of wailing from deep within tortured souls, seeking spiritual release. Everyone, it seemed, was standing and gently swaying, and I sat, unable to stand, trembling, confused, fully engulfed in this unknown force and energy.

But the moment passed quickly as Robinson got a hit, and in an instant the stadium was suddenly transformed into a gleeful, raucous baseball crowd. Familiar sounds that I recognized: the simple joys of the ballpark, "the Cubbies" and "da bums," playing America's game.

The Cubs lost, 6 to 1, and their season record fell to 58-85: good for last place. Clem Labine, a Dodger rookie, beat Bob Kelly, a journeyman pitcher. Oh, well, maybe next year. Riding home, exhausted, stuffed with hot dogs, candy, peanuts, and soda pop, snug in the backseat of Uncle Hub's new Chevy, I dozed dreamily, thinking about the day. I thought about that strange overwhelming moment, unable to comprehend its meaning. What was clear was the overpowering energy that swirled around us for a brief time and seemed to gently envelop the man Jackie.

That day, now over sixty years ago, remains indelibly etched in my memory. I'm not certain I'll ever fully understand or appreciate what happened that day at Wrigley Field. What I do know is that Jackie Robinson was much more than just the Dodgers second baseman. And today, as I reflect on his lonely pilgrimage, I think of another gentle, yet fiercely determined soul, Mohondas Gandhi, the "Mahatma," who, as Jackie, changed a nation.

# A Song for '57

Come listen my friends I've a tale to tell, of a time in our youth that I know quite well. It's a song of you, one and all, a time now passed when you answered a call.

There was no place for me at the local high, my legs were gone and surely a boy can't fly. Two stories up seemed impossible then, but old "DV" sort of chuckled and said, " Oh well let's give it a try."

What would you think was I a burden for you? But with nary a pause you made a reply, "Hey no problem, that's something we can do." Great kindness and debts I can never repay, thoughts in my heart remind me each day.

I was no lightweight and rode heavy wheelchairs, gosh almighty I was hauled up and down a million stairs! Exaggeration you say, but it was surely a lot, who can forget that D.C. trip, humid and wet and broiling hot!

So come and sit with me, we each have a song, you and I, don't hurry, you'll remember if you try. About our lives, what we did, and being together at Dakota High.

Four years of magic, laughter and fun, were we not like young flowers budding in the sun? Parties and sports and cars too fast, does anyone recall a brew or two? Bobby sox, saddle shoes, DA haircuts, gosh, now that's all past.

The girls had beauty, charm and grace, those winsome young lasses causing pulses to quicken and hearts to race. And the fellows, smart and strong, and handsome and tall, goodness it seems we were special, each and all.

Our faculty is a story one should tell, crowded hallways and a rush to beat the bell. Good teachers there were, surely some of renown, but then and again we'd get a clown.

Four quick years that flashed away, a time to study, but oft times play. Children we were, learning the lyrics of life, days that were idyllic and free from strife.

So this is our story, this is our song; it was a time and place when all did belong. My goodness dear friends I'm somewhat aghast, can it be true that those days of serendipity are fifty years past?

Yes time has flown, different songs we've all sung, yet in my heart, forever, we'll always be young.

*There is a time-worn story of an old fellow who seemed to have extraordinary success fishing. Invariably he returned from his always solitary excursions with the limit of whatever he was pursuing that day. He was a crafty old codger and always demurred if asked where he had fished and also, importantly, what bait or lures he had used. A rather haughty young game warden had watched the elderly gentleman return to shore on more than one occasion, and the warden was perplexed since no matter the weather or condition of the lake, the fisherman always had great success. The warden decided to lie in wait for the foxy old fellow and follow him on his next trip.*

*One early morning at dawn, the old man launched his weather-beaten little boat and putted away in a cloud of smoke and fumes. Stealthily, the warden followed, barely keeping the old man in sight. The old man stopped, and shortly the warden heard a loud but muffled thud. Aha, he thought, I'll bet the old bugger is using dynamite. Again there was a major thud, and the lake seemed to shudder. The warden raced toward the old man, shut down the powerful engines of his boat, and glided up next to him.*

*"Any luck, old-timer?"*

*"Oh, sure."*

*"You're quite lucky, aren't you?"*

*"I suppose."*

"It wouldn't have anything to do with how you're catching them, would it?"

"Maybe."

"Well, I think I know your secret. Let's have a look in your tackle box."

As the brash young warden oared toward the ancient fishing boat, the old man reached down, producing a bright red stick of dynamite. He calmly lit the fuse and tossed it into the horrified warden's boat. He smiled broadly at the warden and asked, "Now, look, son— are you going to start fishing or continue to ask stupid questions?"

# The Big Bang

I REMEMBER MY FIRST experience with dynamite when I was nine years old; that is, being in the locale when it was ignited.

My father was building a new dairy barn, and the entire neighborhood joined in what was an old-fashioned barn *razing*, as opposed to a barn *raising*. Dynamite was being used to demolish the original stone foundation walls that were six to eight feet tall.

It was 1947, and I had returned home after a year and a half of hospitalization from polio. I hadn't lost any part of my curious nature, and I made sure that I was close to the activity of tearing down the old barn. The men took turns yelling at me to stay clear of what was indeed a dangerous process, particularly when the explosives detonated. After the blasts, which either toppled or weakened the walls, farm tractors, using cable or heavy ropes, finished the job. One of the neighbors had an Oliver tractor (we thought it was a real wuss of a machine compared to Dad's Farmall M), and it was struggling to bring down a particularly stubborn section of wall. My sisters and I, plus other neighborhood kids, were snickering and making insulting remarks about the tractor, which apparently pissed off the owner/operator. With each unsuccessful backward lunge of the tractor, the driver getting bounced up off the metal seat (likely bruising a *huevo*, or both), his face turned progressively redder, and

35

he started cursing. Initially he swore rather quietly, but with us kids gawking, laughing, and generally being obnoxious, we evidently lit his fuse, and he blew his top. He cut loose with a blast of profanity that would have made the toughest old sea dog wither under the barrage. He reeled off all the local favorites—"son of a bitch," "goddammit," "shit," "bull-shit," "bastard"—and knocked us haranguers off our pedestals with the almost-never-uttered-aloud "F-bomb"! Holy cow, no one used that word in our locale. Well, the incident would be a major topic of conversation among the neighbor kids for several weeks thereafter. Maybe it was all the blasting, the use of dynamite that contributed to the guy unraveling; whatever the case, that event seemed to be an impetus for some of us to explore other uses for the lethal TNT.

We discovered that it was a great fishing aid, as the old fellow in the opening anecdote understood well. Almost every farmer had dynamite, but my father hid the blasting caps; however, we discovered that cherry bombs (powerful firecrackers) would indeed detonate dynamite. We "caught" a lot of fish for several summers, until one sunny day, in the midst of a blasting party, the county sheriff arrived and permanently ended our fishing with explosives.

Dynamite, used appropriately, was a very utilitarian commodity, especially in the rural farming community where I grew up. An individual knowledgeable and skilled in using TNT would regularly be called upon for a job requiring its use. And there was such a man in my neighborhood; his name was Edwin, he was a bachelor, he lived alone on his farm, and we thought of him as an eccentric. Two defining characteristics were attributed to him by locals: he was most likely highly intelligent, and most assuredly he was an expert in handling dynamite. As to the matter of his intellect, my favorite recollection is of his ongoing battle with the local power company. I was never on his farm, and the saga of Edwin versus the power company, as I know it, has been compiled from multiple sources. While the story is doubtless accurate, some of the finer details may be sprinkled with local folklore.

Edwin had lights throughout his farmstead: indoors, outdoors, and in locations that seemed to serve no specific purpose or need. On one occasion he apparently missed or failed to pay his electric bill, and in the ensuing communications between himself and the company, Edwin must have become unhappy as they pressed for payment of the bill; possibly he took exception to what he saw as a challenge to his highly independent nature and also to his integrity. He refused to pay the bill, so the company shut off his power. The evening after his power was cut off, one of his neighbors reported that Edwin's entire farmstead was "lit up like a Christmas tree." The company wasn't amused by his (in their view) flagrant behavior and proceeded to disconnect the power again. I have no knowledge of electrical wiring or what steps the company took to ensure that his service was now eliminated; but I and a whole lot of other folks knew he had been warned not to attempt to restore his power, as advanced technical training, knowledge, and equipment were required to safely turn the power on again. Well, as I'll bet you guessed, a day after the power was cut, the evening sky over Edwin's farm was once again aglow. The power company then resorted to extreme measures and (they thought) eliminated any possibility of Edwin being able to restore the power. They didn't literally remove any overhead lines to his farmstead, but they terminated the power at a main junction box located on what we called the "high line" pole. The battle was now over; there was no way for Edwin to restore his power, except that he did, maybe not in one day, but in a short period his place was again fully illuminated. Edwin had made his point, accepted the challenge, while maintaining his integrity and independence; evidently he reached a compromise with the company, and the saga ended.

As tolerant, nonjudgmental, rural Midwest folks are apt to say, "Edwin was different," as demonstrated by his method of getting his herd of hogs from a field back to the buildings and into their hog yard. My high-school friend Keith, who lived next door, described the scene: Edwin, on his John Deere tractor, going full throttle, was lobbing (probably partial) sticks of dynamite behind the hogs, presumably to hurry them on their way back to the buildings. Now, that really is different! Keith told me he observed these antics on more than one occasion. Notwithstanding this behavior, which might appear at least reckless (he never injured a single animal), the entire community had come to realize that Edwin loved to use dynamite and, further, that he was highly proficient in handling the explosive. He was called upon regularly, and invariably he obliged, to demolish old walls and buildings, blow out tree stumps, and to do a wide variety of jobs that required an expert in handling the material.

On one occasion he used dynamite to blast a tunnel from the basement of a house, through a foundation wall, to an existing water well; I recall the distance was twelve to fifteen feet. The old fellow who hired him was also a "different" sort. I guess you'd have to be a bit unique to hire another guy to blast rather than dig, with pick and shovel, a tunnel under your home! The wife vacated the premises, likely taking her best dishes with her, and she didn't return until Edwin had completed the job and left. His ability to use small chunks of dynamite, strategically placed, to carve out a likely three-by-four-foot tunnel through the foundation (the house not sagging), with no collateral damage, was real testimony to his knowledge and skill in using the dangerous product.

But my all-time favorite Edwin anecdote, related to me by my father, who was a wonderful storyteller in the classic American rural tradition, was number one on the list of Edwin's escapades. It also may have been a "mountain-top" experience for Edwin. My father, who was a dairy farmer, a great herdsman, and really an all-around nice guy, had just completed an early summer evening milking of his high-producing Holstein cows. After being milked, the cows were released to amble slowly down the dusty lane to the pastures about half a mile southeast of the farmstead. Dad would often follow a short distance, to urge along a laggard cow, and then return to close the gate to the cow yard adjacent to the dairy barn.

That particular evening he glanced into a cornfield adjoining the lane and noticed what appeared to be a piece of splintered wood. He crossed over into the field, where the corn was roughly ten or twelve inches high, and retrieved the chunk of mangled wood. It was wood from a tree, and he further noted that it was green, indicating that it had been splintered recently. Puzzled, he began to search the area, and he discovered additional fragments of tree wood. Rather quickly he realized it was a debris field of tree fragments, and he was able to follow the debris back to the site of origin. Even before he arrived at our fencerow that adjoined the neighbor's land, he was chuckling to himself; he already had a pretty good idea how the wood had gotten into our field and, more importantly, who was responsible. Someone had blown a tree stump out of the neighbor's field not far from the property line fence. To my father's amazement, there was a large crater where the old, rotten tree had stood. A powerful explosion had created a hole four to five feet deep and a bit wider across. Dad was certain he knew who the perpetrator was, and he had the opportunity to verify his suspicion several weeks later. He encountered Edwin in the small village of Rock City (population 150), which served the local rural community as a kind of shopping center. My father related that his conversation with Edwin went something like the following:

"Hello, Eddie. How are you?"

"Good."

"Been keeping busy?"

"Yup."

"Say, are you still blowing stumps now and again?"

A slight grin creased Edwin's face and a faint twinkle flickered in his eyes as he gazed at my father and replied, "Yup." Edwin already knew the next question, and my father knew what his reply would be.

"You know, I found some wood from a blown stump not far from my barn and discovered someone had gotten rid of an old tree in Johnny Schlueter's field. Was that your work, Eddie?"

"Yup."

"Man, there is quite a hole there. How much dynamite did you use?"

"Well, I wanted to take it out with one shot, so I used maybe twenty-five or thirty sticks."

Dad was flabbergasted and struggled to come up with a response worthy of the magnitude of Edwin's handiwork, but all he said was, "Really? Well, that did the job all right."

Only Edwin, now gone many years, really knew the amount of sticks of dynamite he had used; was it thirty, twenty, or maybe only ten? I don't think Dad ever told any of the citizens of Rock City what he knew about the explosion, although some folks may have learned the truth from Dad telling the story to others. We can be assured that Edwin told no one, and he probably had many a private chuckle as he overheard townsfolk speculating about the origin of that bomb-like blast.

I once related the story to a brother-in-law in Minnesota, who responded, "My god, thirty sticks would have broken windows a half mile away." Our farm buildings were at least three-quarters of a mile from the blast site, and we sustained no damage. We learned later that many people in the village of Rock City heard the explosion and that doors and windows throughout the town shook. My father never tired of repeating the story and always smiled when he recalled the encounter with Edwin and the crafty old bomber laying claim, with relish, to arguably one of the largest explosions ever in Stephenson County, Illinois.

Edwin lost his driver's license in later years (maybe he refused to retake the test, having already passed it) and drove his John Deere all over the area, winter and summer, rain or shine, standing upright, never seated. In extreme cold weather he wore a leather cap with earflaps hanging down each side of his face. He never fastened the strap under his chin, and on particularly windy days, the earflaps flopped up and down like the ears of a bloodhound in hot pursuit of his quarry.

I don't recall any of the details of his passing, as years before his death I had left the community. My good friend Keith, now also gone, who lived next door to Edwin, said he was very generous. He once gave Keith a new saw, a very practical gift, on one of his birthdays. Keith, with whom Edwin conversed on a fairly regular basis, said Edwin kept track of all the local happenings, knew who most everyone was in the community, but rarely associated with others.

Although I really didn't know him personally, I thought I liked him. I didn't understand why, back then, but today I think I have an idea. He embodied many of the characteristics that I admire: he was intelligent; he was self-reliant, in the best tradition of rural America; he was an independent cuss; he disliked bureaucracy (the power company); he was adaptable (he had no driver's license, so he drove a tractor); he took nothing from the government; he was generous; he went to church; and best of all, he "did it his way." He was likely a person who lived by the maxim, "I don't give people advice, and therefore I don't take advice from anyone."

One day, I too will be in another time and place, and I truly hope I encounter Edwin. I'll know it's him when I see a very thin, ascetic, unshaven, older fellow, standing upright on a weathered John Deere going full throttle, with the earflaps of his leather hat flying in the wind.

With his great knowledge and expertise in the uses of TNT, and with my insatiable lust for fishing, working together as a team, we might cause future scientists to completely rethink the idea of the big bang theory!

*Reminiscences of my youth in the country, of a Jeffersonian world, are memories that flood into my consciousness: a father in the full bloom of manhood, and images of an idyllic time and place. And still today, thoughts, poignant yet serene.*

# My Father in Summertime

Days of Summer, warmed by the Sun, carefree hours, a comforting place and time standing stilll, living things and fruits of the land. The rhythm of seasons; Fall, Winter, Spring, and this Summertime.

A fathers love, his time and all that he has; stories to teach and tales for mirth. Simple truth, the knowledge of years, and wisdom to weave the fabric that binds the generations; a summer tan, overalls and the size of his hands.

Bees that buzz and birds that sing, and millions of things, whining-dancing in the air; a raucous crow high in the sky, the call of a cock hidden in hay.

Calling cattle in the early morn and hushing dogs that bark in the night; a symphony of melodies in the country.

Now Summer has gone and the songwriter writes that the days dwindle down; for there is a harvest of all things. Toil and sweat and a time to rest, and all there is, and we too, shall also pass.

One day two brothers, aged eleven and twelve, decided they had reached an age when they should begin behaving more grown-up. It was, in their minds, a passage from childhood to adolescence. Swearing, they determined, would signal to others this important change in their status. One young boy decided to say, "Oh, what the hell's the difference?"—an expression their mother would use on occasion. The other boy decided to use, "You bet your ass," one of their father's favorites. They felt that beginning their cussing career should start the next day. At breakfast the following morning, the father asked one boy if he preferred corn flakes or Cheerios. Confidently he replied, "Oh, what the hell's the difference? I think I'll have corn flakes!"

The father jerked the startled boy from his chair, bent him over, and gave him several resounding whacks on his rear.

The other boy, shocked by what had just happened, listened carefully to his father, who now asked, "And what kind of cereal would you like?"

The boy thought carefully for a moment and then replied, "Well, you can bet your ass it won't be corn flakes!"

# A Rite of Passage

HAVE YOU BEEN THROUGH a rite of passage lately? Perhaps you didn't recognize the experience or event as such, or maybe you weren't inclined or interested in naming or marking the occasion. A rite of passage can literally be just about anything. However, significant milestones in our lives, such as career moves, marriage, religious ceremonies, passage into adulthood, initiation into fraternal societies, births, and deaths, are almost universally noted benchmarks. One thing is certain: all cultures practice rituals, and we all experience these events repeatedly during our lifetimes.

If you check the Internet, you'll find numerous definitions and examples of rites of passage. A short one from Dictionary.com is, "Any important act or event that serves to mark a passage from one stage of life to another," and that statement seems sufficient for what is to follow.

This is a brief recounting of a rite of passage that I experienced on June 6, 1959, the day I turned twenty-one years old; it was informal, spontaneous, and facilitated by five "brothers of the brush." But importantly, it is also a story of one of those five comrades, a leprechaun-like fellow named Otto Grunder, who for years had been the local blacksmith in my childhood home of Northern Illinois. He would emerge as a mentor for me in what I would later come to understand to be an unquestioned passage into adulthood.

Cultures throughout the world conduct rites of passage for youths from childhood to adulthood. These ceremonies, often elaborate and extensive, are typically guided by elders of the society or individuals knowledgeable of the appropriate procedures to follow. Among some groups the initiations may involve extreme infliction of pain, like adolescent circumcision, usually for young boys, still practiced in many cultures. Judaism practices a much more benign form of infant circumcision as a religious rite, and other cultures do so for health reasons.

The "bullet ant glove" is a particularly diabolic ritual. For ten minutes, a boy must keep his hand in a glove filled with ferocious ants and endure hundreds of stings, with a single bite capable of causing cardiac arrest. The Mandan American Indians practiced the Okipa, a ceremony where young boys were hung by wooden skewers inserted in their chest muscles. Though this is no longer utilized, many more seemingly cruel and highly dangerous ceremonies are still in use today in other societies. By contrast, two very anticipated and celebratory practices seen as gateways to adulthood are the Christian rite of confirmation and, in Judaism, the bar mitzvah.

Some individuals may self-define their own rites of passage into adulthood: a first suit and tie; a driver's license; for girls, "the change"; or simply a parent telling a child, "You are now a man (or a woman)."

For me, a day I recognize as a passage into adulthood—June 6, 1959—happened to coincide with the hundred-year celebration of Rock City, Illinois. The village was founded as Rock Run City in 1859 and later shortened to just Rock City. Typically these celebrations last three to five days. They are common throughout the Midwest and, I'd assume, across America; they feature parades, pageants, marching bands, beard-growing ("brothers of the brush") royalty, entertainment, lots of food, games, and prizes.

As with any community celebration, advertising is a key activity to ensure good attendance. Word of mouth, newspaper ads, radio spots, and posters plastered throughout surrounding counties in gas stations, banks, restaurants, churches, and taverns, and on telephone poles and building walls, were all utilized. Undoubtedly they all had an impact; however, for my money, the quintessential message vehicle was exactly that—the *vehicle!* The caravan! Everyone with time on their hands, looking for an excuse to raise a bit of good-natured ruckus, would meet at an appointed time and place with their vehicles and form a caravan of however many folks showed up; then the fifteen to twenty cars and trucks began a trek throughout neighboring communities to announce and invite the local citizenry to the upcoming celebration. I don't really remember how many vehicles were in the caravan that June 6 evening, but I vividly recall that at about 5:30 PM I was lifted in my wheelchair into the lead vehicle, likely a 1940s or '50s panel truck, with an extremely loud siren mounted on top. I also don't remember whether the exterior of the van identified us as the "Keystone Kops" (which was supposedly our designation). Actually, only two of the fellows were dressed in full 1920s Keystone Kop regalia: Bill Keister, the driver, and Nathan Kubly, who was his copilot and designated siren handler. About the same size in stature, these two had decidedly different personalities. Bill, a mechanic, was very quiet, almost stoic. He rarely initiated conversation that evening, if ever, and that was his general demeanor. People who knew him well suggested he was apt to be more conversant if he was familiar with you. Nate, by contrast, seemed to never stop talking; he was a lively, good-natured fellow who probably never met a person he didn't like. So throughout the entire trip Bill drove, remaining silent, while Nate kept up a running dialogue with the rest of the group.

Along with me, there were three others in the truck. One was my long-time friend Gene Shippy, who had not yet been corrupted by alcohol (he was soon to turn twenty). Also in the truck was Elmer Lapp, a burly bear of a man who related stories of his WWII experiences in the Pacific theater; he had been aboard a navy vessel under attack by Japanese kamikaze, and his description of the terror of the men in the bowels of the ship was chilling.

The last member of the group was Otto Grunder. Although I knew who he was from a young age, I had not interacted with him much before that evening. His daughter, Dorothy, had been a very attentive helpmate to me when I returned to the local grade school after a two-year absence due to infantile paralysis. The Grunder family was a close-knit group, and they were particularly so after they lost their mother at the age of forty-four. The nine children were fiercely loyal to one another back then, and at this writing, in 2011, they still gather on a regular basis. That strong sense of family identity was not coincidental, and Otto, their father, was the key. Helen, another daughter and a friend of my sister Carol, told me Otto had said he was lonely after he lost his wife, but he would not remarry, as he wanted his children to have just one mother. I think this is an uncommon and selfless act.

Otto, born in Berne, Switzerland, in 1897, came to America in 1922 at age twenty-five and spoke only the Swiss German dialect. He was short and stocky with a very dark complexion, and after a day working at the blacksmith shop, it was difficult to tell if he was a white or a black person! It was amazing how sparkling clean he appeared after he had returned home for a good scrubbing.

My early images of him, in addition to being gregarious and soot-covered in his shop, are of him after his evening bath, wearing a white T-shirt and trousers with suspenders and trudging determinedly toward his evening libations with the local gentry. I recall another characteristic of Otto's: he was a master of the ancient and sometimes revered art of cussing. He didn't use a broad range of oaths; rather, he relied on rapid-fire repetition for maximum effect. If he was particularly agitated by a difficult weld on a piece of machinery, a cantankerous horse, or a pushy patron, one might be treated to a scorching diatribe directed at the offending animal, machine, or customer in broken English with a Swiss dialect overlaid. Helen also told me that he said he initially learned many swear words from the locals while in his shop, and he incorporated them into his everyday language, a common occurrence when people are exposed to a new language. Otto's style of interaction was direct, and his use of profanity fit well with his candor and straightforward delivery, leaving no doubt as to his views on a matter.

Our caravan left the small village of Rock City around 5:30 PM with horns blaring, the siren wailing, and much fanfare from the assembled crowd of locals. We headed west through the small towns of Dakota and Cedarville, being as noisy as possible, and we made our first stop in Orangeville, as they had a tavern. It became clear that the boys in our vehicle were heading into the bar, and I assumed I'd stay in the truck, as these bars were typically located in very old brick buildings with multiple concrete steps to the entrance. That wasn't the case. Otto barked, "Okay, men, grab Kent and his chair, and let's go have a drink." I was summarily hauled from the truck and carted up the steps into the bar, to be greeted with astonished looks from the patrons; they got a second jolt when Otto's first words were, "By *Gott*, it's this boy's twenty-first birthday. Let's get him a drink." The assembly didn't respond quickly enough, in Otto's mind, and he followed with an even higher-decibel command: "Well, Jesus Christ, what are we waiting for? My friend and I are really thirsty!" Maybe those weren't the exact words he used, but the message got through, and suddenly the place would erupt with a flurry of activity, and all of the Keystone Kops usually had more than one drink in hand. There were toasts all around, congratulations for the birthday, lots of "hail fellows, well met," and Otto chuckling to himself and giving me a big wink as we departed.

Otto's admonitions were the upside; the downside was that we were in a hurry. If you're country folk, you've seen hogs swill whey; well, like hogs, we swilled our beer and hurried off.

In another small town, Winslow, the childhood home of my Grandfather Kloepping, we followed the same routine. Otto again barked, "By *Gott*, let's get this boy a drink." The patrons did, and they also got drinks for Bill, Nate, Elmer, Gene (who likely had a Coke), and of course Otto. Among much camaraderie, we gulped our drinks, and then we piled back into the truck, with a noticeable increase in hilarity, and again headed west.

Oddly I don't recall what the people in the other vehicles of the caravan were doing while we were in the bar. Maybe some were joining us in our celebrations, or possibly passing out fliers concerning the upcoming centennial celebration. I'm not surprised that I wasn't totally alert to happenings around me; early on, people and places began to blend and get a bit fuzzy. We continued west toward Warren, with Bill Keister at the helm. He was Otto's son-in-law, married to Bertha, affectionately known as "Bert."

As noted earlier, Bill was a quiet fellow, more of a doer than a talker. He was slim and had a dark complexion, with a sparkle in his eyes like his father-in-law. At each stop he accompanied the panel truck crew into the tavern and appeared to drink as much as everyone else. His demeanor didn't change, and he spoke no more frequently, but he did appear to hunch over the steering wheel a bit more, sort of like someone driving in fog or a snowstorm trying to see the road. Interestingly, when no one was paying attention, Otto, who kept track of everything and everyone, asked, "Bill, you okay?"

"Yup," was the only response.

I declined the invitation to exit the truck in Warren, and when Otto returned, he said with a mischievous grin, "Kent, we need a little fortification while we're on the road." He produced a pint of apricot brandy and offered me the first drink. I took a long swig from the bottle, and Otto chuckled and said, "My turn." He wiped the top with his sleeve, took a drink, and passed it back to me. Like a couple of mountain men, we'd take a drink, wipe the top, and pass it back, and soon we finished the bottle. After we had finished our "jug," Otto smiled at me and asked quietly, "Are you having a good time?"

"Why, yes, I am."

"Dat's good," he replied, patting my shoulder gently. "You deserve to be happy."

I didn't respond, as I was a bit caught off guard, not expecting such a genuine expression of concern and kindness. Well, I'll be damned, I thought. Otto is watching out for me. He's going to make sure this truly is a special night for me.

I didn't think about his comments any further, but several days later it occurred to me that Otto had assumed the role of mentor for me that evening, like an elder guiding me through an important passage. He indeed was a soft-hearted man, and he must have loved his children deeply, and I saw a bit of that gentle, caring side of him that evening. But his compassion for others, of which I believe most people only caught a fleeting glance, extended beyond his family. Helen told me Otto had gone to only one local high school basketball game; the coach yelled at the team repeatedly, which upset him, and he never went to another game.

Feeling no pain and seeing everything with a shiny glow, we entered the town of Stockton. I suppose our arrival was a bit exuberant, with horns blaring, our siren screaming, and folks yelling from car windows, for quickly we were met by the local gendarmes. Their cherry tops were flashing and the sirens on their cars were sounding, adding to the general uproar. They were not pleased with our noisy entrance into their city, and after a brief discussion, they invited us to leave, like right now! We complied and headed back east for home, through Freeport.

In Freeport, someone suggested, "Hey, let's stop in at Tiger Woods's place for another drink." No, the bar owner wasn't the chap of golfing fame; this guy was white, about six foot two, and tipped the scales at around three hundred and fifty pounds. He was a gentle, gregarious giant, but he wasn't there. The bartender, a somewhat odd chap, didn't talk, and someone thought he might be severely hard of hearing or completely deaf. Everyone started ordering drinks at once, and the bartender began to gesture sort of randomly with his hands and arms, pointing at one person and then another, his eyes fluttering like a flag in the wind, and then suddenly he was gone.

"Where the hell did he go?" asked Nate, who then walked around the bar and exclaimed, "Here he is, out like a light."

We were unable to arouse him, so we got a pillow and put it under his head. Nate then announced, "Well, men, I believe I'm the designated barkeep, and tonight drinks are on the house." I'm not sure how much liquor we consumed, but it was a substantial amount. Strangely, during our entire binge, which lasted probably close to an hour, no other patrons showed up.

Amazingly, we all seemed to realize at the same time that we had reached the alcohol saturation point, as our ability to speak, walk, and come to a decision concerning the appropriate action on behalf of the still-unconscious bartender were all deteriorating. After several minutes of confused discussion, we just turned off the lights, said good night to the barkeep (still sound asleep), locked the doors, and left.

Gene was the obvious choice to drive, but Bill was adamant that he should finish his job. Otto asked him if he was okay, and Bill replied, "I'm fine. I'll drive."

Otto, still alert to the dynamics around him, simply said, "Okay, Bill, you drive." Gene did ride shotgun, and I think he prompted Bill subtly more than once. We arrived back safely at Rock City, some twelve miles from Freeport.

Gene took me home, a mile and a half north, but not before I emptied the sum total of my evening of revelry on the side of the blacktop road. We all know the expression that sometimes we fear that death may be imminent, but then we begin to hope for it; this was such a moment. Gene waited patiently until I was sure nothing remained in me. Wow, I felt as though in addition to emptying my stomach, I might have started on the small intestine! Gene got me home and into bed, and as he left, I swore I heard a slight snicker as he said, "Well, you really had a good twenty-first, didn't you?"

I don't believe I ever saw Otto Grunder again after that evening, as our life paths simply didn't cross again. I think of him every now and then and smile to myself as I recall bits of that night. It was, without a doubt, a serendipitous happening. Instead of the soot-covered little firebrand I was used to, I encountered quite a different fellow that night. Oh, the impish twinkle was still evident in his eyes, and his creative use of English continued, but beneath that sometimes crusty exterior I glimpsed the soul of a sensitive, compassionate, rather wise, and gentle man.

He was also an immigrant who came to America and found his way; he was resourceful and independent, he provided for his children alone after the untimely death of his wife, and he asked nothing of the government to lessen his burdens or responsibilities. He was a member of the generation that Tom Brokaw called "America's greatest generation." It occurs to me that Otto Grunder, and a few other folks who lived in the community where I grew up, deserve a paragraph or two in Brokaw's book.

I asked his daughter Helen to tell me some things about her father. She wrote me a letter describing her thoughts of him, and two things she said resonated strongly with me. "He was a man of great faith," she wrote. "Many people didn't realize that because of the way he spoke." Maybe most importantly she wrote, "He told everyone he was a rich man because he had a large family who all loved him." That was Otto's wealth: the unconditional devotion of his children, a treasure that money cannot buy.

Helen was right about her father, and he revealed a small measure of the depth of his humanity as he was at my side on that night of passage.[1,2]

*A true friend is someone who thinks you are a good egg even though he knows you are cracked.*[1]

# Friend

I've known this man now for quite awhile, he's pretty straight forward, a fellow of little pretense and not much guile.

I can count many friends, in that I'm a lucky guy; I don't use the term best friend, rather like the "Brits." I think of him as first among equals, and here is why.

It's been fifty plus years since he first gave me a ride, I was ever grateful, it made me feel good inside.

We loved high school and other sports and he always came, I'm not sure we ever missed a game.

Old schools, all steps, nary a ramp for heavy wheelchairs; so get more guys, go up or down, they must have hauled me over 10,000 stairs!

Poker and bately, late nights and drinking too much, but he never failed me, he was there in the clutch.

We followed the Bears, but mostly the Cubs, those boys from

Chicago's' north side; each year they started out fast, but in the heat of summer they began their annual slide.

College, and marriage, and families to raise took us apart, but many fond memories I carried in my heart. High school reunions brought us together every five years, laughter, stories, happiness, never tears.

Now we're older, in our seventh decade, he's had some sorrow, that's made life's luster begin to fade.

He lives 2000 miles away, but we talk weekly, sometimes each day; for it's the Cubs once again  we cuss and discuss, why don't they win, is there simply no way?

Yes, this is a tale of friendship, that's for sure, but life-long loyalty is more what I mean; his brothers liked a cowboy star called Autry, and that's why they agreed to name him Gene.

# Our Old House

Black shutters, white shingles, and a wheelchair ramp with no rails, does it sit on a hill? That old house, a family gathering place, now silent, empty, and still.

Oh how quickly did the days fly away. Joy, and so much laughter, wasn't it just yesterday? But now a mother and father, growing older, and they're closing the doors, they're going away.

Gone are the hearts that made it sing, and now the rest, like blood and flesh from a living thing. From the attic and the basement out through the doors, as life, oozing from it's pores.

A piano and clocks, pictures and books, tables and chairs buckets, toys, dishes, crocks, and sleds. Out in the yard, under the trees, most everything heaped on tables, except the beds.

Piles and rows, a litany of lives. Tools and rakes and honey bee hives. How it all came here, where it will go, the stewards of yesterday and tomorrow, they will know.

Reminiscing, the auctioneer's bark, and tears from the sky, selling the memories from days gone bye. But a house is not a home, only wood and stone, for it's family, and time and all others alone.

To tell its story, what it means to all, happiness and sadness each heart will recall. A family, weary, and some trusted friends, in the gathering darkness, a fire, a few loose ends.

Rest then awhile you stalwart old one, for your time to shelter is not yet done. Smoke and haze, peaceful and yet forlorn, now silently waiting to be reborn.

# II

*College and a Brief
California Interlude*

A blind man was describing his favorite sport, parachuting. When asked how this was accomplished, he said that things were all done for him. "I am placed in the door with my Seeing Eye dog and told to jump. My hand is placed on my release ring for me, and out I go with the dog."

"But how do you know when you are going to land?" he was asked.

"I have a very keen sense of smell, and I can smell the trees and grass when I am three hundred feet from the ground," he answered.

"But how do you know when to lift your legs for the final arrival on the ground?" he was asked.

He quickly answered, "Oh, the dog's leash goes slack!"[1]

# Who Did You Say Was Driving That Car?

I RESTARTED MY COLLEGIATE career at Southern Illinois University, Carbondale, Illinois in the fall of 1959, after a one-semester disastrous flame-out at the University of Illinois in 1957. I have detailed the particulars of that academic and personal debacle elsewhere, in a personal memoir, so it's sufficient to say it wasn't a high point in my life.

I had encountered a new kind of disability culture that fall at Urbana-Champaign that I would describe as "the cult of the super gimp." Emanating from the folks who ran the disability services program and permeating the population of students with disabilities, a myth was perpetrated that disabled students were no different from the rest of the student body at the university. Well, in my view, that was unadulterated bullshit! I mean, who is kidding whom? Unfortunately, I was to learn later that my minority perception of the matter was not appreciated by the "cultists."

To be fair about the issue, maybe their concept of "equal" was meant to signal that as disabled students we had, like our AB (able-bodied) counterparts, transitioned away from Mom and Dad and had become fully functioning "gimpers." That sounds pretty good in

63

principle, but a disability can have a tendency to cause hardships and difficulties in activities of daily living, in social relationships, matters of energy, and the rigors of a fast-paced university environment. I'm not complaining about the fact of disability or loss of ability, as the other side of coin is that persons with disabilities will often have extraordinary attributes ascribed to them. And in fact the general public seems to have an insatiable appetite for "heroic" stories of unexpected achievement by disabled people: a paraplegic climbing a mountain (dragging himself over the ground to the top), blind folks who bowl, wheelchair racers doing the Boston Marathon, a double amputee swimming the English Channel, or other amazing physical feats. But the perception pendulum swings both ways, and there still exists a substantial reservoir of belief that folks with "crippled" bodies likely also have attending mental deficiencies, rendering them overall less capable than the so-called non-disabled population. But hold on, this isn't supposed to be a lecture on psychological aspects of disability; it's intended to be the story of a new beginning in my pursuit of higher education in the fall of 1959.

I had mostly repressed my failures and transgressions of two years earlier and was now a full-fledged student (although on academic probation) at Southern Illinois University. The academic year was a trimester system, but we referred to the sessions as fall, winter, and spring quarters. There was also an abbreviated summer session, which I think accounted for the "quarter" terminology. I did well academically in the fall and winter terms and by the spring quarter had regained most of my self-confidence and self-esteem, and I once again felt secure enough to engage in those non-classroom activities that had contributed so heavily to my earlier academic demise at the University of Illinois: namely, "partying" and poker! But I had learned from my past mistakes, and now I first met my academic responsibilities and then engaged in my favorite dissipation. The lady who was later to become my wife had not yet arrived on campus, and thus the focus of my life outside of the classroom and studying was fun and frolic. A glimpse of those carefree times, often of raucous and unabated frivolity, is also detailed in the memoir I mentioned previously.

One of my dormitory suite-mates (we shared a shower and toilet) that year was a wisecracking fellow named Charlie Brown! He was five foot four and weighed about 115 pounds, and his idioms and style of speaking easily led one to conclude he was from the hills of Tennessee or Kentucky, but he wasn't. Charlie was from Olney, in Central Illinois, home of a population of rare albino squirrels. Even more amazing, we thought, he was the nephew of the university president, Delyte Morris, who would later become a legendary administrator in higher education. Charlie's mother and Delyte were brother and sister, but beyond that fact I never learned (or asked) where he'd acquired what we labeled a hillbilly twang. I never met his parents, and I recall he rarely spoke of them.

Charlie had what only can be described as a prodigious capacity to drink beer; I don't mean for his slight build, but rather in comparison to all beer drinkers. He would often drink eight or ten beers in one sitting, and his behavior, demeanor, and notably his speech never changed. As a child he had tuberculosis, which affected his hip, permanently shortening one leg. He wore a three- or four-inch platform shoe. He walked with kind of a forward-leaning, rolling gait; again, no amount of alcohol affected his gait or his balance.

One evening at a local college beer joint, he introduced me to a couple of fellows, who were also true "sons of the suds." They, like Charlie, could consume large quantities of the elixir they called "barley pop." Dave was about six foot three, and Jerry was probably five foot eight or so; both guys were blind. They were seemingly inseparable, in the classroom, in bars, or walking across campus. I can't say we became fast friends, but I seemed to encounter them on a more regular basis in the cafeteria and in our complex of six residence halls called Thompson Point. They hired me as a reader, as in those days there were almost no classroom materials in any format but print. I read on tape for their later listening, and I read aloud to them, with them sometimes taking notes in Braille; eventually I graduated to reading midterm and then final course examinations.

Now, you will recall that I had earlier briefly discussed the idea that some folks (non-disabled) will at times ascribe particular characteristics or qualities to people with disabilities, simply because they are disabled. Well, I have to believe that was the case with most, if not all, of Dave and Jerry's instructors.

They must have assumed that a blind person acquired or developed an untarnished sense of honesty and integrity (along with a tremendous sense of smell and unmatched hearing acuity). Why else would they deliver the examinations to them, for me to read to them, unsupervised, in a tiny cubicle in the main campus library? Well, old Dave and Jerry were well prepared for these examinations, as they brought along all of their class notes as well as the textbooks. If they weren't sure of an answer, they would refer to their notes or have me check the book. When I asked them if they were supposed to have all these aids for the examination, they vehemently informed me that it was not my concern, as I was simply a hired hand, their eyes, and my question was inappropriate. I needed the money, so I didn't pursue the issue any further; I suppose, if I'm to be honest about the matter, maybe I was committing a sin of omission. They usually did quite well on exams I read for them!

Dave was born blind. His eyes were a milky white color, and

they fluttered continually, a condition call nystagmus. Interestingly, he never wore dark glasses to cover his eyes, which to some folks was a bit disconcerting.

Jerry, who had light perception, had lost his sight in the explosion of a firecracker he was holding in his hand. His standard line, if asked about the incident, was, "Yeah, it blew up and put the lights out." He had residual scarring on his face and hands from the blast, and he also never wore dark glasses.

One Friday afternoon Charlie and I had gone to the Rumpus Room, a favorite college beer bar, and as was always the case, the place became noisier, extremely crowded, and more rowdy as the day crept into the late evening hours. At some point Charlie and I met Dave and Jerry, and we decided we ought to drink the place dry!

Now, Carbondale was heavily influenced by the Southern Baptist churchgoing folks, as opposed to very few of those more liberal American Baptist slacker types. No dancing was allowed in the bar, but by 10:00 or 11:00 PM there were always a good number of comely coeds gyrating on tables, doing some pretty good imitations of a burlesque audition, all of which I described in lecherous detail to my two "blink" (disability nomenclature for blind people) friends.

Closing time was 1:00 AM; feeling no pain, the four of us were reluctant to call it a night. Charlie and I had taken a cab to the bar, but I don't recall how Dave and Jerry had arrived—maybe the bus. But now with the bar closing down, Charlie remarked, "Man, it's too bad we don't have wheels. You know, Skinheads east of Carbondale is open for a couple more hours." Skinheads was another college watering hole.

Jerry perked up, saying, "Hey, no problem. I have a car parked only two blocks from here."

Indeed, he did have a vehicle, and furthermore, he said he could drive it! He was fourteen or fifteen years old when he lost his eyesight. He lived in a small Iowa town and learned, or relearned, to drive out of necessity, transporting his younger siblings around the town, with them giving him verbal instructions to guide him.

Jerry continued, "I'll drive you guys to Skinheads."

"No way," Charlie and I responded.

But he continued to insist that he was sober. And as Dustin Hoffman's character assured his brother in the movie *Rain Man*, Jerry told us, "Guys, I am an excellent driver."

We finally relented, and Jerry clambered behind the wheel, with Charlie riding shotgun. Dave and I were in the back of the four-door sedan, and I wondered what was to happen. He was obviously very familiar with the controls in the car, and he drove us the ten miles east on the two-lane main highway, with Charlie describing the roadway. Jerry was amazingly adept at interpreting Charlie's verbal commands to stop, go, turn left or right, begin to veer right or left, or a little more left or right, and so on.

The entire trip out of town went very smoothly, with the exception of one potential glitch. At the last stoplight heading out of Carbondale, we had to stop at a red light. Wouldn't you know it, a city police car pulled up next to us to make a left turn when the light changed.

"For God's sake," Charlie hissed quietly, "there's a squad car on your left."

"What are they doing?" Jerry asked, looking at Charlie.

"Jesus Christ, man, they are looking at you."

"Really?" said Jerry, and he turned to face them and waved with a broad grin on his face.

"Oh, no," gasped Charlie. "What the hell are you doing?"

But the cops only waved back, smiled, and made the left when the light turned green.

Notwithstanding his already-demonstrated high level of skill in driving, we didn't allow him to drive on the return trip to Carbondale at about 4:00 AM. He protested, of course, but Charlie handled the situation quite diplomatically, I thought.

"Now, look, Jerry," he said. "Being blind and driving is one thing, but being blind drunk is quite another matter!"

That was the only occasion that I rode with Jerry. I don't recall whether I had any other opportunities; maybe one time was enough for me.

But after arriving home safely at my residence hall, there was still a bit more to the story. After my newfound drinking buddies dumped me into bed and went noisily on their way, my stomach began to churn and my head to spin. I assume that the twelve-hour beer binge had a lot to do with the rapid onset of nausea. I quickly got up, slipped on only a pair of slacks, got into my wheelchair, and headed out across campus for a predawn cooling-off run. I lost control of the chair, freewheeling down a steep incline in Thompson Point Woods, and ended up in a muddy and very soft ditch at the bottom of the hill. I wasn't injured, but the doctor at the emergency room, quite disgusted with me (I'd guess because of my evening of dissipation), nevertheless made me stay the rest of the morning in the hospital. Rather embarrassingly, the student newspaper carried the story under the headline WHEELCHAIR CRASHES and included my name.

Jerry would later chastise me, barking, "Kent, it's guys like you who reinforce the belief that blind and disabled people can't drive safely. Maybe we need to do a story in the paper about that trip to Skinheads." We convinced him that we couldn't do the story because he didn't have a driver's license!

*A man was walking down the street when he heard a voice say, "Pssst ... you, come over here!"*

*He looked around and could see no one but an old, mangy greyhound.*

*"Yes, over here," said the greyhound. " Look at me! I'm tied up here. I should be racing. I won fourteen races in my career."*

*The man thought to himself, Oh, my god, a talking dog! I have to have it. It will make me rich! TV appearances and cabaret bookings!*

*So he went in search of the owner. He found the owner and said, "I'd like to buy your dog. Is he for sale?"*

*"No, mate, you don't want that old moth-eaten thing."*

*"But I do," insisted the man. "I'll give you a thousand pounds for him."*

*"Okay," said the owner, "but I think you're making a terrible mistake."*

*Handing over the money, the man asked, "Why do you think that?"*

*The owner replied, "Because that dog is a bloody liar. It never won a race in its life!"[1]*

# California Dog Days

MY WIFE AND I once had a dog named Harry. He was a tricolor black, brown, and white beautiful specimen of the so-called African barkless dog, the basenji.

After completing my master's degree in 1965 at Southern Illinois University (Carbondale, Illinois), we packed all our worldly goods into our trusty 1962 two-door Chevrolet Impala and set out for California, if not to seek fame, hopefully to find fortune. We were much younger then, maybe a bit foolish, and obviously a lot more courageous than we are in the year 2012.

We set out on that five-day cross-country trip with no cell phone, a single gasoline credit card, and no specific itinerary other than our final destination, the home of the Silvas, my sister and brother-in-law, in Santa Clara, California. Most motel accommodations were not wheelchair accessible, and we had no contingency plans in the event of a major vehicle breakdown; but we forged onward and, I think with greater powers riding shotgun, we arrived intact.

Sometime shortly before we left Carbondale, after I had finished my degree, we happened upon a fellow walking three quite unusual-looking dogs. Neither Marlys nor I had ever seen this particular breed before, but we were shortly to learn that the dogs were basenjis, and while the three dogs were unique, so too was the fellow who had them in tow. I didn't know the guy, but I had seen him frequently on campus. I knew he was a graduate student, I guessed in philosophy, and on this day, as was often the case, he was wearing a long, tattered, heavy brown overcoat. He was quite tall and rotund, with a mop of unruly red hair; a broad, cherubic smile; and eyes that seemed to constantly revolve in their sockets; and we both assumed that he was extremely intelligent. We stopped our car, leaned out the window, and asked him about the dogs. He was indeed an expert on the basenji breed, and he was very accommodating, launching into an extensive lecture on the origins, habits, and characteristics of these feisty, assertive, and handsome little canines, adding a bit of folklore. He told us, and we also observed, that they were very muscular animals, about seventeen to eighteen inches at the shoulder. They weighed twenty-four to twenty-five pounds and had erect, pointed ears; a slim, nicely shaped, somewhat elongated muzzle; a wrinkled forehead; a smooth, short coat; a tail that curled tightly over the back; and almond-shaped eyes. He proceeded to detail their finer qualities: they were extremely intelligent; they didn't shed; they were very fastidious, cleaning themselves almost like cats; and they were essentially odorless, attributed to an evolutionary charac-teristic that prevented their detection and subsequently becoming a meal for larger animals (big cats) in their African habitat. The dogs were also called tireless, as they had tremendous stamina and could literally run for miles in pursuit of faster small game, which eventu-ally fell victim to exhaustion. As we listened to his informative spiel and watched the dogs dancing, prancing, and yodeling at us, we both decided independently that one day we would own a basenji.

He concluded his informative lecture on the basenji, and appar-ently noting our rapt attention, he began a monologue on the birds he owned. With a wide, pleasant grin he began, "Now, I also have thirty-two caged birds in my home."

Oh, my, I thought, he probably has unlimited knowledge on all of his birds and is willing to share it all with us. We thanked him for the information regarding the basenjis and politely excused ourselves.

Our sidewalk expert in Carbondale had been very convincing, as not long after arriving in California and getting settled in our first apartment just off Stevens Creek Boulevard in San Jose, we purchased our first basenji. Her name was Sassy, or at least that's what we called her at home; but among the more sophisticated AKC (American Kennel Club) dog show crowd (that is, dog snobs), she was known by the somewhat more regal-sounding name Africannas Sassy Lass!

Her name fit her well, as she was a sassy little rascal. She was a trim red-and-white female, a bitch in proper dog show parlance. We bought her that autumn 1965 from a man named Bob Mankey, a major player in the Northern California dog show circuit. A year later we acquired our tricolor male, Harry, from a colorful lady named Lyla Yocum, who not only bred basenjis, but additionally had a good number of dogs that she showed. Lyla, like Mankey, was terribly competitive, as she expected that her dogs could win every show; second place wasn't on her list of acceptable alternatives.

With Sassy now a year old, we ventured into the arena of the dog show world. The objective of the shows we entered, confirmation class (how well the animal conformed to the standard for that breed), was to earn points toward the ultimate goal of being certified as a champion of the breed. Fifteen points were required to reach that lofty goal, and a different number of points was earned for each win. The more dogs in the class, the higher the points, up to a maximum of three points (termed a major win, usually referred to as simply a major) for one show.

Also, I recall, your dog (male animal) or bitch (female animal) had to have two three-point wins (two majors) in the total of fifteen.

That meant your animal could win, say a hundred one-point shows, but absent the holy grail of two three-point wins, alas, your dog or bitch was a mere pretender, an also-ran, a common mutt! Thus, losing a match that carried the much lusted-after three-point win could cause gnashing of teeth and despondency, but also some unexpected hilarity. At one show, Lyla's male dog did not place first in a group that awarded three points to the winner. Her dog, Fearless Festus, actually the grandfather of our male, Harry, needed one more major to become a champion, but he finished second, which really annoyed Lyla. As she huffily stomped out of the ring, she asked the judge, "Why did Fearless not win? He's a beautiful specimen."

"Well," the fellow replied, "his testicles don't hang level with one another."

"Oh, really?" snapped Lyla. "I'll bet yours don't either!"

The judge, speechless, looked stunned, and a smattering of snickers was quite audible from among the onlookers.

Lyla was an expert handler and very knowledgeable of the breed. She had beautiful animals, but her dogs (or bitches) were not the cuddly family-pet variety. In the show ring, old Fearless Festus behaved like a newborn lamb, but once his appearance before the judge was completed and he exited the ring, he sat silent and sullen, probably hoping that someone would touch him, which, in his apparently hostile mind, was sufficient cause to relieve the offending hand of a finger or two. He really was a ferocious little cuss, maybe even a bit vicious, and folks who knew his temperament gave him plenty of "dog space"!

Harry, our dog, of course had a fancy AKC name, Harama Tamu, which supposedly was Swahili for "sweet bandit." I don't recall if we ever verified the translation, but the dog show sophisticates thought it was a cool name, so if it was untrue, we continued the facade. He was a sweet dog, and he adored my wife, Marlys. Each year he seemed to take his self-appointed role as protector of Marlys more seriously; he was so diligent as the family defender, particularly of Marlys, that at some point he acquired the nickname "Hector Protector"! He most assuredly carried the genes of Festus and would eventually demonstrate that power of heredity.

Now, among the dog show crowd there are many really good people—maybe most of them are. But early on we discovered that some of the owners, breeders, and handlers at the shows were simply snobs. For unknown reasons, being participants in these AKC-sanctioned shows (some held at plush resorts like Del Monte in Pebble Beach) and owning purebred dogs, especially if the animal was a champion, made a few folks insufferable. It occurred to me that sometimes these wannabe blue-blood pretenders behaved as if they were attending Ascot in England and were waiting for the queen and all the other royals to appear; never mind that they had the wrong country and the wrong animals, and some of them were likely descendants of "white trash."

Everyone always brought their newly acquired dogs to the shows to parade them around and, pardon the pun, show off. Appropriate etiquette was to first inquire about the dog's bloodline, and then, after a few mandatory oohs and aahs, ask the dog's name. Simply to be antagonistic, I always said that our male dog's name was just plain Harry! The name was usually somewhat difficult for the more elite types to handle, and it generally served to extinguish any further inane discussion of dog names.

If I was feeling particularly ornery or bored, I might tell the inquiring soul that in honor of my German heritage, we had considered naming him after an obscure old German actor born in 1862, whose name was Gustav von Seyffertitz, as phonetically I thought it had an interesting sound.

We got into the dog show scene quite accidentally. One day at a veterinary office with our bitch, Sassy, I met a fellow named Ron, who had a beautiful male basenji in tow. He looked Sassy over carefully and observed that he thought she might develop into a really good standard of the breed. He was showing the male for a family, and before we left the vet's office, we agreed to meet and talk about dog shows. Thus began the saga of our "California Dog Days."

Ron and his wife, Betty, had four children and lived in a modest home, and Ron was an extremely capable technician in the booming Silicon Valley industry. On the surface they appeared to be a typical middle-class California family, except that Ron oversaw all aspects of the family and household as if he were in charge of a military compound and his role was that of a master drill sergeant! He was bright and extremely conservative (he had me listen to John Birch tapes), he probably never compromised his ideas or views on any topic, and he said absolutely whatever he was thinking. His beliefs and ideas on politics, religion, and "right and wrong" were cast in concrete, and if he was agitated or questioned about his views, he would defend his thinking fiercely, with extensive information and substantial data to support his arguments. He could be a formidable adversary if one challenged him. By contrast, his wife, Betty, was a sweet, gentle lady who understood her role in the family and rarely, if ever, took issue with Ron; at least we never witnessed her openly contradicting his decisions.

In my view, some of Ron's shenanigans were almost legendary. He banked at Wells Fargo and noted on his monthly statement that a minimal fee had been charged to his account. He took great exception to the charge, as he had not authorized the withdrawal from his account. Failing to resolve the matter with bank officials, he proceeded to station himself in the bank lobby and began yelling loudly that this Wells Fargo bank had stolen his money and would likely take other patrons' funds as well. Amazingly they didn't call the police, and after he agreed to stop shouting, they agreed to restore the amount of the small fee to his account.

We began to attend dog shows all over the Bay Area. We went to Sunnyvale, Monterrey, San Jose, Daly City, Cupertino, Petaluma, Santa Rosa, Santa Clara, San Francisco, and as far afield as Stockton, always in the company of Ron, Betty, and their children.

Initially we entered Sassy in "puppy" matches to gain experience and be trained for later AKC-sanctioned shows. Betty, Ron's wife, handled Sassy. The dog (oh, I mean "bitch") did mature into a beautiful specimen and won two majors at Stockton and Santa Clara, six points towards the fifteen to be certified as a champion. We left California before she became a champion, but clearly she would have reached that goal.

Dog shows could really become a drag. For example, if the basenji class was held at 8:00 AM, say in Santa Rosa, we had to leave San Jose at 6:00 AM; if our animal won its class competition (all basenjis), the competition for all hound breeds might not be held until 3:00 that afternoon. That meant seven hours of waiting, "passing gas," telling lies, avoiding dog poop, and pretending you really were glad you were there! I don't recall a single show in which a basenji won the hound group competition. It seemed to me that the larger hounds always won, like an Afghan, a greyhound, a huge Irish wolfhound, or even a borzoi, but never a beagle, a dachshund, or a basenji. Much to my wife's dismay, every time our dog didn't win, I would make disparaging remarks about the wining dog, the handler, and the judge. After spending the whole day waiting and then watching your dog being eliminated in a matter of minutes, it was hard to take. If the handlers were rich old dudes or "dudesses," I'd accuse them of paying off the judge; if the handler was a foxy young chick, I'd assert that the judge (if a guy) had spent more time looking at the hooters on the gal than checking for good alignment of the teats on the bitch. Yes, I was a sore loser! Then the show was over for our animal, and it was two more hours to get back home.

Boring as the shows could be, there was always the possibility of the unexpected occurring with our friend Ron on the scene, like on a trip to Daly City. We were south of San Francisco on a five- or six-lane highway, jam-packed with traffic, with Ron and his family several cars ahead us of at a stoplight. The light turned green, but several rows of cars didn't start moving; horns began honking, and suddenly Marlys gasped, "Oh, my god, it's Ron!" Indeed it was Ron, outside of his beautifully restored old Cadillac, in the middle of the highway, bobbing and weaving like a boxer, apparently challenging the driver in a car stopped behind him to come out and fight. Now, Ron was very muscular and in excellent physical condition, and I thought, *Well, I'll be damned—he reminds me of Carl "Bobo" Olson* (a great middleweight fighter of that era). Well, the guy didn't exit his car, and we learned later that Ron had gotten pissed because he felt the guy was tailgating him. There was another memorable freeway escapade, which we didn't witness, but we heard the entire story. Again a fellow was tailgating (according to Ron) in heavy rush-hour traffic on El Camino Boulevard in Santa Clara. Ron stopped dead, walked to the rear of his car, opened the trunk, and invited the startled motorist, "Now, go ahead. Drive into my trunk." Ron told me the guy cussed at him and then "the SOB flipped me off," which of course led Ron to assume his best pugilistic posture and invite the guy to come out and do battle. The motorist swore at Ron again, rolled up his window, and locked the car doors; undeterred, Ron leaped up onto the roof of the guy's car and began jumping up and down like a crazed human jackhammer! I really don't know how Ron avoided being arrested and hauled off to the slammer for his (I'll be kind) unorthodox public outbursts, but to my knowledge he never did.

In retrospect, the many dog shows we attended with Ron, Betty, and their four children were really fun times and provided lasting memories of our relatively brief stay in California. Either shortly before we left for Arizona or soon after we arrived in Tucson, Ron and Betty had another surprise for us. We had become accustomed to Ron being unconventional, but Ron told us that he and Betty were switching marriage partners with their friends Dick and Wilma, we were floored! So now it was Ron and Wilma and Dick and Betty! Later, when I was living in Tucson, I spoke by telephone with Ron regarding the status of the switch in partners. I don't recall any discussion of divorce and remarrying, which I assumed would be the case, but then again maybe they just agreed on a period of non-binding boinking. With his characteristic cackle, Ron stated that for both couples the results would best be described as "so far, so good." I'm not sure we ever had contact with either of the couples, and for all I know they are still living happily ever after.

We left California in the summer of 1967 for Tucson, Arizona, where I was to begin doctoral studies at the University of Arizona. It was the time of the so-called six-day war between Israel and Egypt, and it took us half that time (three days) just to reach Tucson. Sassy never became a champion, as there were very few shows in Tucson or in surrounding communities. While we were in California, there seemed to be a show almost every weekend; in Arizona it was difficult to find one show a month. We also didn't have the time, money, or motivation to continue pursuit of the certification.

Harry matured into a powerfully built, beautiful specimen of a classic male basenji. We had entered him only in puppy matches in California, as he was not old enough for the AKC shows. He became devoted to Marlys, and it soon became apparent that he was of the lineage of old Fearless Festus. We landed in a seventy-dollar-a-month run-down rental house with a leaky roof, cracked concrete block walls (we could see daylight from the outside), and an ancient cooling system, in a neighborhood of transient, often unsavory, types. Marlys was home alone most days, as I was off attending class or working at my part-time job. Our address was 3946 East Lee Street, and strangely the mail, not only for our house, but also for the five dilapidated rentals behind us, was all delivered to a single box mounted on our house by the front door. A rather seedy dude living in one of the rentals began to tarry a bit after picking up his mail, and then one day he peeked around the door into our house through the flimsy screen door. But he didn't realize that each time he came to pick up his mail, Harry quietly moved to a spot just out of sight by the door. The second occasion the fellow leaned over to look in, Harry lunged at the screen door, emitting an enraged, blood-curdling roar that caused the guy to stagger backward and drop his mail. Harry made no more sound, just silently watched him as he quickly retrieved his letters and sprinted away; he never again peeked into the house.

Harry and Sassy had a litter of puppies, and we sold one to a young woman named Paula, who was a classmate of mine at the university. She became so enamored with the breed that she asked us if she could handle Harry in dog shows. We agreed, and she began training Harry for an upcoming show in Tucson.

As she gained confidence, she became more assertive in disciplining him, and one afternoon Harry took exception to her methods. He didn't bite her, but he scared the holy bejesus out of the three of us with his ferocious roar and lightning-quick ability to gain an advantage. Paula decided to change her training tactics, and she became very cautious and much more gentle with the choke chain. Harry approved, and they got along very well from then on.

I recall her enthusiasm and excitement the day Harry was to make his debut in the Arizona dog show circuit. She left with high hopes, knowing they would win; and her confidence was not misplaced, as Harry was a wonderful representative of the breed. We decided not to attend the show, so as not to be a potential distraction for Harry. When Paula and Harry returned home, he was frisky and delighted to be back, but Paula was downtrodden, almost in tears. Harry had bitten the judge! He was doing splendidly, Paula reported, until the guy grabbed Harry's privates. In a flash he whirled and chomped down on the offending fingers, and with equal rapidity he was summarily booted from the show ring.

While Harry was a true grandson of old Fearless, inheriting his assertiveness, he had missed out on the self-control gene that Festus was able to turn on when he was in the ring. That day was not only Harry's inaugural appearance in pursuit of becoming a champion, it also was the day we decided that the wiser course would be to retire him from any further exposure to episodes of gonad groping.

And so ended the short, happy dog show career of our loyal protector, Harama Tamu, the "sweet bandit" also known as Harry.[2]

*A familiar passage in the King James version of the Bible, the 121st Psalm, reads, " I will lift up mine eyes unto the hills, from whence cometh my help. My help cometh from the Lord, which made heaven and earth."*

*Even if one is a Christian believer, questions can still remain as to how, when, and in what way we will recognize the hand of the Almighty. Who can tell what hearts He may stir to come to our aid?*

# *Helping Hands*

My FIRST FULL-TIME JOB after completing my master's degree at Southern Illinois University in 1965 was as a rehabilitation counselor at Goodwill Industries in San Jose, California. Now, 46 Race Street, where my office was located in San Jose, was not what would be described as an upscale neighborhood. It was a tough part of town, and the office was next door to a wholesale meat-cutting establishment that bathed the entire block in greasy raw-meat odors. The area, a low-rent district, was inhabited by a collection of the flotsam and jetsam of beleaguered humanity: the homeless and street people. One sunny morning as I was leaving the office to do a follow-up visit with a client, I was to become the recipient of unexpected *help*. I sensed that I was in trouble the moment I spotted the two unkempt, dirty derelicts staggering up the sidewalk toward me as I loaded my wheelchair into the backseat of my '62 Chevy. I had loaded the chair literally thousands of times into this vehicle and had the process down pat. Open the door, transfer to the passenger seat, tilt the bucket seat forward, reach out and fold the chair, lift the front end and wheels, and, using the door frame as leverage, pull the chair into the backseat in a relatively easy motion.

But when those two chaps spotted me and realized what I was doing, they lunged forward and yelled, slurring, "Hold on, buddy! We'll help you!"

*Oh, no,* I thought. "Oh, that's okay, fellas. I can manage."

"No, no, no, we'll help."

They both arrived simultaneously at the open door and stumbled into the forward-tilted bucket seat, nearly knocking me onto the floor. They began to wrestle with the chair, arms flailing, pushing and shoving, staggering, slipping, working against each other, and making little progress getting the chair into the car.

"Hold on, guys. Let me show you how to tilt the front of the chair up so it will clear the door sill," I offered. Frantically I grabbed the chair and lifted the front end at the same instant my two helpers decided that one coordinated shove would get the chair in place. It did, and it also ripped a triangular hole in the fabric of the new seat covers, gouged a couple of nickel-sized chips of paint off the door-frame, severely jammed my thumb, and sent both of them halfway into the backseat.

"There you are, bud," they exclaimed gleefully as they got themselves upright.

I felt sick to my stomach and was close to hyperventilating from the pain in my hand; I thought my thumb might be broken. I was able to compose myself and said rather weakly, "Gosh, thanks. Here's a dollar for your help."

They appeared shocked for a moment, but then they chorused in unison, "Oh, no." They shoved the dollar back to me and feverishly rummaged through their pockets, producing a handful of grimy, sticky coins that I counted later; the amount was seventy-three cents. "You take this, bud. It might come in handy."

I was so startled that before I could respond, they abruptly turned, arms over each other's shoulders, and lurched away, chattering like two intoxicated magpies high on pyracantha berries!

What a disaster—torn seat covers, chipped paint, and a thumb and hand that would be tender (not broken) for several weeks.

It was a toss-up as to whether the alcohol on their breaths or their rather rancid body odor was more potent, but no matter. They departed in high spirits, sure in their hearts that they had come to the aid of a disabled fellow in need that bright, sunny morning. After that encounter with those two vagabonds of the streets, I never failed to carefully scan up and down Race Street to ensure that there were no potential "helpers" in the area.

I think God has a sense of humor. One can never tell what manner of souls He will send as good Samaritans in our hour of need.

# III

*Minnesota Summers*

# The Truman Cafe

Truman is a rather nice place to spend the summertime, days are carefree, no axes to grind, life is relaxed, it's almost sublime. It reminds one of a time now past, the purpose of these small towns disappearing fast.

Once there was thousands of these vibrant places, centers of commerce and everyone had familiar faces. Nestled away in the heartland of the nation, rhythms and a pace that is somewhat slow, hard-working plain speaking folks, who don't go for show.

And in this town called Truman, at the Truman Cafe, they often speak of corn and beans and sometimes hay. It's a pleasant old cafe with quite tasty food, and the folks you meet are seldom rude.

For many, it's one of their daily stops, for coffee, a meal, some gossip or talk of crops. There is great comfort in familiar things, that's some of the best a small town brings.

Family, a parade, the flag, a wedding dance, and a little known secret, a game of chance. It's a game with dice and "liars" is its name; two bits, a touch of larceny and you're in the game.

There are the usual suspects who always play; Art and Bud, Carl, Chuck, Kent, Herk and Roger are there each day. Sometimes Jerry and Gerald, David, Eldor and John, and Jim and Dean, also make the scene. They're all sort of mellow fellows, and even when they lose they don't get too mean.

Guile and cunning, with a little luck, is the key to how you win, don't get distracted cause the banter and barbs can prick your skin. Anyone of the fellows is apt to win, but only now and then. Yet one crafty old dude seems to win again and again.

It's Herk, that's what he's called, but that's not his name, but he's a sly old fox and dice is his game. Sometimes your luck is mighty lame, three "horses" and you're out of the game.

Herk wins so much, is it the help of an unknown force? When he does lose, the table might all chorus, " holy cow, Herk finally got his third horse!"

You'll not go broke at this simple game, nor gain notoriety or even fame. But here's to the boys who step up to the plate, win or lose they always handle their fate.

Well that's a short tale of this little place, where almost everyone knows your face. Try it one day, it's really quite nice, salve for the soul and a game of dice.

# The Truth of It

Now Carl Jung was a very smart man, born over a hundred years ago in Switzerland. He had theories few thought true, that we can inherit behavior, you know what we do.

His teacher was Freud, that wild old guy, but behavior through the genes, hey that's pie-in-the-sky. Then, eureka, like a bolt from the blue, I discovered what Jung said was probably true.

Reflecting in the solitude of a Midwest dawn, I realized there is a gene for mowing lawn! For years I had asked, sometimes quite brash, why is everyone always mowing grass?

In swirling dust, it's 95, and storms men should fear, still they'll be out there on a Snapper or Deere. Yes life was good, the grass was green, non-stop mowing, what an idyllic scene.

But alas and alack, the winds turned dry, no rain fell from that aluminum sky. The grass turned brown from lack of rain, mowers were silent, there was genuine pain.

People were listless, they lost their spunk, holy cow, the whole county was in a funk. For mowing lawns and acres more is not an option, it's deep within our core.

As air and water are essential to grow, so life has no quality if we can't mow. Many prayed, and the good Lord sent rain, and mowing at a frenetic pace, began again.

When I was young and not so wise, I thought mowing an obsession in disguise. Shaving lawns and roadsides too, was simply "what one ought to do."

But truth, as for all, has set me free, so I'm getting a 4-foot Wheelhorse and going on a spree. Remember my friends, if you've got the blahs and are feeling low, take heart, crank up that engine, *you need to mow!*

# Crocks

Some folks lust after Red Wing crocks, what they will spend can put you in shock. Why is it they will pay such atrocious prices? Tis a weakness of mankind, one of our mortal vices.

Oh what folly, that for simple clay, we will empty our wallets without delay. Muscles can twitch, your mouth will drool, the need to possess them is downright cruel.

Deep is the passion, how dearly some yearn, for a crock, a bowl, or a butter churn. Alas for me, I, to, am under the spell. Who has bewitched us, was it Beelzebub, that monarch of hell?

I began my quest only a few years past, and there's so much to buy I'm simply aghast. Not only crocks, but jugs, bowls, pitchers, all manner of ware, hard like rock, yet fragile if dropped, oh goodness handle with care.

Now others made crockery you'd find on a farm, but it's the Red Wing that carries a mysterious charm. Why do we covet such cold hard stone? That need, each person, decides alone.

I speak not for others why they desire these things, as for me, it's the memories each one brings. They awaken remembrances of those who've left earthly toil, our ancestors, mostly people of the soil.

So it's part of my heritage, these vessels of clay, essential for living and used each day. Pickles and lard and pork in brine, plump wild grapes for dark sweet wine.

Families and friends, in harmony, lending a hand, storing the bounty of our precious land. Witness to a time that has passed away, oh that they could speak, what would they say?

# Different Names, Special Places

Minnesota is where we hang our hats, about three months at a time; And if there's no fishing or antique sale, what's to do but make a rhyme.

The peace and tranquility is good for the soul, just wandering the countryside with nary a goal. In the south of the state it's corn and beans, and of course everything green. Ritual sameness and a slower pace sprinkle harmony over this idyllic scene.

Wandering alone, sometimes distant, but mostly near, I heard a whisper or a voice that had no sound. Ah, now it's clear what I'm told, there's something unique here, that I should know, it's the name of the town.

Could it be that I've been so blind, why this thought had never come to mind? So for each small town I wrote a rather silly verse. I'd guess some folks will chuckle or laugh, but others, not amused, might even curse.

Let's see, there is *Butternut* and *Butterfield* and a town called *Frost*, leave the main highway and you'll surely get lost. *Odin* and *Ormsby*, they're so close, stand on one main street and the other you will see. *Imogene, Lydia, Petersburg* and *Hector* are all quite small, names of people, and the buildings aren't tall. *Good Thunder, Sleepy Eye,* and *Mankato* we all know, Indian names, so lyrical, the words seem to flow.

Directions are good they fit nicely this refrain; there's *West Sveadahl,* and a place called *East Chain. South Branch,* where we were married is a tiny spot, but about a town named *North Branch* I don't know a lot.

*Godahl, Grogan* and *Guckeen* seem like guttural German in my mind, and speaking of krauts, isn't the town of *Kiester* a term for one's behind?

I said Sri Lanka is the name you must take for this town, don't you folks know that *Ceylon* is quite out of date; they smiled politely and suggested it better for me to leave the state.

Still some names are quite a mystery to me, shouldn't there be "crocodile" before *Dundee*? And I always thought *Granada* was a ballad and *Waldorf* a tasty salad. *Blue Earth* isn't, it's black and brown, and what is *Dar-fur,* some fine down?

Oh I think it's time to finish this frivolous story, but don't you wish we knew these towns past glory? They say we're all welcome in *Welcome,* but I've got to run, I'm heading to *Truman* for a summer of fun. Quaint and nostalgic are these places I roam, quiet solitude and a sense of home.

# Robin Sense

I once heard a short little verse that went;
"Thoity doity boids, sittin on a coib, choiping and boiping
and eatin doity oit woims."
That lingo is "Brooklynese" I'd guess.
Thirty birds, gobs of worms, holy feathers, what
A mess!
You've seen these perky fellows, with round orange tummies,
Always on the lookout for some tasty yummies.
Of course, it's Mr. Robin Red Breast,
Chirping and burping throughout the Midwest.
Now they can't all be "Misters," but how do you check?
Take a peek when they bend over to peck!
Then could you tell a girl from a guy?
Hmm, strange to think that someone might try.
Watch them awhile, they stop-look-listen,
Not for a train, they do it a lot, right after a rain.
They never walk, always run or hop, in Minnesota Talk
It's a "little lunch" is why they stop.
They freeze like stone, don't turn around, listening
Carefully for the faintest sound.
Cock their head, tilt that tail, line up that beak
As hard as a nail.
A rapier strike with the speed of light,
Grass and debris flying left and right.
Pity that crawler, so snug in his "rug,"

He's ripped from the dirt with a mighty tug!
Now in the Midwest Robins abound,
But in the Southwest, they ain't around.
Why no Robins in that hot, dry land?
Oh, I think it was Mother Nature's plan.
Simple to say, it's the dirt you see.
Sand and clay, the natives call Ca-li-che.
It comes in layers that's hard as stone,
Whack it with a pick and it'll jar your bones.
No crawler, bug or mammal could dig a hole,
None I can think of, well now, maybe a mighty tough mole.
Caliche's tough, grows neither weeds or grass
But Robins are clever they're not brash.
These birds know there are no worms in hot dry sand,
So who would leave the Midwest, that idyllic land?
Only a "bird-brain" might want to roam,
Be wise, stay at home, don't leave that deep, dark loam.
Dirt and grass full of worms,
Everywhere they turn something squirms.

# The Reminiscence Bell

I bought a bell today, from deep in the rural Minnesota countryside. Odd, I thought, to want this cup-shaped thing, and further what joy could it possibly bring?

As I pondered and gazed upon this bell, I chanced to think of a lady I once knew, who's name was Vernelle. Ah, then I understood, what I had found was a reminiscence bell!

It's a small golden bell and it's song was so clear, yes, it will remind me of many whom I once held dear.

For when we ring this enchanted bell, it will rekindle names from the past and salve our souls with gentle memories we wish to hold fast.

For my Mother, my Father a bright young lad named Rick, now all gone, oh so quick. And my friend from Nippon, the land of the Rising Sun, for Masako told me that Yoshimichi's life now was done.

There are many more that we could name, most as me, just ordinary, but some of fame, let us not forget them, twould be a shame. So harken my friends to the song of the bell, a reminder to all of a story to tell. For it is true, don't we know, it's ordained from birth, that from this life we must go.

And today, as you sing, work, or play, listen for the bell, you may hear it at the break of day. It can brighten your spirit as you find your way.

Each day, in this journey of life, is a gift for both woman and man, so we must use every one as best we can. For remember my friends there's coming a day, we cannot see, when the bell will toll for thee and me.

# IV

*Fishing*

*There was a story reported by Ripley's Believe It or Not concerning a man who could hypnotize fish. Upon hearing the tale, a thoughtful fellow pondered three questions. First he wondered how it was done. Secondly, how do you determine that the fish is actually hypnotized? And third, he thought, why would anyone bother to do such a thing?*

# The Garage

HERBERT WEST ANDERECK WAS his name, but everyone called him "Hub." He was my uncle, married to my mother's only sister, Esther. I got to know him well during what amounted to an on-the-job training stint as a bookkeeper at his Chevrolet dealership (Andereck Chevrolet) in the small village of Juda, Wisconsin. I was embarking in a new direction, as I had not lasted a semester of my initial year of college (fall 1957) at the University of Illinois. I was summarily dismissed, expelled, or kicked out (take your pick) for, among other transgressions, an abysmal grade point average of .767. An "A" was an average of 4.0, and a "D" was a 1.0 average. You get the message. The only positive spin I could put on the matter would be to point out that I had an "F+" average. I won't go into any gory details (I did in another book), and the only disclaimer I could add, à la Benny Hill, the rowdy English comedian, would be "It wasn't all my fault."

So now it's 1959, and I'm a fallen warrior hiding out in a small town, licking my wounds, trying to learn the rudiments of the General Motors Acceptance Corporation (GMAC) accounting system from my aunt. My job was to balance the receipts and expenses for the day. All transactions were recorded on a cash register tape that seemed to be fifteen to twenty feet long by the close of business.

I often wondered if the job had been created with the objective of helping me salvage some vestige of my ego and self-worth. My parents kept me busy around home, doing what I could, but working at the garage was an actual job. Whatever the case, Esther was a great teacher who rarely, if ever, made an error, and she had an uncanny sense for discovering the source of any discrepancy in the tape. For example, if we were ten to twenty-five cents off, she had long before my arrival figured out that Hub had filched some change from the till to get himself a Baby Ruth or an Almond Joy.

They paid me fifty cents an hour, probably more than I was worth, but eventually I got the hang of the job and could usually balance the tape. It was during the early stages of my on-the-job training when I realized that Hub was an avid fisherman. In fact the town was filled with guys who seemed to be off fishing multiple times each week. My office—that is, the desk I worked at—faced the main intersection of the town, and through the large, almost floor-to-ceiling windows, I could observe the majority of both pedestrian and vehicular traffic through town. Early on during my tenure at Andereck Chevrolet, I noted a daily parade of cars and pickups with long cane poles in the beds of the trucks or protruding from car windows. The more sophisticated of the anglers (usually meaning the younger guys) most often carried rods and reels as their weapons of choice. Hub was an exception to the older cane pole crowd, as he had multiple rods and reels.

Almost invariably, anytime someone had a good day fishing, they ended up at the garage to show off their catch. They were always a bit coy and evasive in telling the assembly of locals exactly where (I mean what bend in the river or creek) and what bait or lure had done the most damage. Some of the more notable local fisherman were fellows with good German names (maybe some claimed Swiss ancestry) like Fritz Goebli (also his wife, Esther), Art Ludwig, Johnny Wuetrich (and his wife, Leola), Glen "Peg" Dunwidde, Wayne Vanderbilt, Eddie Jordan, Wayne Gempler, Hank Norder, Uncle Hub, and a mechanic who worked at the garage, Orlin Haas. Each one of them was quite unique, having been steeped in the spirit and woven in the fabric of small-town rural America. I really didn't know most of them that well, but it seems evident that each one of them was fodder worthy of a chapter in a volume of unforgettable souls.

Orlin, Hub's mechanic, was one of the most accomplished cussers I have ever encountered. His everyday speech patterns were punctuated with a barrage of profanity. He didn't have an extensive or diverse repertoire of curse words; rather, he relied on old, reliable expletives such as "hell," "damn," "shit," "son of a bitch," "bullshit," "Jesus Christ," and "goddammit." He rarely, if ever, used what we termed vulgarity, like the "F-bomb," references to male and female anatomy, or crude descriptions of sexual activity. Oddly, he seemed to have a somewhat sophisticated style in using profanity, which really had the effect of camouflaging the flames and making his language seem not all that offensive. He was a likeable cuss, and maybe it was his good-natured demeanor, his quick, raucous laugh, and his lively approach to his work that made his linguistic lashings seem almost benign.

Some mornings as I arrived for work, there would be a faint blue haze gently cradling the valley where the village of Juda was nestled, which I assumed was due to the high level of humidity in the air. But in retrospect, I wonder if in fact it might have been the remnants of a tirade of profanity from the previous day, the source not being difficult to discern. But I digress.

For as long as I could remember, I had assumed that Hub had always been an avid fisherman. Along with the almost daily display of catches at Andereck Chevrolet, there were endless discussions on where the fish were biting and what kinds of bait should be used, and revelations of amazing new lures and scents just on the market, "guaranteed" to catch fish. Hub regularly purchased these assortments of can't-miss lures and scents, mostly advertised in "yellow journalism" publications: lures that buzzed, hummed, vibrated, hopped, dove, popped, glittered, or sparkled; lures that were lifelike—grasshoppers, minnows, nightcrawlers, flies, frogs, beetles, bugs, grubs, and chubs. He had cheese baits, stink baits, exotic scents, and all of the above seemingly in the full array of the colors of the rainbow.

Fishing was not always Hub's sole passion, as Aunt Esther told me that in previous years Hub was also an aspiring golfer, but fate intervened in his budding PGA career.

One day Hub and his next-door neighbor, Wayne Gempler, who happened to own the other garage in town (not a dealership), decided to go fishing together; more significant, however, was that they decided to shadow one of the local fishing gurus, Hank Norder. Hank, it seemed, *always* caught fish, and his wife, Erna, who often accompanied him, was also an accomplished angler. Well, one fine day, Hub and Wayne began following Hank as he fished on the Rock River near the Newville Bridge in Southern Wisconsin. When Hank moved, they moved; they hung onto Hank like glue on flypaper. If he was casting, they would cast; if he trolled, they trolled; and they probably knew what lures and size of hooks or bait he was using and when he passed gas. Eureka—the sleuthing paid off handsomely; Hub landed not just one, but two five-pound catfish! That one day of great fortune resulted in two major life changes in Hub; it launched him on a lifelong, passionate fishing career, but it also ended his fantasy (or maybe real) pursuit of tangling with the likes of Arnold Palmer or Gary Player. Not only did he buy Wayne's boat, but he also put his brand-new set of golf clubs in the closet and never again played a round of golf! He had swallowed the fishing bug, hook, line, and sinker. Over the remaining years of his life, he would display an unbounded enthusiasm and also an unbridled optimism for the manly pursuit of angling. I have described elsewhere (in a memoir I wrote) some of the highlights (or lowlights, if you prefer) of my personal experiences fishing with Uncle Hub. At the outset I must state emphatically that no more upbeat, more agreeable, or more helpful fishing companion did I ever have. When it came to his expectations of the outcomes of our joint fishing ventures, they would surely be embodied in the ancient supplication of all fishermen: that "today we're going to land a whopper." The reality, in our many trips, would probably be best described in the vernacular as a mixed bag.

One of my earliest trips with Hub was to a lake south of Madison, Wisconsin, named Lake Kegonsa. I always thought that was a cool name for a lake. Everyone was catching monster bullheads (a pound or so). Essentially they're like a smaller version of catfish, and in our area they came in two varieties, black and "yellow-bellies." We fished from shore, and Hub cast out my line loaded with a juicy, squirming nightcrawler; there were enough lead weights (sinkers) on the line to get it halfway across the lake. Well, I suppose the distance was closer to fifteen to twenty yards. Of course, unlike all the reports that Hub had been getting, these fish were behaving like good orthodox Jewish folks on the Sabbath; they weren't doing anything! It was on this day that the fictional character Joe Btfsplk from the *Li'l Abner* comic strip came to mind. Joe always had bad luck, and I wondered if my uncle was sort of a living incarnation of that unlucky fellow. No, I actually got a bite; more than a bite—a large black bullhead had swallowed the bait and the hook. Hub was thrilled that I got a fish, and in his haste to land the slippery, tasty fellow, he didn't crank in the line with the reel; instead he pulled in the line hand over hand. He got the fish on shore, a dandy black one-pounder, and also a mass of fishing line so tangled and knotted that he had to cut some ten to fifteen yards off the reel. We had probably fished for two or three hours, and we were feeling kind of low, but the catch washed away the gloom. I was really happy, and Hub was equally elated for me. Ah, sweet success. But wait, as old Paul Harvey would intone—now here's the rest of the story. We were going to have the tasty fellow for supper, so step one was to skin and gut the fish. Hub put the fish in a large pan of cold water and set it outside the kitchen door on the cement front stoop. He went back inside to get a sharp knife and cutting board. I was sitting about fifteen feet from the fish, and when Hub exited the stoop, a large black neighborhood cat entered the scene.

"Hub!" I yelled. "There's a cat sniffing at the fish!"

As Hub ambled out the door, the cat pounced, snatching the fish in his jaws and leaping off the stoop. "Oh, no!" yelled Hub. "You come back here!" He ran after the streaking cat. Hub was a portly fellow, not really built for speed, and the race was over after the first step. The likelihood of him catching that cat was about the same as one of our farm draft horses catching Seabiscuit in a fifty-yard dash. The cat vanished, and Hub trudged back with a terrible, dejected expression on his face. He was so forlorn that I felt much worse for him than I did about losing what had been my prize catch. We both recovered rather quickly, but this was not to be the last of our misadventures.

News of the "cat caper" eventually got back to the garage at Andereck Chevrolet, and all of the cronies of the fishing society heard the full story. Hub was really a good sport and endured the good-natured ribbing without getting angry or losing his dignity.

For many years, the garage had been a local meeting place and general hangout, the center for not only the latest gossip, but additionally for legitimate items of local news. There were regulars who stopped in daily and loitered most of the morning; many others came in for brief periods to pick up the latest gossip or news; this latter group had a tendency to inject some well-chosen incendiary comments (of the "late-breaking" type) that had the effect of adding fuel to ongoing debates, leading to some new rumors, or simply agitating the assembly of mostly old guys. My mother aptly described the daily banter that swirled throughout the garage; she described the rhetoric as "embroidering on the truth." It was the accepted modus operandi among the locals; they weren't telling lies, but rather degrees of truth, like maybe true, somewhat true, likely true, 99 percent true, and occasionally completely true! It seemed that the regulars who were there daily had created a sort of "sleight of speech" technique that made it difficult to determine the actual degree of truthfulness of the presenter. A fellow named Glen Boyer was, in many respects, "first among equals" in his storytelling. Daily he delivered (or concocted) barely believable narratives. Hub mostly ignored his sometimes-outlandish monologues, but every now and then he would quietly say as an aside, "What a windbag!"

Aunt Esther told me that when she and my mother were attending high school in Juda from 1928 to 1932, the garage was already a gathering place to swap stories; she said that two notable daily visitors of that era were Joe Bradley and Judd Davis. Joe was a retired farmer, and Judd was Esther and Mom's uncle. Eldrege Andereck, Hub's father, owned the garage then. Interestingly, the original sign on the garage that came into being in 1915 was spelled "Andreck," missing the first *E.* Joe and Judd sat in car seats in the office where I worked thirty years later, watching the traffic at the main town intersection. Back then, the garage had apparently also become the location where the more creative practical jokes were hatched. Today the art of concocting complicated schemes to confuse and confound the unsuspecting seems a lost art.

Often the shenanigans were spontaneous, as was the case when one of the loiterers decided, without much thought, to insert a rake handle into the latch on the outdoor privy adjacent to the garage. The old fellow who was the victim finally became quite irate, and when the decibel level of his cursing and yelling reached a crescendo, he was released.

One of the more creative pranks was the effort of Hub and his mechanic, Orlin. The local tavern keeper, Gerald Sawdey, and another local named Elmer Matzke had spent the better part of a morning talking to one another in the entrance of the garage. Both Hub and Orlin grew weary of the incessant loud yammering and took action; they poured oil into the carburetor of a vehicle that was in the garage, idling. The resulting acrid, billowing smoke engulfed the entire garage, but it had the desired effect of flushing the two nonstop talkers from the premises. I'm not aware whether any explanation was given to Gerald or Elmer, but they avoided the garage for the rest of the day.

As I discussed earlier, fishing was a primary recreational activity of many of the locals who hung out in the garage. Hub, Orlin, and I were no exception. One humid June evening, Hub closed a few minutes early, hoping to beat a predicted thunderstorm that was approaching from the west. We had heard (in a news flash by one of the guys who dropped by the garage) that bullheads were biting at a place called Indian Ford on the Sugar River. Among knowledgeable fishermen it was axiomatic that an approaching storm with low pressure would likely result in a feeding frenzy of the ugly little devils. In his haste to beat the storm, Hub couldn't find his 6-12 Insect Repellent. Mosquitoes could be ferocious as evening approached, and without some means of warding off these miniature vampires, one might need a transfusion by morning.

Hub did find a can of Raid bug spray and liberally soaked both arms. Even with the threat of facing those nasty critters, Orlin and I declined the Raid. We arrived before the storm, and Orlin parked as close to the river as he could, on an earthen dike. In short order we caught several of the slippery yellow-bellies. Then I got snagged, and while Hub was redoing my line, Orlin also got hung up and had to break his line. With the lines replaced, all of us cast back into the river. Snagged again! Orlin exploded, launching a magnificent barrage of epithets, annihilating all semblance of Sunday school English. When he finished his tirade, he walked down the embankment into the river, which was only two or three feet deep, and began searching underwater with his hands.

"Aha!" he exclaimed as he raised an eight- to ten-foot woven wire gate out of the water, covered with dozens of hooks and lures. Well, there is no way to sanitize his next outburst. "I'll be goddamned, some dirty son of a bitch threw this gate in here on purpose." He continued his ranting and only ceased when the skies suddenly opened with a thunderous boom and a driving downpour of rain. Hub scrambled to retrieve rods and tackle boxes, and Orlin began pulling me backward at a gallop to the car. Dry dirt turns to mud with the right amount of water, and there was a sufficient amount of both on the way back to the vehicle. Mud began to stick to the wheelchair tires and then build up, and by the time we reached the car, my chair appeared to be sporting two medium-sized car tires! No matter; I dove into the front seat, the rods and poles were thrown into the backseat, and my chair with twenty or thirty inches of rich Indian Ford soil went into the trunk. We were soaked and had lost a number of hooks, line, and sinkers. Orlin cussed during the entire trip back to Juda, vowing revenge on the "bastard" (his mildest adjective) who had thrown the gate into the river. Hub, with his seemingly inexhaustible reservoir of optimism, remarked, "Well, we didn't have much luck, but I didn't get a single mosquito bite!" The application of Raid had been effective in warding off the bugs, but it did produce another outcome. Both of his arms swelled to double their normal size and turned red, and Hub said they itched "like the devil." The symptoms disappeared within days, with no later residual problems. Fifty-plus years later, I still have vivid recollections of that ill-fated adventure to Indian Ford.

There were other misadventures but also many good times fishing with Hub, which really deserve a chapter of their own. He would continue to fish for many years after my days at the garage, at times finding success, but on other occasions courting near-disaster. He and Esther once took a brief vacation to Lake Tomahawk in Northern Wisconsin. The morning after their arrival, Esther heard the motor on their rented fishing boat roar to life and then abruptly stop. Although she was curious, she did not leave the cabin to investigate; Hub suddenly appeared at the cabin door, soaked and dripping with Lake Tomahawk water and a few strands of lake weeds. "My gosh!" she said. "What happened, Hub?"

He replied rather sheepishly, "Well, you almost lost a husband!" The motor clamps hadn't been tightened sufficiently to the boat, and when the engine came to life (unfortunately in gear), the boat had lurched violently, throwing both Hub and the motor into the lake. He was dumped into two or three feet of water close to the pier, with the major damage to his ego, fortunately for him as a non-swimmer.

I often think about experiences fishing with my Uncle Hub and my days in that on-the-job training experience at Andereck Chevrolet; the memories are always permeated with a sense of fondness. And whenever I think about those days with Hub at the garage, my mind frequently carries me back to an earlier time, the beginning of the 1940s, and the artesian well at the base of the southeast corner of the building. Returning from Monroe and the Saturday night movies, we always stopped for a drink of the cold, clear, bubbling spring water. Our family had discovered a new snack food, corn Fritos, and we all devoured them voraciously, creating a parching thirst. A refreshing drink from that little concrete well quenched my thirst, and then when I climbed into the back seat of our old Chrysler, the water seemed to give me an uncommon sense of security and serenity, and I quickly drifted off in peaceful slumber. So I think the affection I developed for place in the late fifties got a head start some ten or fifteen years earlier.

When I began this tale, I envisioned it as a story about the adventures and misadventures of fishing with Uncle Hub, which it is. But it's much more than that; it's about a unique place. Older guys in the Juda community actually hoped they would have car trouble so they could go to the garage and spend the day. Andereck Chevrolet was a place that epitomized the people, culture, and values of vintage small-town rural America. You knew everyone and most of each other's business; it was hard to fool most folks, even though there was a good amount of benign energy to that end. People were friendly, outgoing, and generally upbeat. This is a story about what I think was optimism, persistence, and hope. My Uncle Hub, the central figure of this story, embodied these ideas as well as anyone I ever met. He just knew in his heart that tomorrow the fishing would be better. His attitude was infectious and permeated the culture of Andereck Chevrolet in 1959.

Lastly, and most important for me, it wasn't until 2009, when

I started penning these words, that I began to understand, maybe clearly for the first time, that in fact I was describing a time and an environment that began the process of repairing my severely damaged ego and helped me restore a modicum of my self-confidence.

*An Irish priest loved to fly fish. So far this year, the weather had been so bad that he hadn't had a chance to get his beloved waders on and his favorite flies out of their box. Strangely, though, every Sunday the weather had been good, but of course Sunday was the day he had to be in church. The weather forecast was good again for the coming Sunday, so he called a fellow priest, claiming he had lost his voice and was in bed with the flu. The other priest agreed to handle the sermon, and the fly-fishing priest drove fifty miles to a river near the coast so that no one would recognize him. An angel up in heaven was keeping watch and saw what the priest was doing. He told God, who agreed he would do something about the matter. With the first cast of his line, a huge fish gulped down the fly.*

*For over an hour the priest ran up and down the riverbank, fighting the fish. Finally he landed the monster-sized fish, and it turned out to be a world-record salmon. Confused, the angel asked God, "Why did you let him catch that huge fish? I thought you were going to teach him a lesson."*

*God replied, "I did. Who do you think he is going to tell?"*[1]

# Deep-Sea Fishing, Episode Two

My INITIAL DEEP-SEA FISHING expedition was in the Gulf of California at San Carlos, Mexico, in 1968, which of course would be episode one. Although I have written a brief tale of that adventure, I have not included it in this collection of stories. The adventure of which I now speak was seventeen years later, in 1985, with big Jim Jorgenson at the helm, off the Washington state coast in Puget Sound.

I had traveled with my wife, Marlys, and my son, Matt, to the great Northwest in our twenty-two-foot Chevy motor home, in the company of our friends and neighbors Merle and Sharon Jensen. They traveled in their two-door Buick, and we stayed in close contact with the then-popular CB radios, which was prior to the arrival and mania of the cell phone era. Merle and I did most of the talking on the radios, and I recall that in the lingo of the CB crowd, his handle was "Tomato Red" and mine was "Golden Rod." His name was relevant to his expertise with tomatoes as a horticulturist. As for Golden Rod, I don't remember the origin; maybe I was laboring under the illusion of some kind of Freudian fantasy! We had traveled through Arizona to the North Rim of the Grand Canyon, through Utah, visiting Bryce National Park and Zion National Park on our way to Yellowstone.

On our first day on the road, near Page, Arizona, we had what initially appeared to be a major emergency, as the interior of our motor home caught fire. I slammed on the brakes and yelled, "Mayday, mayday!" into the CB for the Jensens. Matt leaped from the vehicle, and Marlys and I looked blankly at one another, both, I think, wondering if we were about to become crispy critters.

Merle arrived and exclaimed, "It's the microwave!" Somehow it got turned on and had ignited a book housed in the microwave. We had literally cooked our cookbook! That was the end of the emergency and also the cookbook.

After leaving Yellowstone we headed into the state of Washington and stopped in the quaint little town of Winthrop. We ate buffalo burgers, Sharon and Marlys went shopping, and we had another minor emergency. The ladies "overextended" the time allotted by Merle, and he went a tad ballistic!

As Matt and I sat chatting leisurely in the motor home, a wild-looking guy raced by, face beet-red, hair flying as he leaned out the window; he made a sharp U-turn down the street, only to reappear shortly. "Hey, Dad," chirped Matt, "that's Merle." It was, and he was frantically trying to locate the gals.

After another pass or two he eventually located the wayward shoppers and hustled Marlys back to our motorhome. He was frazzled, his face was bright red, and he wanted to leave immediately. He had heard on the radio that the forecast called for rain or snow in Deception Pass over the Cascades, which could have caused a significant delay in our trip. Of course Merle was right, as the weather did deteriorate, but we were ahead of it and got to our destination, Lynden, that evening.

Merle's parents, Harry and Ruth, and other relatives lived in the area and were to spend several days with us until we headed out on our fishing expedition. The crew of fishermen consisted of Merle; his father, Harry; Matt; myself; and a cousin of Harry; who had just arrived from Denmark, a slightly built seventyish fellow named Ingeman Jensen. Old Ingeman had flown for twenty-five hours from Denmark and gotten to bed around midnight, and four hours later he was jolted awake from a deathlike slumber to head off to the sea! We were to meet big Jim Jorgenson, our fishing guide, at 6:00 AM to begin our quest for silver salmon. Merle, always keeping close track of time, tried to dissuade his father from stopping for breakfast, but to no avail. As Norm, the husband of a pregnant wife, Margie, had insisted in the movie *Fargo*, Harry said with authority, "You gotta have a good breakfast."

We ended up at Denny's, and, I'd guess out of kindness, Harry ordered Ingeman one of the well-known greasy gut-busters, a "Grand Slam": fried eggs, bacon or sausage, hash browns soaked in grease, and toast saturated with butter. Being a thoughtful host, Harry encouraged Ingeman, "Eat up, now. We have plenty of time." We really were behind schedule, and Merle was getting a bit agitated, but Ingeman finished the entire meal like a good soldier, and Merle raced us off to meet our guide at Blaine Harbor. We were late, and Jim showed his displeasure with a less than cordial welcome aboard. Merle huddled with him as we left the harbor, and their verbal exchange thawed Jim's icy demeanor somewhat. Maybe he told Jim that old guys and gimps had to eat breakfast, or they might faint or even pass out.

We scooted full throttle out into Puget Sound, some ten or fifteen miles from the harbor. I noted that the twenty-five-foot cabin cruiser was spotless, all the gear was neatly stowed, and the metal fittings were polished and gleaming. Jim barked out orders as to where he wanted each of us to be stationed. We arrived at our designated location, and Jim shut down the powerful twin inboard engines and switched to a ten-horsepower Honda trolling motor.

"Okay, guys, sit tight while I get the poles ready."

Jim, maybe in his mid- to late thirties, was amazingly adept and efficient in baiting and setting up five poles. His every movement was almost machinelike, with no wasted activity, and in short order we were on the hunt for those delectable silver salmon (wonderful grilled over alder wood). The ten-horsepower Honda purred ("Best trolling motor I ever owned," remarked Jim), and we all began to relax after the past hour of sometimes frenetic rushing. With a slight breeze in combination with the speed of our trolling motor, our boat began a gentle but quite evident rocking motion, bow to stern. The motion was actually very comforting and relaxing, and I was enjoying the hypnotic effect; but I happened to glance at Ingeman, and I thought, *Gosh, he has a strange pallor. Must be the light reflecting off the water.* No, he had turned almost a green color; holy smokes, I had an idea what was coming next. I nudged Merle and quietly suggested that he have his father attend to Ingeman.

"Dad, you'd better check with Ingeman. Is he okay?"

Well, Ingeman wasn't okay. Harry began to say, "Now, Ingeman, are you—" but he stopped as the old fellow lurched for rail, emitting a cry as if having a grand mal seizure, and relieved himself of the Denny's Grand Slam breakfast.

I hadn't noticed, but Matt had sidled up to me. He asked, "Wow, Dad, did you see that?"

"Well, yes," I replied. "Everyone did."

"No, no," Matt said. "I mean his teeth."

"What about his teeth?"

"Well, he caught them."

"What do you mean?"

"Well, he opened his mouth, kind of yelled, his torso heaved violently, his false teeth flew out of his mouth, and he grabbed them just before they sailed overboard."

Sure enough, when Ingeman's stomach exploded, the Vesuvius-like eruption and torrent that followed had blown his teeth out of his mouth; but he had snatched them in mid-air as they were on a downward course into Puget Sound, likely for eternity. Amazing reaction. Thirty years later I still marvel at how he was able to snag those choppers—both of them!

Man, was he sick. He spent ten or fifteen minutes completely emptying the remaining contents of his stomach. Even out on an open deck, the smell was pretty rank. Matt and I tried to cover our noses unobtrusively, Merle was snorting, Harry was trying to comfort poor Ingeman, who was softly moaning, and Jim just looked pissed! They got Ingeman onto a cot, down in the cabin, and shortly he fell asleep.

We did catch some salmon; when one was on the line, Jim sprang into action, helping or hauling in the fish himself, and immediately tossing it in a large cooler filled with ice.

An hour or so after he retreated to the cabin, Ingeman emerged, teeth in his mouth, with a normal-appearing skin tone, and in his broken English communicated that he was feeling much better—in fact, quite well. But his apparent full recovery was only temporary. I don't know if it was something that Ingeman said to Harry about his feelings of well-being, but whatever the nature or content of their discussion, it triggered some deep-seated nurturing response in Harry.

Harry proclaimed excitedly, "Great, Ingeman! Now let's get some food in that empty tummy of yours, and you'll be 100 percent."

Merle startled visibly, jumping up and turning a bit pale. He protested, "Oh, no, Dad. His stomach is probably pretty queasy. Maybe a sip or two of soda, but no more food."

But Harry insisted that to return Ingeman to full recovery, he had to get food into his stomach. Whether Ingeman wanted to eat was unknown, but he complied at Harry's urging and downed a sandwich, a cookie or two, and some coffee. Merle sat silently, obviously perturbed, watching Ingeman closely for any change in his color or behavior, and he didn't have to wait very long. Ingeman suddenly emitted a pathetic-sounding cry, spit his teeth into his hands, bolted for the boat rail, and projectile vomited into the bay. He must have been in pretty good physical condition, as that liquefied mixture of baloney, cheese, and Oreo cookies arched a good three to four feet out from the boat. We watched him—everyone, that is, except our guide, Jim, who had turned his back to the group and was staring silently at the distant horizon. Ingeman was again in the throes of agony as the process turned into the dry heaves.

At one point, Harry, wringing his hands, uttered a barely audible "Oh, dear."

Ingeman once more retreated to the sanctuary of the cabin, out of the reach of Harry and his force-feeding cure methodology, and dozed off.

Although we did end up with six nice silver salmon, Jim expressed disappointment, as he had expected to land at least a dozen, maybe more. We might have gotten a few more, but we had lost one fisherman to the gentle motion of the sea (as Ingeman never ventured from the cabin to potentially face another of Harry's "cures"), and we may have spooked fish for miles with all the ruckus aboard ship and the pollution hitting the water.

Jim told (almost ordered) us all to have a seat, as he didn't need any assistance. He expertly filleted the fish and wrapped them in paper, and we put them in our ice chests for the trip back to shore and on to Lynden. Jim retrieved all the poles, stored them securely, washed down the deck, wiped off all the metal fittings, rinsed out the rags he used for cleaning, and hung them in a predetermined location. We all

121

watched in silence, as in addition to being a bit subdued by Ingeman's suffering, we probably all thought that maybe we hadn't been Jim's all-time favorite fishing group.

We later had a backyard picnic with lots of members of the Jensen clan, featuring fresh salmon grilled over alder wood. The fish was absolutely wonderful. I can honestly say that I have never again had fish that tasted so good!

Notwithstanding the outcome of Harry's "food cures all" philosophy, I thoroughly enjoyed what in reality was a "deep-bay" fishing excursion. I have not had the opportunity to go fishing for salmon since, but I believe the memories of that trip from Blaine Harbor will last my lifetime. Jim Jorgenson was a great guide, but I still chuckle at times when I recall his sometimes near Gestapo-like demeanor and efficiency in orchestrating every aspect of the adventure. Maybe even more memorable, improbable, and extraordinary was old Ingeman's eye-hand coordination in snagging those pearly whites in mid-air.

There were three fellows lost in the desert; one of them was an amputee, the second man was in a wheelchair, and the last guy was blind. They were dying of thirst, but the fellow who was an amputee kept urging them on. "Keep going," he admonished them, "or we will surely perish."

When they were exhausted and ready to give up, an oasis suddenly appeared over a gigantic sand dune. "Oh, praise the lord!" shouted the amputee as he staggered ahead on his crutches and plunged into a pool of deep, cool water. He drank deeply of the life-giving water, splashing exuberantly for several minutes. He emerged from the water and immediately exclaimed, "It's a miracle! My leg has been restored."

Indeed it had been restored, and he implored the man who was blind to dive into the pool. The blind fellow did and drank deeply, and as he exited the pool, he cried, "I can see! It is truly miracle water."

The two then lifted the fellow in the wheelchair and dumped both the man and the chair into the water. He was full of joy as he thrashed about ecstatically in the pool. Then his two friends lifted him and the chair from the water. It was another miracle: he had a brand-new set of tires on his wheelchair!

# One Fine Day

"HOLY MOTHER OF GOD, Kent, now I know why you have handicapped license plates. You drive like a disabled person."

"Oh, relax, Bill," I chuckled. "You seem a tad jumpy this morning."

"Well, my gosh, Kent, we're barely out of the city limits, and you almost got us killed!"

"Ya, that's right," chimed in one of the other two passengers.

The other one said, "Maybe you need to let one of us drive, or maybe call this trip off."

"Hey, you guys, cool it. And Bill, don't let that Irish imagination get away from you. Furthermore, that jeep had all kinds of room to pull off the road if he had to, which he didn't."

I did have the 360-horsepower Chevy engine cranking pretty good, and when a little jeep coming toward me had pulled into my lane to pass a car, I had slowed only slightly, and the guys got excited and accused me of playing chicken.

It was spring break of 1991 at the University of Arizona, and even before we left town, I had a premonition that these guys were going to get out of hand. Maybe we were an hour into our inaugural fishing trip together—three colleagues from the university and me. I thought, *My friends, that's a heck of a way to show your confidence in my driving abilities.* Tongue in cheek, I admonished them, "I hope this attitude I hear doesn't reflect hidden and unspoken views about persons with disabilities as being less capable, not fully functioning people."

"Oh, cut the crap," barked Bill. "Don't try to use your disability as an excuse. You're just a piss-poor driver, and we want to survive this trip."

This trip was to be a "guy thing": no wives, male bonding, all agendas on the table, no shirts or ties, no deadlines, no meetings, and best of all, escape from those twittering sycophants that infested the university community.

We were rocking and rolling up old Highway 83 in my twenty-two-foot cab-over Chevy motor home, past the Tom Mix memorial (he met his demise here in a single car accident; I don't know about Tony) on our way to Roosevelt Lake.

"Bill, now that I think about it, I believe all you Irishmen are alike. It's genetic, you know. Like Carl Jung said, personality traits are passed on to later generations through the genes. Your somewhat frazzled nerves may have come down from your ancestors hanging out in smoky, dingy pubs, drinking too much stout, and looking over their shoulders for the damned English."

Bill shot back, "Oh, is that like all black folks like watermelons, or Indians can't handle alcohol—you know, firewater?" I heard a lot of snickering behind me, and when I looked back, Josh and Glen were grinning like a couple of Cheshire cats. I deemed it advisable at this time to remain silent.

Bill was a stocky, pugnacious, balding fellow with a crew cut. He was associate dean of students at the university, and although he hid his feelings well, he was disheartened, having been passed over for promotion to dean of students, even though he had a long and distinguished career of service at the institution. The official reason he was not elevated was that he did not have a doctoral degree. What really happened was that the new vice president brought in his own people (even with the charade of "competitive" interviews), passing over the old guard.

Glen, a powerfully built African American was an assistant dean at the university. We became friends very quickly based on only two conversations. The first time I met him was after he came to the university to interview for the newly created position of director of minority student affairs; although he had developed a similar program at another major university, he didn't make the top-five list. "How is that possible?" I asked. "You created such a program!"

He smiled a Machiavellian grin and replied, "Well, I think I was one shade too dark."

He was right, of course; that the university would only hire a person who was Hispanic was a "secret" that everyone knew. Bill hired him, and as our friendship grew and I experienced his honesty in dealing with people, I found the courage to tell him that referring to Americans who were black as African Americans made no sense to me. He asked me what I felt was appropriate, and I told him, "Americans who are black, or black Americans."

He said, "Fine."

"You're okay with that, Glen?"

Very matter-of-factly he replied, "Of course I am. I know where you're coming from."

And there was Josh, also an assistant dean, a tall, dark, sometimes enigmatic American Indian. Early in our relationship he excused me from using the supposedly politically correct and again inaccurate descriptor "Native American," which he may be; but so am I, along with millions of other Americans who are white, black, or of Asian descent. Josh was extremely proud of his ancestry, and in his veins flowed the fierce heritage of the warrior clans of the Southwest, the Comanches. "Lords of the plains," he liked to remind us.

With his strong, rugged features and deep black eyes, he could look a bit fearsome with his early morning I-don't-feel-like-talking glare. I told him on one occasion, "It's no wonder white men were spooked by you Comanches if they got that look!"

I was the fourth member of the party, and I was sometimes accused of being too outspoken in advocating for disability rights issues, even by my three cohorts who called me, in my capacity at the university as the director of the Center for Disability Resources, "the head gimp." The four of us had a propensity (and I suppose viewed as the audacity) not to follow the company line. We were at times labeled non-team players for expressing views inconsistent with policy. I didn't ingratiate myself with a scathing editorial for what I saw was a failure in many instances to not include persons with disabilities in not only policy decisions, but also programs and services. I cynically suggested grouping disabled folks together, like in a fraternity, rather than integrate them across campus; I proposed that the fraternity name could be "Gamma Gamma Gimper." Gee, I thought it had a nice ring. It really pissed off the vice president and other higher-ups.

We had left town quite early that morning, maybe 5:30 or 6:00 AM, and already they were ragging about my driving. We had high hopes of catching a ton of fish, having a fish fry over a campfire, and partying into the night. But three of us carried a veiled ache inside, for Glen had been diagnosed with a rapidly progressing neuromuscular disorder, the disease already ravaging his once-muscular frame. On a number of occasions we had talked about taking a fishing trip together, and then as the destruction of his body began to accelerate, Josh, Bill, and I decided it was time to act.

I had rented a spacious pontoon boat several days earlier, and upon our arrival at 8:30 or 9:00, we unloaded enough food and fishing gear for a weeklong stay. Someone made the remark (not me) that getting all our supplies and equipment, with me and Glen on board, was so disorganized that it was like a Chinese fire drill. Wow, that set off a storm of protest and tongue lashings at the remark being racist and insensitive toward Asians; "Oh ya, like you guys never said that," shot back the offender.

Before getting under way, we almost lost Bill. He was a curious fellow and noisy, too; he was jitterbugging all over an artificial fish habitat of old open pit ore truck tires tied together at the marina. He was yelling, and loudly, "Wow, look at the size of these tires! Check them out. This is really neat." He almost chucked himself out into the lake before Josh collared him.

Well, fishermen we were not, as we caught two very tiny bass, two or three inches long, during seven or eight hours of covering, it seemed, the entire lake. Glen and I got the fish. Josh, playing the aloof Indian role, alibied his performance by allowing that Comanches were hunters, not fisherman; he added that white people fished, and probably a lot of women did too. Bill had no luck at all; in fact, he had to borrow tackle from us. He had gotten a "great deal" on a thousand hooks for only five dollars. He didn't inspect them at the store, and on the lake he discovered that none of them had an eyelet for line! He got a good bit of ribbing, which he took with characteristic good spirits.

We completely bombed out with our fishing but made up for it with enough good-natured bantering to last for a good long time. Throughout the entire day, the dialogues were laced with a minimum of facts, near-truths, and downright fabrications, none of which went unchallenged. Glen's stomach was sore from laughter, as I suspect was the case for all of us. So while we brought home no fish, we had in fact achieved great success with the trip. The trip was for Glen; we all admired him immensely and suspected, correctly, that this would be our one and only trip together. We had, for the day, tried to give up all vestiges of cultural, ethnic, professional, and personal bias we may have held, and communicated openly and honestly in genuine, supportive friendship.

That evening we met a group of fellow fisherman that I knew for a steak cookout; one man was Glen's personal physician. They were great guys: two MDs, a businessman, and the father of one of the doctors. Almost immediately after joining the other guys, the dynamics the four of us had shared that day changed dramatically, not only within our group, but also in relation to the other four. Josh became quiet and watchful; Glen seemed to be tense and became mostly an observer; and even Bill struggled to initiate conversation. I was confused; only later did I think that maybe a special bond had been forged that day, and when we encountered others, the serendipity of the day ended. We ate and left, probably before 10:00 PM, for the short walk to the motor home. It had been a long day, and none of us was inclined to join in the alcohol-driven partying and pretty uproarious shenanigans of these fun-loving fishermen. We had already accomplished our mission—yes, fishing, but more, the support of a friend and colleague whose life was now in peril.

We were parked adjacent to the motel where the other four guys were staying, and all of us had drifted off before their revelry ended. As dawn broke, Glen suddenly sat upright, I think for an instant unsure of his whereabouts. Bill, who seemed never to sleep, instantly quipped, "Hey this is wonderful. I have always wondered what a black guy's hair looks like in the morning." He continued, "Gosh, Glen, you're lucky. It looks just the same as when you went to bed last night. Us white guys really have a problem, as our hair is a disaster in the morning."(Bill had a crew cut.)

"Wait a minute there, Bill," Glen replied. "Give me about five minutes, and I'll show you how much work it takes for a nice 'do!" Using a pick, he diligently fluffed, preened, and shaped his thick, glossy black hair, which was nearly an Afro. When he finished, he gave Bill a pretty fair Bill Cosbyish grin and asked, "Well, now what do you think?"

"Well, I'll be damned," replied Bill. "It doesn't look any different!"

Bill's outspoken candor set off a debate and discussion on hair: black folk's hair, the hair of white people, Indian hair, Asian hair, and the hair of Irishmen. The discussion ended with no consensus and no conclusions and really amounted to a final free-for-all dump of whatever came to mind.

We got ourselves organized, sort of. I ran over Josh's reel and broke it. ("God, you're dangerous," he offered.) We headed home. Going through Globe, Arizona, a local gendarme pulled me over for speeding. I gave him my best "poor handicapped fellow" routine. As I was exhausted from doing all the driving and being distracted by my passengers, it worked: he only gave me a warning. As he left, the howls of indignation reached a crescendo. They were all talking—no, yelling—at the same time, vilifying me with what I felt were outrageous and unwarranted attacks on my character.

The arguments went something like this. "See? All you handicapped people take advantage of your disability. Boy we hope never to hear you accuse blacks, Indians, Mexicans, women, or any minority of such behavior." The final insult was, "Boy, people get pissed about the *race card*. What about the *gimp card?*"

We never went fishing together again. Maybe we just never found

130

the time; then again, maybe none of us wanted to risk altering the memory of the dynamics between us on that trip. Black culture in America coined the term "soul brother." I sometimes think back to those two special days and wonder if what developed among the four of us was something like that. Does the concept cross racial lines? I was always going to ask Glen, but I waited too long; he died less than two years later.

I have bittersweet memories of back then, and today some feelings of sadness. Glen is gone. Bill lives in a close neighborhood, but I rarely, if ever, see him; I believe he still carries the scars of what the university did to him. And I've lost touch with Josh; I've tried to communicate with him, but it doesn't work; I'm puzzled about what reason he has for what appears to be a withdrawal of his friendship.

I still love to go fishing. I had a pontoon boat, but I sold it; now I think that was a rash decision. Often, when I still owned the pontoon, drifting gently across the lake, I'd recall that time with a smile and think to myself, *Well, we didn't get any fish, but it sure was one fine day!*

# V

*Foreign Affairs*

*Eccentricity is not, as dull people would have us believe, a form of madness. It is often a kind of innocent pride, and the man of genius and the aristocrat are frequently regarded as eccentrics, because genius and aristocrat are entirely unafraid of and uninfluenced by the opinions and vagaries of the crowd.[1]*

# A Man Called Spice

THE BELL ATOP THE old schoolhouse was ringing cheerfully as we rounded the last curve into the tiny hamlet of Noke, England. Henry Spice, our host for the day, laughed heartily as he announced that the bell rang only for "distinguished guests to the kingdom."

In 1990 my wife and I had traveled to England with our friends Merle and Sharon Jensen, and we were staying with their great English friends David and Peggy Churchill. This day we had gone to visit Henry, a horticulturist like Merle and David, to see his plot (nursery). It was his life's work, but now, sadly, it was showing signs of having a caretaker who was no longer physically able to keep up with the acre of plants collected from around the world; years of heavy smoking had begun the insidious work of ravaging his lungs. Upon meeting him, it quickly became apparent that Henry was not the average, run-of-the-mill Englishman. In a brief period of time we had an extended discussion on churches, "quite a profound discussion for so early in the day," he observed.

Henry also provided a brief but very informative lecture about the Enclosure Acts of England, many during the 1700s and 1800s. They were acts of Parliament, on behalf of wealthy folks and the nobility, that literally fenced in lands previously open for everyone for grazing animals, cultivation, and mowing hay and grasses. Two locals in the area of Noke, Tame, Brill, and Beckley who were caught tearing down a fence were put in the jail at Oxford. Some villagers stormed the jail and released the men, and the authorities went asking about their whereabouts. After relating the story, Henry recited a ditty about the event that revealed who had informed on the two escapees:

They came to Noke, and no one spoke.
They went to Tame; it was just the same.
They went to Brill, and they were silent still;
So they went to Beckley, and they spoke directly.

Two hundred years later, the locals are still annoyed with the folks from Beckley.

Henry, seemingly always in motion, said, "Well, let's show you the plot." He made the statement in a tone somewhere between those of a drill sergeant and the leader of a scout troop on a field trip. In fact, he was wearing the shorts to his scout uniform, which was fifty years old. "Still in fine shape, don't you think?" he chuckled as we trooped off into rows of plants in the plot. It was damp, even muddy, but Henry insisted that we see every plant, tree, and shrub. In almost eloquent terms, he described the origins of the species, where he had obtained the particular plants, and more often than not he had a rather lengthy anecdote to share concerning the unusual circumstances, and especially the bargain basement price, in getting the plant. He paused frequently, struggling to regain his breath, and in reply to my inquiry, he reassured me, "Oh, I'm quite okay, old boy." He wasn't, but he deflected my concern with his cheerful demeanor, quick wit, and infectious enthusiasm when giving us the tour.

"Ah, there's Fat Boy. He's a beautiful conifer, isn't he? He was smuggled into England in the bottom of a suitcase," Henry offered with a sly twinkle in his eye.

Tour complete, we spent twenty minutes washing caked mud off wheelchair tires and shoes. Henry produced a half dozen pairs of worn shoes, offering them to his guests while theirs dried. It was time to wash for lunch, and Henry led me to his "work washroom" through a large room jammed full of fifty years of seemingly everything he had ever acquired.

"You like wine, don't you?" he asked.

"Yes," I replied.

"Well, look here," he chuckled. "Do you think this will last us?"

There were easily three or four hundred bottles stacked in groups of thirty or more throughout the room.

"I get these great buys on burgundies and Cabernets—I buy out the store." Yet before lunch, he served a drink of the finest single-malt scotch whisky. "Uncivilized to drink those blends," he advised.

Lunch was an adventure: fish and chips wrapped in paper, and a wonderful fresh garden salad of lettuce, tomatoes, radishes, and fresh asparagus, on the back patio. Oops, Henry forgot the silverware.

"Oh, dash!" he exclaimed. "We don't need knives, forks, or spoons. That's why you have hands. Eat it with your fingers. No dressing on the salad—ruins the taste."

So everything was finger food and inexpensive wine (not cheap;— that's vulgar) of quite good quality, and more than one could drink. Henry was attentive to everyone's needs, gently chastising anyone who attempted to usurp his role as a gracious host for his guests, while sharing his intellect, wit, and warm hospitality.

He had bought the old schoolhouse and made only minimal changes to accommodate his needs. Everything was secondhand; he needed nothing new for his ascetic lifestyle. Books and papers were scattered throughout the premises, from the classics to the latest scientific research in horticulture. He insisted on a final tour of the old church next door, circa twelfth century.

"Do you attend services, Henry?" I inquired.

"Never set foot through the door, my boy, except as a tour guide." But he knew the history of the place intimately.

We went on a day trip to see Salisbury Cathedral. Henry noted on the way, "You know, you Americans tend to say Sals-*berry* rather than *bury*." We had been doing so, but we corrected our pronunciation with some coaching from Henry.

He was indeed a unique fellow, an obviously intelligent, fiercely independent bachelor who had a rather distinctive wardrobe. On this trip he wore a bright red shirt, brown slacks, black socks, rather tired-looking shoes, and a food-stained yellow plaid sport jacket with a gorgeous red rose from his garden in the lapel. Someone suggested that he might be "worth a fortune," but whatever his economic situation, early on, we saw a true eccentric of the best sort, a kind, genuine individual, a person completely satisfied with who he was, without the need for pretense.

Henry would serve as our tour guide for one final excursion to Blenheim Palace (birthplace of Winston Churchill) and a region known as the Cotswolds. Always in rare form, he noted two large stone balls at the entrance to the palace. "Very common," he remarked. "A sign of fertility at manorial houses. Come to think of it," he mused, "they do look like testicles, don't they?"

In the short period I had known Henry, it was apparent that he had a large appetite for alcohol, his tastes ranging from excellent malt whisky to his bargain-basement reds. But to folks who didn't know him, he was apt to present the facade of a local deacon or cleric. At Blenheim Palace, as we were leaving a bookstore, free samples of an excellent cream sherry were being given to visitors. But when the plump matron offered one to Henry, he put on his most sanctimonious face and rather sternly replied, "Oh, no thank you, my dear lady. I'm a complete teetotaler!"

Later that day, on an extremely narrow one-lane road, with large hedges only a matter of inches from each side of the car, Marlys suddenly asked, "My gosh, what would you do if you had a flat tire and had to stop? There's no place to get off the road!"

Henry appeared puzzled for a moment, and then in quintessential English understatement replied, "Well, my dear, let's try not to think about that."

We returned home after a long day, dropped off Henry, and said our good-byes to him. We were all a bit overcome with emotion, as beneath that sometimes curmudgeonly appearing demeanor, we had glimpsed the heart of a gentle, caring soul.

I returned to England several years later for a proposed international conference relating to legislation for persons with disabilities. Unfortunately, the primary organizer, the guy handling the money, absconded with the funds. A European, an Englishman, and I constituted the "international conference" that met for one half day. The week I was in England, I stayed in a once-magnificent old manor house, toured the countryside during the day, and at night drank scotch with the German and our English host Gordon.

On my last day in England, I stayed with David and Peggy Churchill, and David took me to visit with Henry, whose health had rapidly deteriorated. He was on oxygen twenty-four hours a day, and when we arrived that mid-afternoon, he was dressed only in pajamas and a robe. David left us, as he said, "so you two can have a good visit."

Henry's breathing was labored, his eyes sunken back in their sockets, his cheekbones pronounced, and his complexion sallow; it was an Auschwitz-like mask. "Well, old boy, we must have a drink," he told me.

I thought how destructive alcohol would be for him, but his dark, piercing eyes looked at me, reading my thoughts. He smiled a gentle warning not to speak of his struggle.

We drank fine Scotch whisky and washed it down with warm English ale for two hours or so.

Not long before we parted company, he suddenly asked me if I was a "believer."

"Yes," I answered.

"Well, I could never quite get it," he said softly, and he drifted away momentarily.

He gave me a packet of bean seeds when I left. "They're special. I think you'll have good luck with them."

I left England and never again saw Henry, as not long after I was gone he too left—his earthly struggles.

# A Roo A-Wooing

In the land "down under" on a lengthy holiday, with George at the helm, barking "right on regardless," we rarely lost our way.

But we had roamed the land, both far and wide, in search of that elusive lot, a kangaroo, the Aussies say, a name that means "I forgot!"

Then, finally, at Pebbly Beach where lorikeets screech, and sit on your blooming hat, and kangaroos abound to our delight, we stopped for a friendly chat.

There were dozens of roos roaming the beach, and oh my gosh, a lorikeet pooped on my hat.

Twas bread we brought that so ardently they sought, and beckoned those rascally buggers, but they all came at once, and jumped on us, those bloody little muggers! I waved a loaf to a "mob" and up hopped a large male gray, he grabbed my arms, assaulting me, as I tried to hold him at bay.

On Marlys' chair, in Joyce's hair, on George and Sharon too, but Merle the most from head to toe, was covered with kangaroo. He danced and hopped, and laughed a lot, there wasn't much else he could really do.

Now a comely roo caught my eye, as she clung to a squirming Merle. A pleasing beast with fur so fine, aha, surely it must be a girl. She nipped his ear, and clawed his chest, and hopped his leg twelve times. Good Lord my mates, now we've seen it all, she's trying to ring his chimes.

But she backed away with a look of dismay and ambled off in disgust, cause a Dane can't do what a roo must do to satisfy that lust. Yes it was clear, to that doe and also to us, when it came to kangaroo love, old Merle was no doubt a bust!

# Along the Shores of Lake Nillah Cootie

Traveling one day in this land down under, the day was bright, no rain or clouds, or signs of thunder. It's time for lunch of pies and biscuits and Toohy Blue; so we ate and drank by the shores of Nillah Cootie where giant red gum trees grew.

What a life, the food, our friends, sipping tea, all so soon we must go, but first, lets take a wee. So I pushed my wheelchair to that privacy place, ah, this trip will bring a smile of relief to my face.

Alas and alack the door is too narrow, it's giving me fits, no worries mate, in Australia you use your wits. Don't worry, fret, yell, or shout, keep your cool, relax and look about. What to do, where to go, I better think of something quick, my bladder's about to blow.

So I slid from my chair onto the ground, checked to see that no one was around. I have to hurry, find a spot, somewhere in the shade, the sun's too hot.

Some tall weeds, a ditch, I looked to the heavens, and then I knew. Yes, those trees so tall and wide, anything I have they'll easily hide.

I watered the grass in no time flat, and gave a sigh and straightened my hat. Back in my chair, "Hey lets look for a roo, and how about another Toohy Blue?"

In America, if your wheelchair wouldn't fit in, "no access" would be the hue and cries, but the Aussies, a bit more laid back, just smile, wink, and improvise.

*In the mid-1800s two imposing figures exercised their many-faceted diplomatic skills across the European political stage. One man, French, was Charles Maurice de Talleyrand, and his primary antagonist was Count Klemens von Metternich of Austria. Talleyrand was a brilliant practitioner of the art of deception; no one could ever be certain whether the policy he was advocating was his true agenda or a complicated facade for a hidden objective. By contrast Metternich was recognized for his legendary ability to see through even the most sophisticated schemes that sought to obscure the true intent of a course of action. Thus Talleyrand and Metternich were destined to become adversaries at the highest levels of diplomatic intrigue in Europe. Metternich, keenly aware of Talleyrand's trickery, became obsessed with uncovering the wily Frenchman's real goals in their encounters across the diplomatic table. So all-consuming was Metternich's scrutiny of Talleyrand's motives that when Metternich learned that Talleyrand had suddenly died, Metternich was alleged to have said, "Now, I wonder what he meant by that?"[1]*

# *Diplomacy*

WEBSTER'S NEW COLLEGIATE DICTIONARY defines diplomacy as "the art and practice of conducting negotiations between nations, as in arranging treaties." Also, "artful management in securing advantages without arousing hostility; address or tact."

I cannot claim any degree of expertise in the realm of diplomacy, but it seems that a key idea underscoring the concept of diplomacy is the existence of stalemates; that is, two opposing ideologies or objectives, unresolved by war, boycott, or capitulation, which eventually bring the opposing factions to the bargaining table.

Diplomatic endeavors among nations have been documented throughout recorded history. In the modern era, dramatic and critically important examples of diplomatic missions are evidenced in so-called summits, which indicate that it is the national leadership of nations who are negotiating in attempts to resolve existing conflicts. In my lifetime I recall instances of world leaders coming together to forestall potentially momentous consequences, or to negotiate a settlement: the Korean War peace talks of the 1950s, the conclusion of the 1967 Six-Day War between Israel and Egypt, Richard Nixon "opening" China in 1972, and the Camp David Accords of 1978. There are, of course, many other ongoing negotiations between representatives of nations and governments that would be labeled as "diplomacy" that never reach the level of general public awareness.

What are qualities of men and women essential for successful resolution of conflict? Furthermore, what are nonhuman factors that can enhance or facilitate movement toward agreements? Such variables as the setting, environment, rules of negotiation, schedule, and food and other amenities can all have a major impact on the outcomes of diplomatic missions.

There are many individuals in history who have been recognized for their skills and ability to successfully negotiate the resolution of conflicts. There are differing names on lists, but there is not always consensus on whom should be included; however, a brief listing that would find much agreement would include, of course, Metternich and Tallyrand, Ben Franklin, Thomas Jefferson, Henry Clay, Abraham Lincoln, Otto von Bismarck, Eleanor Roosevelt, Richard Nixon, Henry Kissinger, and Anwar Sadat. Occasionally some of these individuals are referred to as "statesmen," a term of highest respect.

Notwithstanding all that has been written about the complexity of factors leading to successful diplomatic outcomes, I personally experienced two critical variables that I am thoroughly convinced are major, if not essential, ingredients for effective diplomacy; they are singing and alcohol— yes, *songs* and *sauce!*

In November 1991 I traveled to Prague, Czechoslovakia, to attend an international meeting entitled "System of University Studies of Visually Handicapped Students." The previous year, Dr. Jan Halousek, a professor from Prague, had visited selected programs in American universities that had well-developed support services for students with disabilities in higher education. He visited the University of Arizona and subsequently invited me to present papers at the conference the following year. The conference was held from November 24 to 27, 1991, at the Crystal Hotel in Prague. Given the name "Crystal Hotel," I envisioned a luxurious facility with all the latest amenities; however, in a word, it was a dump! The communists had used cheap materials throughout; windows and doors were off center and didn't fit; appliances and fixtures were junky; carpets were about a quarter inch thick. The hotel had thin walls, and elevators shook and rattled, with wind howling in the shafts as in a wind tunnel. Workmanship and materials combined, the construction was a disaster!

But the conference moved ahead with an international cast of representatives from America, Czechoslovakia, Germany, England, Italy, Belgium, and (still at that date) the USSR. All of the sessions were simultaneously translated into six or seven languages. Halousek, our host, was determined that everyone should attend all of the meetings; at times he would go in search of missing participants.

We did have free time, and we got in a fair amount of sightseeing. Among other attractions, we visited the famous Charles Bridge, built in 1357 by Charles IV, Czech king and Holy Roman emperor; Hradčany Castle, the largest ancient castle in the world; and Wenceslas Square, the old Jewish quarter, the home of the famous writer Franz Kafka.

It was during these recreational excursions that we got to know our fellow conference attendees more intimately; in particular, we spent a good amount of time with the group from England: Gordon, the director of the Royal National Institute for Blind (RNIB), along with David and Peter, two young fellows who were blind. Joachim Klaus of Germany and Oliver and Gayle from New Orleans were also frequently with us in these informal social gatherings, often somewhere in downtown Prague. Alcohol was always a featured beverage, most notably the many varieties of excellent Czech Pilsners and ales. Testimony to the high quality of Czech beers was a tour bus full of German nationals we met who were on holiday in the country with the primary objective of drinking Czech beer!

At this juncture, I trust the reader has not completely lost track of the definitions and questions with which I began this brief tale; that is, on *diplomacy*, and the qualities and skills of individuals and other variables that contribute to successful diplomatic outcomes. I'm sure studies and in-depth analyses have been undertaken to identify critical elements of the processes of diplomatic missions; however, I have not researched the subject matter. I must confess that I purposely avoided any literature review that might have served to blow my theory out of the water. But that's not suggesting I'm incorrect in my assumptions and observations. Rather, my purpose is to postulate what I believe are two crucial ingredients in establishing constructive relationships with members of diverse international types—in a word, diplomacy. This serendipitous enlightenment of which I write began rather innocently one evening when Gordon Dryden from England asked me, "Kent, have you ever tasted Cragganmore single-malt Scotch whisky?"

"No," I replied. "I've had Glenlivet and Glenfiddich, but never Cragganmore." "Well," said Gordon with a gleam in his eye, "come up to the seventh-floor lobby of the hotel tonight, and we'll have a short one."

I decided to take along some excellent Czech beer, six or eight large bottles, and rode the rattletrap elevator up to the seventh floor to meet Gordon. He was waiting with Joachim from Germany and the Americans Oliver and Gayle from New Orleans. I noted immediately that the other invited guests had also brought along an assortment of alcoholic beverages. The Cragganmore was excellent; not everyone tried the scotch, but there were ample supplies of beers, wine, schnapps, and bourbon to satisfy all tastes. It wasn't long after the initial group assembled, with the alcohol flowing freely, that someone began to hum, likely a favorite song. The response was as if a match had been tossed onto a gasoline spill.

Almost instantaneously several folks joined in, asking the hummer to name and sing the song. Although not everyone knew the words to the song, everyone joined in, humming, making up words, and ad-libbing in any fashion they could, creating the impression that they had memorized the entire song. One song led to another, and suddenly doors down the corridors began to open, and sleepy-eyed folks came to join us.

David and Peter (the blind fellows from England) yelled from their room, "Where are you? We want to join up!" A contingent of Russians arrived, with vodka in hand, as did a few Czechs and Wolfgang, a tall, blond, blue-eyed, Aryan-looking fellow wearing a trench coat. He indeed was a son of the "Fatherland," and the thought crossed my mind that he sure fit the image of a prototype member of the *Schutzstaffel*, the SS of WWII Germany. But I kept my curiosity silent, as frankly his demeanor alone was more than a little intimidating.

The hour was now likely close to midnight—time had begun to blur—and the partying accelerated with renewed vigor with the arrival of a last guest, Miriam, from Belgium. The focus of the group had become twofold: consuming and sharing alcohol and singing. The majority of the songs were done in English, as most of the participants had some level of ability in my mother tongue. The decibel level of our combined screeching seemed to increase with each rendition of the next favorite tune. Maybe because it was the holiday season, Christmas carols were in high demand. The

Germans, even the somewhat sinister Wolfgang, particularly liked the carols.

I'd guess we sounded godawful, as some folks sang completely off-key; there were spontaneous attempts to "solo," with hair-raising assaults on one's senses; and there was complete disharmony, with a variety of different words for the same song. Then suddenly, out of the cacophony of chaotic sounds, emerged a wondrous tenor voice; it was David from England. Everyone stopped singing to listen to him, and for a while, interspersed between what was arguably the absolute worst chorus to ever hit Prague, David would sing an old Irish or English ballad and bring the troops close to tears.

As the drinking and singing continued, another dramatic dynamic began to flow among this now well-oiled international set. It began with toasts, to one another, then to country, to prosperity for all, and to brotherhood, sisterhood, family, and finally anything one could conjure up from addled minds. This "camaraderie quotient" continued to escalate upward, and now folks, total strangers mere hours before, from distant and diverse cultures began to hold hands, give high fives, drape arms across shoulders, hug one another with exuberance, and exchange effusively sentimental platitudes. A oneness of spirit enveloped the group of revelers; differing cultural and ethnic traditions and political ideologies evaporated as smoke on the winds. With the last rendition of *White Christmas*, an overpowering aura of goodwill permeated throughout the seventh-floor lobby and corridors. Business cards were exchanged. I traded American dollars for USSR currency. To a person, we committed to keeping in touch, and even to visiting personally in each other's homelands. Finally, out of the chaos emerged the idea of holding an international meeting in England the following year.

No one really wanted the evening (now mid-morning) to end, but we had run out of booze, couldn't think of any more songs to sing, and had difficulty remembering the words of tunes we had already sung, so reluctantly we trudged off to our rooms.

I returned home after the conference and over the years lost touch with all those one-night comrades, including the Americans.

I enjoy history, and this past year, 2011, I attended a series of lectures (on DVDs) entitled *Diplomatic History of Europe, 1500 to 2000.* One lecture, maybe spotlighting Tallyrand or Metternich, rekindled memories of my time in Prague and that memorable evening, now two decades past, on the seventh floor of the Crystal Hotel. At that time, November 1991, Czechoslovakia was in the throes of internal conflict that threatened the dissolution of the country that had been born in 1918. There was much sadness among the Czech nationals at the prospect of an impending schism of the country. In fact, they were unable to overcome their differences, and in January 1993 the country split into two independent nations, the Czech Republic and Slovakia. As I reflected back to Prague, I think I experienced what might be called a "eureka moment." Holy cow, I thought, the solution to the troubles of Czechoslovakia at that time was at hand! If only the leaders of the two opposing national factions had been with us that evening on the seventh floor of the Crystal Hotel, today there still might be a united Czechoslovakia!

Now maybe the reader will think it a bit ludicrous to suggest that booze and ballads might have saved a nation or that the two in combination are critical variables in the realm of international diplomacy. I will acknowledge that my hypothesis (alcohol and singing as key ingredients in diplomacy) is based on a single experience, but I do have a statistical foundation for my assumption. Cliff Abe, a fellow doctoral classmate of mine and a brilliant student of statistical analysis, once presented a powerful argument on the validity of drawing conclusions based on small sample sizes, maybe even a sample of one. Unfortunately Cliff passed away at a young age, so I don't have my trusted friend to support or defend my assertions.

I suppose legitimate students of diplomatic history and process might take exception with me equating the stakes and the players involved that evening in Prague to the magnitude of the issues confronting those legendary figures Tallyrand and Metternich as combatants, for example, at the Congress of Vienna in 1814.

I did begin this short story admitting I had little expertise in the subject matter of international diplomacy. So I can't assert with 100 percent assurance that alcohol and songs have an important place in diplomacy, particularly at the international summit level; however, I'm not willing to completely discard my ideas; rather, I'm going to test out my theory concerning the efficacy of lyrics and liquor for mediation at the local level.

For example, my wife and I, like many couples, don't always agree on issues relating to managing our household, in such mundane areas as who left the milk out, why was the cap left off the toothpaste, emptying the trash, cleaning up after the dog, playing the TV too loud, and other such (in reality) frivolous annoyances. To address these household mini-crises, I propose that utilizing several shots of a fine single-malt Scotch whisky, or another libation of choice, and a soothing rendition of *What a Wonderful World* by Louis Armstrong might be a quick and effective means of resolving these domestic deadlocks.

# VI

*Dogs and a Cat of Note*

*A burglar enters a house and notices a flat-screen television. As he is about to pick it up, he hears a voice saying, "Jesus is watching you." He then notices a wallet stuffed with bills on the sideboard. He picks it up and again hears the voice: "Jesus is still watching you."*

*He looks around with his flashlight and spots a parrot in a cage in the corner of the room. He approaches the parrot and asks, "What's your name?"*

*"Solomon," the parrot replies.*

*"Who would be dumb enough to name a parrot Solomon?" snorted the burglar.*

*"The same person who calls a Rottweiler Jesus," chuckled the parrot.*

# *How to Build a Doghouse*

IN 1972 MY SON was born on December 23, sometime in mid-afternoon. Now, children are born every day, literally every minute, maybe every second; someone surely has that figured out. His birth, a joyous event, as they all are, was really kind of miraculous, if not a miracle. He was six weeks early, but Dr. Foreman and Dr. Perry got their heads together and decided, *Dude, it's time to show up.* My wife, post-polio and a wheelchair user, had some disadvantages in being pregnant and attempting to carry the baby to full term: high blood pressure, which is not compatible with a cesarean section; significantly reduced respiratory capacity; and the matter of trying to function in a wheelchair with essentially a bowling ball-sized bump in her belly. The good doctors monitored her progress closely, and on a Saturday, with her blood pressure going up, they decided it was time to start the countdown to "lift-out." Matthew came in at a bawling four-pound, thirteen-ounce bundle of fury. Actually both he and his mother were pretty laid back and worn out for a few days. But a couple of really exceptional physicians and a whole lot of good people pulling for them made it happen.

But this is a story about a doghouse, which I began writing in 1999 and then waited another thirteen years to finish now in early

2012. So what does my son's birth in 1972 have to do with the story of a doghouse?

The impetus for writing this tale began the week of May 24, 1999, when I began to dismantle the old, weather-worn doghouse that had been sitting in our backyard since December 1972. I had expected the deconstruction of the house to take several hours; in fact, it took the better part of a week, with me working several hours each day. I'm slower than most "non-gimps," but I was still amazed it took so long. I finished around Memorial Day, or, as my father called it, Decoration Day. Oh, yes, speaking of Dad—Dale Kloepping—he has a prominent place in this brief tale, as he was the individual who built the doghouse in question.

I sat under the Aleppo pine tree in our backyard, usually in early morning, and slowly and laboriously began to extract nails and staples, one at a time, from the house. Without really thinking about the disposal of the nails and staples, I tossed them into a five-gallon bucket close at hand. As I worked, it dawned on me that this doghouse had not been constructed hastily as simply an afternoon project; no, this *bowser box* was much more than just four sides with a door for the two little beasties to call home.

I began to wonder about what he was thinking as he started building the doghouse. I recall he didn't rush the project; in fact, he spent a good amount of time (I thought excessive time) planning and thinking about what he wanted to do. His tendency, maybe more accurately a personal philosophy, was that when he built something, he would say, "Well, I want it to last my lifetime." I think what he meant was, "If I'm going to expend the effort to do it, I'm going to do it right." I started to chuckle as I tried to envision his thought processes in approaching the project. I laughed aloud as I realized that he must have decided that this project was a matter of great significance and that he needed to marshal his resources to ensure a finished product equal to its importance.

In 1999, as I resumed the task of deconstruction each morning, I found myself drifting back to that time twenty-seven years earlier, and I could see him, wearing OshKosh bib overalls and with a floppy, white milk hauler's hat pulled low over his eyes, sitting comfortably in a lawn chair, deep in thought about his creation at hand.

I believe that one morning I began to understand the meaning of his methodical, almost contemplative, approach to building this doghouse; it wasn't simply a building project; rather, it seemed to have become a personal mission for him. You see we had basenjis, the African so-called barkless dogs. Having grown up in the rural Midwest in the company of countless varieties of dogs, not only ours, but all the neighborhood mutts, I saw myself as being quite knowledgeable in the ways of most canines. But I had never encountered a basenji. If you happen to own one, it has a *major* impact on your life; in our case, we had two. We had learned the ways of the basenji during the five or six years we owned them; given their extreme rambunctious nature and the approaching birth of Baby Matthew, it was clear that our two precious companions Harry and Sassy needed their own private and separate space. They had been our "babies" and had always been indoor hounds, but now they were to be banished from the house like a couple of street mongrels. Dad recognized that we were probably way overboard in essentially treating them as almost equal partners in our family. I think he decided that this project was not only a matter of creating a home for the dogs, but also a quest for him to lessen the trauma of demoting the animals to their appropriate status as dogs.

Moving them outside was not a frivolous decision, as they were so active, nimble, and strong that we were afraid they would hurt the baby—unintentionally, I believe, but the mind of a basenji is a mystery, and in their sometimes maniacal exuberance, in tandem, they could wreck a room in a matter of minutes. At times they spontaneously began to career through the house at full tilt; Harry was particularly adept at using the living room rug as a springboard, landing onto the couch, and literally accelerating horizontally across the back of the couch, leaping back to the carpet, continuing down the hallway, doing a complete circle in the bedroom (over the bed), and then racing back up the hallway to the living room to repeat the process. On one occasion I was sitting on the couch and decided to intercept him as he sprang from the carpet; he had already developed terrific momentum, and he knocked me completely off the couch to the floor. I was sore for a week, but Harry showed no ill effects from the collision. I shuddered to think of old Harama Tamu (his name in Swahili) using Baby Matthew's tummy as a trampoline for launching himself off of the couch. Oh, my god, I thought, get those beasts out of here!

In the chapter "California Dog Days" I have detailed how we were first introduced to basenjis, how we acquired Sassy and Harry, our experiences in the California dog show circuit, and our move to Tucson. Reading that short tale will provide the reader of this story a glimpse of the importance and impact of these feisty two mutts on our family.

So with the imminent arrival of Baby Matt, Dad agreed to build a doghouse for our hounds. It can get very hot during the summer months, but at a twenty-five-hundred-foot elevation in the desert, temperatures can often drop below freezing. "I'll insulate their house," he had offered early on, as if to allay our concerns of them being exposed to extremes in temperature. "You wait and see what you think."

In May 1999, before its demolition, I carefully took measurements of the structure. The house was thirty-six inches long, twenty-six inches high, and twenty-four inches wide. The arched opening at one end was eighteen inches high and ten inches wide. A double layer of bath towels covered the opening to eliminate drafts. The rear of the house had a twenty-by-twelve-inch window, double-hinged, with a strap lock so it could be opened for ventilation in the summer and closed in the winter months. That window that opened and closed was really quite unique in design. The hinged frame was recessed about two inches into the back wall and was insulated with two inches of tightly packed old newspapers. The window opening had a quarter-inch wire mesh for strength, and that was covered with a fine screen to keep the bugs out. It took me over two hours to take it apart. All four sides were of double-wall design and had two inches of insulation in them. I noted the dates of the newspapers when I removed them: December 10, 1972, to January 2, 1873, a total of twenty-three days. He must have begun the project earlier, maybe a week or more, and finished sometime after the second of January. If he had started on December 1 and finished around January 10 or 11, he would have spent essentially *six weeks* on the project! I'll bet he did spend all of that time. Like he said, "When I do it, I'm going to do it right!"

The roof, which was removable, was also recessed about two inches into the box. The top panel, or lid, extended three inches over the house on all three sides, with a six-inch extension over the front door. The entire structure sat on a three-by-six-foot platform that was elevated two inches off the ground to eliminate the possibility of water getting into the house. When construction was complete, we trekked down to Home Depot, got a good quality of lime-green marine paint, and gave it two coats. Wow, this was some doghouse!

Dad obviously recognized how attached we were to our dogs, and thus he made sure they would be living in the lap of luxury—warm in the winter, cool in the summer, and safe from the summer monsoon rains. It was quite an event the day Harry and Sassy were introduced to their new home. Without any hesitation, Harry boldly approached the house, stuck his nose through the door curtain as if he had done it a hundred times before, and went in. Sassy was more reluctant to enter, but eventually we coaxed her to enter and exit, and everything seemed copacetic. But all was not well in this new basenji mansion; Harry quickly decided that the house was to be his exclusive domain. He simply would not allow Sassy to enter when he was in residence. We didn't realize that he had expelled her until the morning after they took possession of their new bungalow; but when we saw her curled up sleeping on top of the house on a quite chilly January morning, we knew there was a problem. We were very surprised, as the pair had produced two litters of puppies, and with a family of eleven offspring, we assumed that their relationship was intact. But there had been a major change in their life—actually, in Harry's. He had become more aggressive as he aged, and we decided that he probably needed a personality alteration; that is, to be neutered. He had the surgery, and interestingly he was stitched up with a single long metal suture. Most likely because the vet knew Harry's temperament, he suggested (really requested) that we remove the suture. I had to laugh, as like myself, I'd guess the vet was also wary of Harry's unpredictable nature. Marlys, who Harry liked and trusted the most, volunteered to remove the suture. (Actually, I was afraid.) True to form, when she began the process, Harry uttered a fearsome, deep rumble of warning, but then he very gently clamped his jaws on one of her hands. She spoke softly to him in a reassuring tone, explaining what she had to do. Although he squirmed a bit and did whine some, he did not exert any further pressure on her hand. It was an amazing demonstration of trust and communication between human and animal.

No amount of coaxing, cajoling, or threats would move Harry to allow Sassy in that house when he had entered first. If she did sneak in when he wasn't looking, he'd soon discover her missing and race to the house; once inside, what ensued sounded as if both animals were being torn to shreds; when they exited, both were intact, but the honeymoon was definitely over. Apparently, with the loss of his *huevos*, he had also lost his compassion for his partner.

Dad went back to the drawing board and built another doghouse. This one was much smaller, just big enough to accommodate one dog, obviously Sassy. He mounted her home atop the roof of Harry's much larger bachelor pad. She quickly adapted to her new residence, easily jumping onto Harry's roof and spending tranquil nights unmolested by her increasingly crotchety ex-mate.

Both dogs lived to be sixteen or seventeen years old, and as with all of our family pets, it was difficult when we lost them. The smaller doghouse, where Sassy resided, was really an afterthought of necessity, not intended to last forever, and I don't recall when or how we disposed of it. But the big house that became Harry's private pad was another matter. Once I had the house completely taken apart, I spent some time looking at the old comic strips that Dad had used as insulation. For some unknown reason I kept a few of the comic sections; now, forty years later, a few of the faded, rain-soaked, tattered sections still remain tucked in one of my backyard storage sheds. I notice them now and again, and although disposing of them crosses my mind, invariably I decide that I can do that another time.

Remember early in this brief tale when I mentioned tossing the nails and staples I extracted into a five-gallon bucket? With the demolition of the house complete, I carried the bucket into the alley to throw them in the trash barrel. I looked into the bucket and started to laugh. I said aloud, "My god, I wonder how ..."

Without hesitation I carried the bucket back into my yard, dumped them on a table, and began sorting and counting. Here are the totals, types, and numbers:

| Nails | Staples |
|---|---|
| 1 1/2": 162 | 1/2": 18 |
| 2": 56 | 1": 95 |
| 2 1/2": 54 | 2": 6 |
| 3 1/2": 11 | |
| Total nails: 283 | Total staples=:119 |
| Grand total: 402 | |

Yes, the total of all the nails and staples used in the project was a whopping 402! If I hadn't decided to take it apart, I'd wager that, now forty years past, it would still be there, sitting under the Aleppo pine tree. Maybe Dad didn't expect the doghouse to last a millennium, but his rules for building were almost axiomatic. He had admonished me more than once in my life about his guidelines, and in particular on the occasion of this project. Today I can still recall his firm yet gentle lecture: "Now, Kent, if you are going to build something, make sure it will last." He most certainly accomplished that objective in building the doghouse!

# To Remember

Never was a friend so loyal and true,
A rambunctious big fellow, who gave all his love to you.

Powerful and ferocious some thought him to be,
But a strong, gentle heart, he showed to me.

Yet fearsome was that rumble from his massive chest,
Twas an ominous warning no stranger would test.

Jaws like a vise and a gut of steel,
Amazing to think he once made a backpack a meal!

He was smart as a whip, and listened quite well,
But when cousin Mina came visiting his behavior might go to hell.

His antics and energy our souls he could mend,
But all God's creatures, like us, has a life that will end.

Hearts will break, tears will flow, his spirit floats away, as a
Falling leaf;
But have courage we share your grief.

Life is but a brief journey to a better day,

He did his work well, now he's on his way.

Today his spirit is soaring, he's free as the lark
That rascally gentleman, you called Barc.

# The Lament of Prairie Dog Percy

Well scratch my fleas and duck for cover those redneck dudes are coming back. I'm a lovable varmint, don't ruin my day, skedaddle back home, and give me some slack.

Camouflage gear and weapons galore, god almighty these guys are planning a war!

.22's, a .223, .308, and a .30-06, my goodness all the guns they've got. Why not a howitzer, you could wipe out the whole town with a single shot.

We're social creatures and greet each other with sort of a kiss. Whoa there, it's Bubba with his .30-06. Kapow, what's that? Oh no. it's "pink mist!"

I'm a rodent, not a dog, who gave us that name the dirty louse? Oh yes it's the genus, CYNOMYS, it came from the Greeks and means dog-mouse.

The French called us dogs cause we often bark, but we also chuckle, scream, snarl and even growl. Sadly, prior to my early demise, I was perfecting a howl.

Lewis and Clark thought we were barking squirrels and the old settlers called us sod poodles; these folks were obviously misguided souls and frankly, I think, out of their noodles.

I was going to the annual Prairie Dog Blues Festival in Prairie Du Chien in August 09. Those fiddlers are great and their music sublime, but here I sit, my life is past, old Dick ended it all with one mighty blast!

*A little girl asked her mom, "Mom, may I take the dog for a walk around the block?"*

*Mom replied, "No, because she is in heat."*

*"What's that mean?" asked the child.*

*"Go ask your father. I think he's in the garage."*

*The little girl went to the garage and said, "Dad, may I take Belle for a walk around the block? I asked Mom, but she said the dog was in heat, and to come to you."*

*Dad said, "Bring Belle over here." He took a rag, soaked it with gasoline, blotted the dog's backside with it, and said, "Okay, you can go now, but keep Belle on a leash, and only go one time around the block."*

*The little girl left and returned a few minutes later with no dog on the leash.*

*Surprised, Dad asked, "Where's Belle?"*

*The little girl said, "She ran out of gas about halfway down the block, so another dog is pushing her home."[1]*

# Neighborhood Dogs

LOUIE WOULD LIKE TO kill me; I'm sure of it. I don't think he means to have me for lunch; rather, it's just his desire to savage me and tear me apart limb from limb. Anytime he hears me coming, he begins barking—actually more like yapping. He peeks at me through the crack in his backyard gate with a single crazed-looking eye and goes ballistic. His yaps are always in series of three: yap, yap, yap. He then executes a 360-degree spin and looks to see if I'm still there; then there are three more yaps, another 360-degree whirl, and on and on. I hustle off after the second or third spin, before he has a stroke, ruptures a kidney, or miraculously scales the six-foot fence and assaults me. Ferocious, I guess he is—all twelve or fifteen pounds of him wrapped in a black and tan miniature pinscher body. I never did anything to him to warrant such unbridled hostility toward me.

I was a licensed psychologist in the state of Arizona for a number of years, but I put my license on hold when I retired from the university. I got to thinking about Louie's obvious anger and thought maybe I should renew the license, start practicing dog therapy, and invite Louie to be my first client; I wouldn't even charge him. Then again, maybe I won't do that.

There's an old adage that suggests dogs often emulate the personalities of their owners; maybe some do, but in Louie's case, his owners are really nice folks.

Over the past several years I've personally met thirty-six canines that live in my neighborhood. I have encountered these pooches almost always in the company of their owners, often on my daily "metallurgical exploration" forays or when simply cruising through the neighborhood, being nosy. Ostensibly the humans are walking the dogs—or is it the reverse? The dog taking the person for a stroll?

While I have become very well acquainted with a good number of the dogs, with others, I know only their names and breeds, but nothing more. Likewise, some of the folks the dogs have in tow I don't know, and we simply greet one another as people we recognize from the neighborhood. I do have some well-established relationships with a number of members of the *Homo sapiens* class, like Brenda and Cheryl, two close neighbors, who are both Pima County deputy sheriffs and key partners in "metallurgical engineering" with me. Their dog is a beagle named Guinness. He has a very loud voice, kind of a combination bark and yelp, which I think technically is called a bay. He's a bit stand-offish and really is not too interested unless you have a treat for him.

Sylvia, who lives south across the street from Guinness, has a miniature schnauzer who goes by Uno ("one" in Spanish). He's really a cute little fellow who seems a bit nervous at times; he trembles and, on occasion, will whimper a little. Maybe he could benefit from therapy too.

East across the street from Guinness lives my former administrative assistant from the university, Helene, previously known as Laurie. She has three pooches that go into a frenzy of barking when I get within forty or fifty feet of their carport. One time I decided to peek over the carport gate at them, but as I approached the gate, they all yipped frantically and scattered. I have never seen them, but they all have fancy names. Miss Lyla Belle is a chihuahua, Schyler Mae is a rescue Yorkie, and *Tzipiya* (Hebrew for "hope") is a Carachon! Say what? Well, I didn't know either; it's a cross between a Bichon Frise and a King Charles Cavalier.

My neighbor across the street has a dog named Abbey. She's a collie-shepherd mix, a real sweetheart; one ear points up and the other down. We're good buddies, me and Abbey, and Al too.

Al's brother Sam has a dog named Minnie that I think should be on TV, on *America's Funniest Home Videos*. Minnie is a nervous wreck (hmm, maybe I should be thinking about group therapy for a number of these pooches), but her method of urinating or "laying a little log" is truly unique. When she has the urge (number one or number two), she lifts her back legs and torso completely off the ground and proceeds to walk with her front legs while wetting or fertilizing the ground. Without exception, she utilizes this unusual technique. Sam doesn't recall why or when she started, and all I could think of was maybe she once peed or pooped on her tootsies, and once was enough.

Thinking back to Louie, it occurs to me that he isn't the only neighborhood dog who exhibits what can only be described as hostility toward me. Do they sense some innate character flaw in my person? No, I don't think so; it is, I believe, that they have a whole lot of unresolved anger in them.

Let me see, there's Sandy, who lives down the street—part schnauzer, part terrier, about 75 percent aggression—who was badly abused before Ruth rescued him. How about Lovey? Wow, what a misnomer! Her mother, Chenille, lives in the same household and is a wriggly licking machine, but Lovey charges, barks, retreats, and usually will not allow you to touch her. She's part dachsie and something fuzzy, and she reminds me of a mechanical toy scooting forward and backward.

Sam is a black and white "lopsided A-hole" (also known as a Lhasa apso) who looks benign and cuddly, but get within a foot of him and he snarls and lunges. His housemate Tuffy, also a Lhasa, is fifteen, pure white, and legally blind, with a pussycat temperament; their owner, Bob, has to watch Tuffy carefully, or he walks into the cactus. Sophia, a white chihuahua, belongs to Jessica, who lives on our block. The closest I've been to Sophia is when she is in a car driving past me on the sidewalk. If she spots me, she goes off, clawing at the car window and barking hysterically; one time she got a paw out of the almost totally closed window, and I'd swear she gave me "the bird" with a toenail!

There are also two dogs who live about two blocks away, a standard schnauzer and an unknown type with huge, upright ears; when I wheel by, they charge the wrought-iron driveway gate, yapping incessantly until I'm out of their sight.

Now, those six dogs have some real issues, not only with me, but also in general, I'd guess. I've worried about them and their seeming unbridled aggression. I think I have the solution: they all need anger management therapy. I'll do it as group therapy, and hopefully they will be willing to set aside their inclination for savagery and behave as civilized canines. I do have a trump card to play, to ensure order in the group if any of the troops want to get out of line. His name is Jinx: a quite large, docile-acting, male Rottweiler who will serve as a stabilizer and enforcer to maintain a tone of civility in the group. He doesn't bark when you go by his house; he just stares very intently, and somehow one gets the idea that it might not be a wise course of action to rattle his cage. I think he will bring a quieting influence to the sessions.

This could become a new cottage industry and be quite profitable. Let's see; fifty dollars a dog, times six, equals three hundred dollars. These guys need two sessions a week, minimum; that's six hundred dollars a week, or twenty-four hundred dollars a month, not bad. Wow, I need to get my psych license renewed ASAP!

As long as I'm going to begin my therapy practice again, I might as well start a second group for some of my more timid, nervous friends. It will be an ego-enhancement group. Minnie would be a good fit; maybe her self-image has been a bit bruised with folks gawking and pointing at her when she does her potty thing. Uno could use some help in more fully embracing his masculinity. Lady Belle, an absolutely darling Jack Russell, who leads her master, Eli, around the neighborhood, could use a few tips on what constitute appropriate occasions and objects to bark at; currently she will bark at birds, trees, clouds, large rocks, butterflies, and often mysterious things, unknown and unseen. Coco, a tiny poodle who lives with Dick and Joyce, seems a bit withdrawn since the arrival of their second dog, Midge, a beautiful, classy-looking golden retriever. Rex, another golden (who seems lonesome, as Mark and his sons are often off at work and school), earnestly desires female companionship. I may have to sprinkle a little saltpeter on his Alpo to minimize his overzealous amorous tendencies. Also in this group I'll have an Australian shepherd named Blue sit in, as his presence will undoubtedly have a soothing effect; I mean, Blue is Mr. Serenity. He's so mellow that his owner, Jamey, is going to use him as a therapy dog for people; this group will be good experience for him. Every time I go past his house, I stop to say hello, and he pushes up tightly to my chair and gazes up admiringly as if I'm his best friend. Yes, this should be a productive encounter for all concerned.

Most folks have favorite dogs: their own, or others they have met;

I am no exception, as in my neighborhood there are a number of really neat mutts. Scoobi, an old black lab who has lived in England, Australia, California, and the Midwest (now Tucson), is a happy, overweight, still highly energetic lady of twelve years, with her tail in constant motion. Her owner, Bill Bailey, has to hustle, as she seems to want to make sure he comes home!

Speaking of overweight, Bubba is a massive English bull who is really a round mound of lard. His mistress, Tanya, I noted, was also very large, but she had an excuse: she was pregnant, I'd guess one day short of nine months. But old Bubba, like me, apparently has difficulty pushing away from the dinner table. I've only spoken to him twice; on the first occasion he rumbled, woofed, and smelled me all over. But our second meeting was completely cordial; he waddled some twenty feet down his driveway to greet me, plopped down as though worn out from the trip, panted, puffed, slobbered, and smiled up at me in quintessential bulldog fashion.

Judy and Fred walk Barnum and Bailey, two frisky black poodles, early every morning. Judy's father worked for Barnum & Bailey Circus, hence the names, and he also had a marvelous collection of miniature circus animals, people, cages, wagons, etc., many figurines carved by him, that were displayed in local restaurants here in Tucson. Chloe, a golden, moved to Maryland so that Rob, her owner, could attend medical school there. We really miss her, Chrissy (Rob's wife), and the little girls, Katie, Sarah, and Baby Audrey. Whenever the family returned from a day trip, Chloe was let out of the house first; she greeted the family exuberantly, howling with glee, running zigzag patterns in the yard, barking and jumping, delighted that her charges had once again returned home safely.

Although I can name almost all the local dogs, there are a few people that belong to the dogs that I don't know. An unknown elderly woman walks a really excellent young female basset named Belle. Another fellow, sort a of different guy, walks greyhounds, up to six at one time. I approached them on one occasion, asking beforehand if they were gentle. "Oh, sure" the fellow replied, but as I got close to them, the large male suddenly snarled, bared his teeth, and lunged at me.

Shocked, I blurted out, "Hey! What is that?"

The fellow sort of smiled and said, "Well, he's the boss." That dog needs to be in my therapy group—maybe the guy too! Since that time, I've given them a wide berth.

I love dogs, as many folks do. Losing a beloved pet can really hurt. A particularly poignant example was the recent passing of Angel. She was a tiny (six to eight pounds) mixture of chihuahua and "who knows" that resulted in a coal-black fur ball with pointy ears; she looked like a stuffed toy. I first saw her on a leash, walking ahead of an elderly gentleman who was riding a tricycle. I later learned that he was legally blind and Angel "walked" him daily, guiding him safely on his tricycle down the sidewalk.

Tragically, she suddenly sickened and passed away. The old fellow was devastated and inconsolable. The loss of one of those creatures full of unconditional love can be heart-wrenching.

On a more uplifting note, I cannot fail to acknowledge a hound of renown, our dog, Taz. She's a salt-and-pepper, almost forty-pound standard schnauzer who, almost every day, jumps onto my wife's lap and rides throughout the house or backyard. We previously owned a miniature schnauzer named Mina, and be assured the two sizes are nothing alike. Mina was sweet and cuddly, but Taz has nonstop energy and tremendous agility, is a terrific leaper, and really I'm not overstating here, has great intelligence. Isn't a dog owner's favorite line "smartest animal I ever had"? Although we spoil her something awful, she is exceptionally well behaved. She does, however, have a few flaws. On a leash with Matthew walking her, she really doesn't like to be bothered by other dogs. She will mostly ignore them, but she has a seeming permanent dislike for a pooch named Corky, a dachshund-basset mix who appears to be pretty laid back, but she also appears to have a grudge against Taz. When they see one another, they lock eyes—it's instant hate! I think, as a throwback to the heritage of standard schnauzers, Taz also has a tendency to leer at little chihuahuas; schnauzers are known to be great ratters, and as I see it, she must think they resemble oversized rodents. Whatever her issue, my son judiciously avoids close encounters with dogs like Minnie, Cici, or any other smaller-than-average pooch. Recall that I stated that she is a very bright animal; testimony to her high level of brain-power was the afternoon Rio appeared at the end of our alley. Rio is a huge, muscular, magnificent Doberman pinscher, with DOBERMAN in capital letters. My son and I were maybe forty or fifty feet from Rio and his owner, Lisa, who was walking him. "Wow," I exclaimed, "he's really a beauty."

"Would you like to meet and pet him?" she asked. Noting that he was wearing a muzzle, I declined, suggesting I'd meet him at another time. The point of relating this incident is Taz's behavior when Rio appeared. She was in the yard, but she would observe "dog traffic" by peeking through knotholes in the redwood fence. When a dog walked by, she was hidden behind the fence, and she'd "ambush" the dog with ferocious growling and raging as she raced back and forth along the fence; she essentially had a dog's version of a conniption fit. But this day there was total silence from behind the fence. We looked into the yard, and there she sat, completely motionless, peering out through a hole in the fence at Rio. She didn't make a sound, not even a whimper; nary a whisker or an eyelash moved until he disappeared.

Even though she and Rio were separated by a six-foot fence, she was taking no chances, for somewhere in that primitive brain she quickly and correctly processed that on this occasion, complete silence was the better part of valor.

I feel that I would be remiss if I did not mention Tipper and Ripley. They belong to a Professor Wilson who taught Middle East history at the university; I took classes from him, and we occasionally see one another in the neighborhood. Tipper is a poodle, and Ripley is a chihuahua. But Ripley is so old and so fat that if it weren't for his two little pointed ears, he'd look exactly like a baby seal; his coat is a light tan, almost white color, and he has two beady, very shiny black eyes. Furthering the illusion that he might be a seal is the fact that Ripley doesn't go for a walk, he goes for a "carry"! With him cradled in Wilson's arm, one sees no feet, only an obese little critter, and absent his ears, he would be a great imitation of a seal!

Dale Carnegie once wrote a book entitled *How to Win Friends and Influence People.* It was arguably one of the most influential business books of the twentieth century. While this tale concerns my neighborhood dogs, it is also about the folks who either own the animals or, from the dogs' point of view, are lucky to be living with their dogs. I don't know if I've influenced either dogs or people in my local environs; but in my daily treks I have met many fine canines (although a few who have some unresolved anger issues) and a whole lot of really nice neighbors. I'm not sure if making friends with a dog influences people, or making friends with people will influence the hound. Now, as the cooler fall temperatures creep into the Southwest, I shall enjoy my daily encounters with both persons and pooches even more.

Now, let me see, where did I put that telephone number for the state psychological association license renewal?

# Whisper Park

NESTLED AT THE FRONT of our home is a rather smallish flagstone patio abundantly adorned with a variety of Southwestern plants and a few imports that reflect our Midwestern roots. Born of violence, it is a cool, tranquil spot shaded with the filtered light of a blue Palo Verde that greets each new day's sun. A mid-sized bottlebrush sits south, adjacent to the Palo Verde, and on its right flank is a very large olive tree that seems to have a year-round supply of the black, bitter fruit hanging in profuse clumps. Millions of silver-green petals face the midday sun, providing a sun-blotched spot that is restful, belying its near-tragic genesis.

The only saguaro died, but in remembrance of an old friend suddenly taken, its blackening hulk remains. The immature ribs, never to reach the magnificence of the giants, now are appearing, a skeleton, emerging as the horny skin drops away. The barrel cactus thrives, with short, stubby fishhook tentacles ready to slash the unwary. A plump, spineless prickly pear, now ten to twelve feet tall, completes the circle of guardians of this small oasis in the desert.

The house protects the western exposure of the enclave, with a porch swing for comfort, a chiminea for a touch of warmth, an old wagon wheel (a memory from Minnesota days past), and feisty hummingbirds dashing in and out. A spindly, purple-flowered Mexican sage graces the northern gateway to the patio, a fragile, gangling, fragrant native that welcomes all who pass. Precious water gently pours from the mouth of a Mexican pot, inclined on its side, into a small, rock-filled basin—now the favorite watering hole for all manner of winged creatures, quail, lizards, an occasional squirrel, and the neighborhood cats. In the blazing heat of summer days, it is a small haven, a source of life-giving water.

At first there was mostly only bare desert, with the front yard lamp post surrounded by eight large, overgrown sea green junipers: a hiding place for stealthy killers, the neighborhood cats, stalking, following ancient and instinctual codes. The spreading bushes provided excellent cover for ambush, especially against groups of Gambel's quail, running pell-mell to feed on dried olives, chorusing, "Chicago, Chicago, Chicago" and announcing their arrival to all the cats, particularly Whisper, a large, black, long-haired feline with peculiar mannerisms and a taste for quail.

Whisper lived across the street, and I discovered that he had begun to spend his days lying quietly hidden beneath the junipers waiting for the noisy quail. One morning as I watched the approach of a dozen or so of the squawking little morsels, Whisper suddenly struck from ambush, a black flash of lightning, pouncing into the center of the closely bunched covey. Quail screeched, feathers flew, my heart leaped, and birds exploded in every direction! Suddenly all was still; Whisper, spitting soft down, had missed! No front claws— aha! I raced out to the patio and chased off the black villain. Within ten minutes I had my pruning clippers in hand and was lopping large branches of juniper to the ground. I worked several days cutting down the eight large junipers, and the massive root systems finally yielded to the power of a four-wheel-drive vehicle.

But out of the chaos of Whisper's attack was born an idea: a patio, a flagstone patio, now surrounded with amaryllis, pansies, daisies, Cape honeysuckle, autumn sage, Mexican heather, agave, and mums. It's a place to relax and chat, sip coffee, and watch your neighbors go by. Daily birds and quail congregate and drink—cats too, to slake their thirst. But the feathered ones are now wise and watchful—each day old Whisper trundles over, stopping in the middle of the street to engage in strange gyrations, then proceeds to the watering trough, drinks his fill, eyes potential victims, thinks better of it, and departs peacefully.

He's a strange cat, but his behavior was the impetus for this tiny oasis; it's really not big enough for the name, but we call it Whisper Park.

# VII

*Positive Mental Health Activities*

*There is a story of three clerics: a priest, a Pentecostal type named Billy Bob, and a rabbi. They all served their flocks at a university in Northern Michigan and weekly met to discuss how their ministries were progressing and to share ideas on how they might convert additional souls to the faith. One morning it occurred to them that humans had always been the focus of their efforts, and they wondered about saving the souls of animals. As there was an abundance of black bears in this northern territory, they decided to attempt to convert bears.*

*The priest volunteered to be the first to venture into the woods to find a bear. He returned a week later horribly scratched, one ear almost chewed off, and bruised all over his body. He reported, "I encountered a bear and held up a crucifix, but he charged and began to maul me. I then sprinkled holy water on him, and he immediately became calm. Next week the bishop is arriving to give him his first communion."*

*Next, the Reverend Billy Bob set off to locate a bruin and convert him to his charismatic style of religion. Billy Bob returned in worse condition than the priest; one arm was in a cast, a patch covered one eye, and both ears had been shredded. He said, "I found a bear, raised my bible, and shouted, 'Come on, bear! Let us wrestle with the Lord!' He jumped me, and we rolled and kicked and fought and ended up in a creek. I quickly baptized him, and he stopped fighting. We went to the shore and spent the rest of the day praising the Lord."*

*Finally the rabbi left on his mission of conversion. He did not return to the university; instead Billy Bob and the priest were summoned to the local hospital. There lay the rabbi, bandaged from head to toe, IVs in both arms, both eyes black, and missing an ear. "Holy Mary!" exclaimed the priest. "What happened, friend rabbi?"*

*In almost in a whisper, the rabbi replied weakly, "You know, in retrospect maybe I shouldn't have started out by trying circumcision!"*

# Monday Morning Irregulars

EVERY MONDAY MORNING AT 8:30 AM sharp, for the past eight or nine years, I have traveled a couple of miles north to Bruegger's Bagel Shop to meet with three other fellows that I know as friends. This weekly gathering of self-labeled "Monday Morning Irregulars" has risen close to the top of the hierarchy of meaningful activities in my life. This Monday morning ritual is much more than simply a matter of old retired dudes flapping their gums; rather, there are significant underpinnings and a sound rationale for meeting together. Allow me to try to enlighten the reader.

Norman Cousins (1915–1990) was a journalist, professor, author, world peace advocate, and editor of the *Saturday Review* from 1942 to 1972. He may be best known for his book *Anatomy of an Illness*, published in 1979. He lived significantly longer than the medical profession predicted he would, surviving heart disease, a heart attack, and a painful, debilitating disease called ankylosing spondylitis, a deterioration of the connective tissue of the spine. He attributed his longer-than-expected survival to four major steps he undertook: a change in diet, including massive doses of vitamin C; getting off drugs; exchanging a hospital bed for a hotel room; and importantly, renting a movie projector and watching old Marx Brothers movies. He related that he literally laughed himself back to health. He had hypothesized that if negative emotions could contribute to poor health, why couldn't laughter and joy have the opposite effect? So humor and laughter became a daily antidote for Cousins's health issues, and it worked for him.

In the 1990s he came to the University of Arizona as the keynote speaker for a conference on health and wellness; I attended his presentation, which included many examples and stories of people who survived catastrophic illnesses that the medical community had said would kill them quickly. I have always enjoyed humor, and hearing Cousins strongly reinforced my belief in the healing power of laughter.

I now realize that initially I did not understand the truly powerful impact that the weekly gathering of the Monday Morning Irregulars had on me, for humor and laughter is a primary ingredient that punctuates and permeates the one-and-a-half to two-hour session each week. The quintessential humorist is Ron, a tall, innocuous-appearing, white-haired fellow, whose sparkling blue eyes often carry a leprechaun gleam, and in rare moments his demeanor and humor approaches the Machiavellian! He seems to have an unlimited fund of anecdotes. Some are quite appropriate for all-male groups, but others would make even hardened truck drivers turn pale. He frequently has a number of "thoughts for the day," most often in question format, and usually unanswerable:

"Why do we *drive* on a *parkway* and *park* on a *driveway*?"

"If you spend the day doing nothing, how do you know when you're done?"

"If a vegetarian eats vegetables, what does a humanitarian eat?"

"If the temperature is zero degrees today, and it will be twice as cold tomorrow, what will the temperature be?"

He has hundreds more! If he happens to repeat an anecdote (which are often lengthy), he has the uncanny ability to use the exact wording and phraseology that he did the first time he told the joke. Roger, Gordon, or I, the other members of the usual foursome, will also occasionally throw in a story, most often myself.

Roger and Gordon are Catholic, Ron is a Methodist, and I'm a "biblical" Lutheran, which is one who views the bible as *the* foundational text of Christianity, as opposed to those Lutherans who do not adhere to biblical text inconsistent with their social agendas. Agree or not, this question and many other theological issues are often thoroughly hashed out on Monday mornings. Humor relating to religion is fair game, no matter the variety of belief. These jokes are not vicious or intended to be demeaning (like the opening anecdote), and neither is the vast majority of other kinds that find their way into the discussions.

Notwithstanding this, I must point out that Ron is very adept at dredging up "disability humor." I know it's coming, as he gets a wicked look in his eyes; it is expected, of course, and I do my best to express sham outrage, admonishing him for those insensitive and politically incorrect blasphemies against us "gimpers"! That doesn't stop him; rather, it spurs him on to even more outrageous jokes, most of them pretty hilarious; I then add a few I know.

Sometimes Ron will reach to the bottom of the barrel for a simply awful story. Roger has become the designated member of the group to pass judgment on these unseemly tales, as he has a repertoire of readily available adjectives for labeling these stories; he uses such choice descriptors as "depraved," "perverse," "deplorable," "cruel," "despicable," and "downright evil"! When I return home, my wife, Marlys, invariably asks me if Ron told another of his unspeakably bad stories; if I answer in the affirmative and repeat the story, she blurts out something like, "Oh, that's awful! And what did Roger say to him?"

For a good number of years, but no longer, there was a group of guys, between eight and ten of them, who were also present every Monday morning. A majority of the group was of Italian descent, and we affectionately referred to them as "the New York Mafiosi." There was also a "Jewish Mafkowitz" (Howie's terminology) contingent as part of that group; roughly half of the group was from New York or other parts of the East Coast.

Our group, the Mafiosi, and the Mafkowitz types never sat together; we each had our designated locations, but there was a good amount of good-natured banter across the room. Regular participants in that group were Tom, Rick, Charlie, Howard (friends call him Howie), Moe, Jim, Joe, Billy, and a guy named Al. Al, in his seventies but who could pass for fifty-something, plays for TOTS, the Tucson Old-Timers baseball team that has members still playing who are in their nineties! These Monday morning regulars were a loud, boisterous, argumentative bunch who thoroughly enjoyed themselves; their free-flowing interactive style created a sense of familiarity one might experience in a family restaurant or a neighborhood joint. Now they no longer come on Monday morning. There is, however, a visual reminder that they were once a vibrant part of the scene: a plaque hangs on the wall in the northeast corner of the restaurant, above the tables where they always assembled. The inscription is as follows:

IN MEMORY OF GAETANO S. MAURICI
"TOM"
OCTOBER 18, 1942–JUNE 12, 2010
"BA-DA-BING"

Tom, a jovial, heavyset fellow, one of the leaders of that band of rascals, had passed away. He had a number of ongoing health problems, not the least of which was diabetes. He loved to eat, and I think he drank a bit, and the combination of health issues and his lifestyle finally overwhelmed him. The group continued on for a period after Tom died, but eventually they drifted away to another location. Periodically a few of that old crowd will stop in on a Monday morning, but now their corner is mostly quite subdued, often occupied by a few sedate older gals.

There is, however, one exception to the disappearance of the Mafioso group, in the person of Howie. I once mistakenly labeled him as belonging to the Italian clique, and he quickly corrected me, saying, "Well, actually I represent the Jewish Mafkowitz connection." Howie was in fact the person responsible for having the plaque mounted on the wall in honor of Tom. I never inquired, but it seemed surprising that a chain restaurant would allow a plaque commemorating a patron to be permanently affixed to the wall. I can only speculate that he must have exerted some Jewish muscle to accomplish the task.

Each Monday Howie always greets us in a cheerful, upbeat manner. He usually has a word of wisdom to share, on any number of topics, often including his latest review of local fine dinning establishments. He dutifully tolerates a lame joke or two, then gets his morning coffee and bagel and retreats to a table to read his newspaper. We have asked him to join us, but he demurs, smiling pleasantly, saying he's going to do the paper. As a side note, and at the risk of sending a wrong signal, I must say that he really smells good! Of course I expressed that observation in a totally masculine manner, and my voice, I noted, was about an octave lower than usual when I told Howie. His scent reminds me of a friend of mine who was black, and the interaction of his cologne and body chemistry also produced a gangbuster fragrance.

The two other irregular stalwarts of the Monday morning gathering are Gordon and Roger. Gordon, who is the senior member of the foursome, occupies a kind of pseudo elder statesman role in the dynamics of the group; that is, he is a great listener, one who appears to carefully follow the particular conversation at hand and eventually has some sage words to sprinkle into an often bubbling political stew or other controversial topic. I'm arguably the most politically conservative member of the group, and although I do try mostly (honest!) to avoid being too confrontational with my more left-leaning colleagues, I admit that at times I pontificate a bit in pointing out that "to drink the Obama Kool-Aid and get on his socialistic train is to ride the rails to national ruin!"

Whether it's commentary on sports, religion, or politics or a particularly outrageous anecdote by Ron, Gordon very often will add a voice of clarity or reason when the discussion becomes too helter-skelter. He is a knowledgeable and astute follower of the sports world, and although I see him as a loyal Wildcat, he also bleeds pretty heavy doses of Buckeye red and white on occasion. In his life he has endured some heavy personal tragedy not of his making and survived intact, and now, I believe, he finds the camaraderie, humor, and straight talk a medicinal elixir in meeting the exigencies of life, as we all do.

Roger, is sometimes difficult for me to read; that is to say he is an enigma. He's without doubt a great family man, with six children and a host of grandkids. I once told him I grew up knowing that Catholics really multiply prolifically, having only in recent years been replaced by the Mormons for the size of families. He simply ignored the observation. In my view, he sometimes attributes more optimism to what I label as the liberal-socialist ideology of our current national political administration. He counters that I sound like a right-wing thinker, uncaring for the have-nots of our country. We've had spirited discussions on such matters, and just when I think I have him cornered, he will express a point of view that is close to conservative and wreck my argument! I've suggested that in reality he's a closet conservative, but I haven't discovered enough evidence to make the label stick. He has a knack for uncovering little-known facts and information. At the height of the exposés of abuse by Catholic priests, amid all the negative publicity, Roger dug up similar stories on those "fallen" Catholics, the Lutherans! He will, on occasion, bring in a story that appeared in a local publication that none of us had seen. He does give excellent advice on movies and worthwhile TV specials; however, I don't share his views on *60 Minutes*, as the only guy I liked was Andy Rooney. I haven't figured him out completely, but I have begun to understand that on occasion, when he expresses what I consider to be an outrageous liberal viewpoint and I react (or explode) and he merely smirks at my ramblings, he was simply jerking my chain!

Occasionally a chap named Jerry, a former colleague of Ron and Roger at Tucson Medical Center, will join us and share another of his interesting international travel adventures, along with the latest news and prices on Southwestern textiles (Indian blankets) and other collectibles. He is extremely knowledgeable in the fields of Indian artifacts, pottery, and Western artists. He has, on occasion, organized and conducted tours throughout Southwestern Indian reservations, providing detailed and intimate knowledge of the cultures of these first peoples of the area.

Over the years the four of us have come to know the majority of the Bruegger employees on a first-name basis, and we recognize many other patrons who also frequent the establishment on Monday mornings. On rare occasions we invite our spouses for a "ladies' morning" with the boys. Having them join us is always pleasant; we have to ratchet down the raunchy jokes a bit (not Ron), and we four sit in our designated places and the ladies are grouped at the other end of the table.

While I have tried to make a case for these Monday meetings being a therapeutic "health and wellness" gathering, with humor a primary vehicle for enhancing our well-being, these weekly encounters also serve another critical need for men. I have described elsewhere that newly discovered concept called TEAM; that is, *Testosterone Enhancement Among Men*. Without question, we four guys are beneficiaries of the TEAM experience, as is true for all men.

Having attempted to characterize my three friends in some detail, comrades I enjoy and admire, I feel a need to offer a disclaimer for them and for the reader: I would label my writing skills as not bad— but in the same breath, not too good. Thus in describing people, physically, personality-wise, behaviorally—in essence, who they are—I am limited by my level of writing expertise. Talking about someone, either verbally or on paper, is fraught with potential for misunderstanding in meaning and intent. For any observations I have made that might cause consternation, I would ask for your forbearance and trust in my motives.

I was thinking recently about the long-term benefits of humor, laughter, and joy. I wondered if the positive effects on one's health and physical being might be cumulative; that is, could sufficient amounts of humor and laughter actually increase one's longevity? Holy cow, how much longer could we extend our lives? Forever? Oh, probably not, and if one is a person of faith, that's really not a bad thing.

In an article entitled "The Healing Power of Laughter," the author states, "Ultimately laughter may represent the rapture of the human spirit, and in finding this rapture we also find our way back to health."

That sounds right to me; I think I'll join the Irregulars again next Monday.[1]

There is a story of a prominent gynecologist who upon retirement decided he needed to learn about and understand the workings of the internal combustion engine, aka the motor in his car. He enrolled in a trade school, completed the course, and took the final exam, which had a perfect score of 100 points. When his exam was returned to him, the instructor had awarded him 150 points.

"How is it possible that I got 150 points?" inquired the puzzled doctor.

"Well, you see," smiled the teacher, "you got 50 points for correctly disassembling the engine, 50 points for putting it back together again, and I gave you an extra 50 points for doing it all through the exhaust pipe!"

# *Lifelong Learning*

HAVING ENTERED THE EIGHTH decade of my life, it occurred to me that the majority of my friends, guys and gals I hang with, and folks who might drop in for a visit, are close to my age. My wife and I do have younger friends, but this message is more intended for the Metamucil, Polident, and Viagra crowd. The subject for your consideration is the matter of *lifelong learning*. Your early elementary school days and secondary and higher education years should only be seen as preparation for the challenges of ensuring that one's brain doesn't, from lack of exercise, solidify into a mass like old-fashioned head cheese. Yes, to keep those batteries charged and the synapses firing, engaging in critical, analytical thinking and participating in crisp, meaningful debate is the key. Life itself is like a university, and its curricula are endless. We can study art, the stars, plants, people, poetry, dogs, cats, astrology, anatomy—any science—flies, fleas, or bees, even fruits and fruitcakes: literally almost any subject or topic one can think of or observe. I'd like to share with the reader some examples of my current educational pursuits that have been not only stimulating but also invigorating for the old gray matter.

Every Thursday morning I motor across the "old pueblo" (Tucson) to St. Andrews Presbyterian Church (15.6 miles) to watch lectures on DVDs, many from an organization named the Learning Company.

There is a group of TEAM guys (see TEAM article, p. 201) who purchase the DVDs for their personal libraries or share the cost for the common collection. We meet at the church only because one of the fellows from the church founded the group, and the facility provides the space.

Almost without exception, the lecturers, many of them distinguished professors, are excellent presenters, top in their fields, and wonderfully knowledgeable of the subject matter. We have watched lectures on ancient history, the Roman Empire, and the history of Byzantium, and an outstanding survey series on the lessons of wisdom from history. We've seen origins and ideologies of the American Revolution, the American Civil War, WWI and WWII, Abraham Lincoln, the diplomatic history of Europe (1500–present), and US-Middle East relations (1900-present). At this writing, we are finishing a thirty-six-lecture course on the rise and fall of the British empire.

I've also had the privilege of attending live lectures by Dr. Richard Cosgrove, a retired professor emeritus of history from the University of Arizona. His specialty is English history, and the two-hour lectures are presented in four-week sessions. He has covered early medieval England, the Tudors (Henry VII, Henry VIII, Edward, Mary, and Elizabeth I), the Victorians, church and state, English common law, and other equally interesting aspects of the British empire.

While I have always enjoyed history, I have recently embarked on a quite different field of inquiry that has become a new passion for me: *metallurgical engineering!* It's hard to believe that I, a liberal arts type, would become fully embroiled in a truly hard science. There are different areas of emphasis for study, such as theory, research methodology, ore analysis, and exploration. The latter category, *exploration*, has been my area of concentration. This area of study has been so invigorating that a number of local folks, some neighbors, spontaneously joined with me in this exciting endeavor. Two former Air Force pilots, two deputy sheriffs, my barber, a retired educator, a dental hygienist and her partner, and a single father are just the beginning of what I envision as a growing (to borrow a line from Ken Burns) "Corps of Discovery." This field of activity has many upsides, not the least of which is a likely designation as an environmentally green program. I haven't heard from Al Gore or any of his assorted lunatic cronies, but I can envision a call at any time. Well, green or not, metallurgical exploration is very satisfying and in fact does have a positive environmental impact.

Daily, my metallurgical forays find me cruising the local environs in my trusty Storm Series Torque SP Power Wheelchair. I've not tested the limits, but the manual claims it has a range of fourteen *miles*!

My journeys take me to Udall Park, St. Pius Catholic Church, and bus stops, and through alleys, parking lots, and vacant lots. One must carefully look under shrubs, scan yards, and check metallurgical receptacles (aka trash barrels). These treks of discovery not only provide a healthy dose of fresh air and allow me to meet many new folks, but each outing filled with anticipation can also be quite profitable.

When I initially began my explorations, the material I recovered netted me forty cents per pound. Now, in the summer of 2011, the value of this commodity has skyrocketed to eighty cents a pound! Yes, by now you may have discerned that it is the elusive aluminum can that is the object of my daily quest. Now, lest you feel that this brief tale is frivolous, I can assure you that there is an art (maybe not at the level of science) to this endeavor. One must be alert, carefully scanning the landscape, anticipating where some indolent teenager littered the environment or a street person disposed of a twenty-four-ounce container of potent malt liquor. At times my daily excursions result in some unexpected happenings.

Recently one morning, as I was leaning over to pick up a can at the bus stop by Walgreens, a hand from behind me suddenly landed on my shoulder. I froze momentarily, as several months back, a visually impaired fellow was attacked and stabbed repeatedly from behind at 6:00 AM. The perpetrator was never found. *Oh, no,* I thought, *did that dude nail another gimp?* But a ponytailed fellow only remarked, "God bless you, my son," as he strolled by, eventually entering El Camino Baptist Church two blocks west. I later decided that he was on his way to bible study and, seeing me, had stopped to offer encouragement to a downtrodden (in his mind) handicapped person.

On two separate occasions, women pulled out of traffic, exited to a street in front of where I was on the sidewalk, left their cars, and came walking briskly back toward me to offer assistance. One thought I had dropped my wallet, and the other said groceries, as I was bending over to retrieve a can. There are good Samaritans out there, and I was a bit sheepish explaining what I was about. Lastly, a portly fellow sitting on the Walgreens bus stop bench, arms folded across his ample waist, remarked rather dully, "Thanks for helping keep our community clean," as I leaned over to pick up a can.

My growing cadre of metallurgical enthusiasts rarely, if ever, accompanies me in search of my elusive quarry. Rather, each member of the group has his or her own method of delivering cans to me.

One young father has his son bring them to my house in a five-gallon plastic bucket. I usually don't know when they are coming, but I open my front door, and eureka, there they are. The deputy sheriffs bundle them in neat packs of eighteen or twenty, and I pick them up from their driveway. Other folks accumulate a large number and then drop them off periodically in large plastic garbage bags. Arguably the most unorthodox means of receiving cans is by drive-by toss. This neighbor, I think responding to an inner need to litter, throws his empty (usually Coke) cans out the window of his truck onto my front yard as he drives by. Later, when I notice the can, I retrieve and crush it, adding it to my ever-increasing cache. But this agreed upon method of delivery can cause consternation to the unsuspecting. A young stealth bomber pilot who was visiting the former Air Force pilots Rob and Chrissy across the street, observed the drive-by neighbor throwing a can into my yard as he was sitting outside in their front yard. I happened to be looking out my front window and decided to retrieve the can immediately. The stealth pilot watched me come out to get the can; we didn't speak, and he went into Rob and Chrissy's house. Later I learned that he was outraged, sputtering to Rob, "What kind of damn neighborhood is this, anyway?"

"Why?" asked Rob.

"Well, some asshole just drove by and threw his soda can into the yard across the street. Then a chunky old dude in a wheelchair came out and had to pick it up!" Once Rob explained the arrangement, the visiting pilot and the rest of us had a hearty laugh.

Well, there you have it: two fun-filled, rewarding activities that never lose their appeal. The study of history provides endless data for future bloviating (a Bill O'Reilly word) at "wisdom groups" or plain old BS sessions. Metallurgical exploration keeps my synapses firing at high levels, as I am continually scheming and trying to devise new strategies for enlisting new converts into my "Corps of Discovery" and outwitting little old ladies who might be my competitors in the daily dash for cash. And along the way, there have been a number of humorous happenings, with surely more to come.

A serendipitous result of my explorations is that I've about become a compulsive hand washer. After every expedition I scrub, disinfect, and sanitize my hands; gosh, I can't recall the last time I had any kind of bug.

*Two innocent young children, a Catholic girl and a Methodist boy, were walking to church one Sunday after a morning rain shower. They came to a flooded stream that they had to cross. "Oh, no!" exclaimed the little girl. "Mama will be very angry if I soil my new pink dress."*

*The boy replied, "I know—let's take off our clothes, wade across, dry off, and put them back on," which they did.*

*As they were dressing, the boy eyed the girl with a perplexed expression on his face. When they set off again toward their respective churches, the boy smiled and remarked, "You know, I never before realized there were such big differences between Catholics and Protestants."*

# T.E.A.M.

## (Testosterone Enhancement Among Men)

THERE ARE FEW OCCASIONS, if any, in the lives of men and women, when we have a eureka-type experience; *i.e.,* "I have found it." It is that sudden, out-of-the-blue dawning of awareness, the unraveling of one of life's mysteries. I recently had such a moment: a sudden illumination of understanding.

Throughout my life, I have been inclined to observe the world around me—people, events, circumstances—and ponder the meaning of what is out there or what has transpired. Most often the true nature of the workings of our environment and the motivations of mankind remains obscure, undefined by the limited reasoning of mere mortals. But there are breakthroughs in divining the mysteries of the universe, and it is the unraveling of the meaning of human behavior that is the subject of this treatise.

It is literally after a lifetime of careful empirical observation (free of cultural biases), diligent research, and seemingly endless testing of hypotheses that I am now able, with a high degree of confidence, to announce a heretofore-unknown axiom of human behavior. Having withstood the rigors of my strict scientific research methodology, it is my great pleasure (and, I think, boon to mankind) to unveil the concept of TEAM! This is a paradigm of human male behavior and, although operational over the centuries, it never before had been postulated. I am today a participant in TEAM, a living testimonial to this eons-long phenomenon. This social-psychological concept is defined as "Testosterone Enhancement Among Males." This dynamic of male behavior is so widespread in cultures throughout the world that it seems incredible that it has never before been described. It is the practice of men gathering together to recharge their testosterone quotients: to elevate the testosterone barometer, refill their reservoirs that have been depleted, diluted, or essentially neutralized. The primary factor in the loss of testosterone is *estrogen*; that is, over exposure to women. Estrogen, while not negative itself, is pervasive in the environment, and long-term exposure can result in toxic levels for males.

Men and women are inherently different—anatomically it is apparent—but the need for testosterone renewal relates to the emotional responses of men under stress. John Gray, in his 1992 bestseller, *Men Are from Mars, Women Are from Venus*, sort of danced around the concept of TEAM, with his idea of men "retreating into their caves." He suggests that men under stress sometimes literally go to their garage or spend time with friends (guys, I'd wager), which allows them time to work out a solution. All of his reasoning may be valid, but I would also submit that the excess buildup of estrogen can cause great stress and result in men fleeing to find a TEAM experience. Thus my hypothesis is not necessarily antithetical to what Gray states; more likely, my concept is a specific kind of reaction to his more general thesis of stress. But I am not completely convinced that the need for TEAM is predicated on presumptive evidence of stress. (Wow, is that a line of BS or what?) Seriously, further research is required, which I have undertaken, and I suspect that the need for TEAM may in fact be in the male genetic makeup.

Many hypotheses need to be tested. A couple that immediately come to mind have biblical and Freudian roots. In the bible we learn that God created Eve with a rib from Adam. Do you suppose this made the male vulnerable to estrogen in the environment, entering the body by osmosis through the gap created by the absent rib? What about the matter of the Oedipus complex of Freudian psychology? Old "Siggy" may have totally missed the boat in failing to fully understand or explain what happens to boys who are unsuccessful in totally eliminating the complex. Maybe that psychological barrier, so necessary for resolving feelings about Mom, was never completely erected and there is feminine leakage—estrogen—permeating the wall. Of course this is only speculation at this juncture, but in the spirit of true science, we must not discard any ideas.

Uh oh, it has suddenly occurred to me that by this point I may have raised the ire of some of those folks who are my opposite gender. Now, before the feminists of America, stay-at-home moms, "church lady" types, female felons, or ladies of the night become irritated or even hostile toward me and my revolutionary concept, I will state unequivocally that women and estrogen *are not problems*! It is simply, as Gray asserts, that women and men are as different as beings from different planets. The question may legitimately be raised whether women are similarly vulnerable to testosterone poisoning. I cannot respond to the likelihood of that potential, as I have no expertise in the area. Moreover, I would challenge women of all ages and persuasions to investigate the question, of course utilizing a rigorous scientific methodology. Who can foresee what they might discover?

Now, hopefully having extracted myself from a potential black hole of gender quicksand, I shall continue my discussion of this new concept. It will appear clear to all thinking people that without TEAM, men may experience serious deleterious consequences. Thus ancient man instinctively recognized the need, the absolute necessity, for ongoing and repetitive TEAM experiences. As TEAM activity has likely been continual since the dawn of mankind, it would require years and take volumes to adequately address the subject. An attempt at a comprehensive review of the topic would probably make Will and Ariel Durant's *The Story of Civilization* (eleven volumes) seem like a first-grade primer in comparison; therefore, only a cursory review of examples of TEAM can be provided.

In the distant past, Neanderthal man and Java man most likely hunkered down around a fire, deep within the safety, sanctity, and seclusion of a cave to ostensibly plan the hunt, while in reality it also served as an early example of a TEAM encounter. Wars and warrior societies in the ancient world, in medieval times, and into the modern era were predominately male-oriented and may represent an extreme form of TEAM enactment. I must concede that given the overall magnitude of wars, TEAM as a primary impetus for these conflicts is only a tentative hypothesis. But it surely appears true that with the differing motivations for war, TEAM seems evident in the rush to sign up, and in references to "comrades in arms" and "bands of brothers." I also think about the rise of monasticism; which came first, a commitment to serve God, or an escape into the sanctity of maleness?

In past centuries, all-male organizations, schools, hunting clubs, and learned societies flourished. While each of them espouses a purposeful and legitimate rationale for its existence, I would submit that TEAM is a pervasive theme for these assemblies of men.

In the modern era, the incidence of TEAM seems more apparent in fraternal organizations such as the Masons, Knights of Columbus, Woodmen of the World—(yikes, even the KKK)—college fraternities, and innumerable groups under the title "Brotherhood of ____." This, of course, is just the tip of the iceberg. Think of the concept at the international level: surely Indians deep in the Amazon basin, the

Sherpas in Tibet, Celtic descendants in Wales, and maybe billions of dudes in China and India also have their TEAM days.

As I stated earlier, I am a regular attendee at TEAM gatherings. Every Monday morning, rain or shine, snow or frost, I meet with my comrades (collectively known as the "Monday Morning Irregulars") for lively debate and discussion, covering a wide range of contemporary topics. TEAM is a major benefit of regular attendance. But one weekly dose of that crystalline compound (testosterone) is not sufficient for me. Each Thursday morning I drive across town to join an all-male group to watch excellent DVDs on a variety of topics, predominantly history. I'm also looking for a monthly poker night with the fellows to supplement my TEAM exposure.

Today, across America, there are countless numbers of men meeting, some daily, to reap the benefits of TEAM. A classic, time-honored, almost mandatory example is the morning coffee get-together. I doubt there exists a single community in America (okay, scratch Utah) where you would not find the men having coffee. Yes, it is not only a sublime thought, but it is also living testimony to the concept of TEAM.

# Quotable Quotes

What should we say to tickle your fancy and pass the time?
Why of course, the fruit of sage minds, some nifty sayings, and a
  silly rhyme.
Pondering some axioms to brighten your day, tis surely a sign of our
  intellect, wouldn't you say?
Some are old, some you know, mine are new, study them leisurely,
  give them their due.

## Think on These

1) The art of medicine consists in amusing the patient while
   nature cures the disease--Voltaire.

2) Virtue has never been as respected as money--Mark Twain.

3) Disability just means kinky sex is OK!--K. Kloepping

4) I always keep a supply of stimulant handy in case I see a
   snake, which I also keep handy--W.C. Fields.

5) Aim at Heaven and you will get Earth thrown in, aim at
   Earth and you will get neither--C.S. Lewis

6) Don't overestimate the decency of the human race--H.L.
   Mencken

7) For people who park illegally in disabled spaces, we should
   hope for events that would soon legitimize their eligibility-
   -K. Kloepping

8) Obscenity is whatever gives the judge an erection--anonymous.

9) People will swim through shit if you put a few bob in it--Peter Sellers

10) Alimony is like buying a dead horse hay--Groucho Marx.

11) Even though the politically correct crowd have a need to label me "physically challenged," I must confess that Polio actually left me "crippled!"--K.Kloepping.

12) A woman drove me to drink, and I never even had the courage to thank her--W.C. Fields

13) A friend is someone who knows the song of your heart and can sing it back to you when you have forgotten the words--Unknown author.

# VIII

*Tucson People*

*Men have called me mad; but the question is not yet settled, whether madness is or is not the loftiest intelligence—whether much that is glorious—whether all that is profound—does not spring from disease of thought—from moods of mind exalted at the expense of general intellect.*[1]

# Blue-Collar Czech

"KENT, YOU'RE ACTING LIKE a sausage-head. Stay out of it. I talked with the boys at City Hall, and it's all taken care of."

That was John, my neighbor, standing defiantly with his arms crossed, reading me the riot act!

Another neighbor named Sharon and I were going through the neighborhood with a petition that asked the City of Tucson to amend the plan for a proposed street exit from a 150-unit townhouse development into our one-block-long street, Adams Drive. My home was immediately adjacent to the proposed exit. I had a three-year-old son, who had found his legs and could unexpectedly scoot away from my wife and me in a flash. The prospect of the townhouse traffic pouring out into our street was frightening.

Additionally there were a dozen or more young children who lived on the block, and many of us parents felt the mix of cars and kids was a recipe for disaster. Also, there appeared to be more obvious and reasonable options for directing the traffic into other adjoining streets. But John didn't see it that way. Indeed, he had visited with city officials, and out of that encounter he had concluded that the increased number of vehicles on our street was not a problem.

"But John," I had protested, "we have a block full of kids. The

211

city has other alternatives. Let's not unnecessarily endanger the children—they are frequently in the street, or crossing it."

"So you teach the little dummies to look for cars," John retorted. "The streets are for cars, not kids. Back in the city *(Chicago)* we were smart enough to get out of the way when cars or trucks came along. What's the matter with kids and parents today? Don't they have any sense?"

That was essentially the end of the discussion. John obviously wouldn't sign the petition, and he had fired his "sausage-head" volley as I was exiting his driveway.

We had moved into our new home on Adams Drive in the spring of 1971, and the now infamous "sausage-head" encounter occurred around 1975. John was about sixty-one years old at the time, and I thought I knew him reasonably well; but that encounter was the first occasion that I experienced what I was later to learn was a predictable pattern of behavior with him when a controversial topic was under discussion. Conversations with him almost always began on a positive note; however, any comment that he sensed did not support his views on a subject could quickly cause him to become flustered. Failing to agree on the matter could rapidly lead him to become agitated. He would raise his voice several decibels; begin to question the intelligence, integrity, and sanity of his perceived adversary; and deteriorate into a generalized episode of ranting and raving. After being the "beneficiary" of just a single incident of his argumentative style, I became much more cautious of the nature and content of our conversations. My next-door neighbor also became expert at derailing subjects that John might bring up that were clearly headed for a major explosion.

Despite his volatility, he was a great neighbor, as the majority of the time he was really quite a genial fellow. He was the neighborhood busybody, and any activity or gathering of folks on the sidewalk or street would attract him with his characteristic question: "Okay, so what cooks?" He was slight of build, with salt-and-pepper hair combed straight back, European style; he wore glasses, often repaired with Super Glue and hanging low on his somewhat long, pointed nose. He often wore plaid shirts and trousers (often with patches), and he always had a handkerchief hanging from a back pocket. If he'd worn a leather apron, he would have presented a good likeness of an old-world Jewish tailor or cobbler. He was very bright and seemed able to fix almost anything. He had an ancient gasoline-powered lawn mower that sputtered, popped, clanged, and bucked, but ran just like fresh out of Sears Roebuck.

John and his wife had been born and raised in Chicago and had moved to Tucson sometime in the 1950s. Over time, as we became friends, we learned of their history in Chicago and of their initial years in Tucson. Ann, John's wife, had used the term "nervous break-down" in reference to their decision to leave Chicago and relocate to Tucson. John had been a tool and die maker, a highly skilled artisan, and lost his job, which evidently caused some serious mental health issues for him. I never heard the full story of what had transpired back in Chicago, but John frequently made reference to his former workplace and the circumstances that led to him leaving his job. He had worked for a firm that had government contracts, and he alluded to practices of some companies (he never directly implicated his firm) of overcharging the "feds," and company higher-ups pocketing the excess. Speculation on my part led me to conclude that he discovered such a scam and threatened to blow the whistle or demanded to be included in the kickbacks. On one occasion Ann had stated, "They made John a scapegoat, ruined his career, and forced him out." To what extent John's mental health issues were related to any alleged shenanigans of a former employer is still unknown. John would frequently bring up the topic of that period and job, and if my neighbor or I was unsuccessful in getting the subject changed, or in suggesting a beer as a diversion, he could go into a full-blown rant. I must say that he was really pretty creative in his choice of slurs aimed at these former adversaries. Some of his favorite disparaging terms, which I thought sounded "old world," were labels such as "punks" (one of his favorites), "peasants," "commies," "Bolsheviks," and the ever-popular "Polacks."

A story he told me on more than one occasion concerned a particularly loathsome co-worker that he suspected had been a part of the plot that had cost him his job back in Chicago. In almost ecstatic vengeful tones, he would describe drinking a six-pack of *cheap* beer, going to the cemetery, and "watering" the now-deceased fellow's grave. The story invariably ended with a gleeful cackle on his part, and truthfully I also chuckled at the story.

John had a substantial reservoir of work-related skills to offer an employer; however, by the time we had moved onto Adams Drive, some twenty years after he had come to Tucson, the local block folklore was that he had held over two hundred different jobs since his arrival in the city two decades earlier. I always believed it might have been true. I'd guess he followed a similar pattern with each job he had: get hired, quickly learn the job, decide how the job tasks could be performed more effectively and efficiently, push his ideas, meet resistance (which only fueled his resolve), become confrontational and then combative, become a bit wild and crazy, get fired, exit, calling them "punks" and "peasants," and look for a new job.

His wife, Ann, was a wonderful cook, especially when turning out delectable pastries, cookies, and other goodies. Then they met an old guy (I believe in his nineties) who was sort of a healthy-eating guru

214

type. He was in terrific physical condition for his age, and both John and Ann became disciples of his dietary regimen of fruits, nuts, vegetables, grains, and little meat. Both of them lost significant amounts of weight, particularly John, who began to look like an escapee from Dachau! They would fast on fruit juices and water for a week, getting so weak that they would stagger when walking. Their new diet ended one of my favorite pastimes with John, beer-drinking and Limburger cheese-eating orgies that we engaged in on a regular basis. Eating the potent Limburger and drinking a few brews was very relaxing for him. Often, during one of our impromptu Limburger feeding frenzies, he would reflect, in positive terms, on his life in Chicago. I can still remember his gleeful cackle as he talked about buying Limburger, putting it in a fruit jar, adding some sesame seeds, and storing it in a warm place. He was never allowed to eat it in the house; he would grin and exclaim, "Yes, it was pretty potent!"

John was the neighborhood handyman, and it seemed he was continually assisting the neighbors, both kids and adults, with small household repairs and projects. He was especially creative in addressing problems that required some ingenuity or fabrication. He regularly made replacement parts for his ancient gasoline lawn mower, and even an engine part for his '57 Mustang. He solved a major headache for my wife and me, as we were unable to reach the air-conditioning switch located on the ceiling of our twenty-two-foot cab-over motor home. He looked at the problem, went home, and several days later arrived back with a U-shaped piece of metal welded onto the end of an old golf club. It worked perfectly. "No charge," he chuckled, self-satisfied, "or maybe a beer later," he added, as he knew I would insist on some sort of payment.

Speaking of golf clubs, he and Ann were avid golfers. He had learned his way around golf courses in his youth in Chicago, caddying, often, in his words, for "the mob." Telling me the story, he remarked, "We all knew who they were, but no one ever asked a single question. Gosh, they tipped well."

While he loved the game, he must have been a weekend hacker, but if he played poorly and someone razzed him about his play, he could become very upset. I recall such an incident; one afternoon after he arrived home, he immediately came to my house, very distraught, and said "Let's have a beer. I saw those f—king punks from Chicago on the course today." He hadn't, but some young guys made fun of his game, and he apparently temporarily lost a bit of focus on reality. After several beers, he began to calm down and could accurately identify his tormentors as simply "young punks." I really felt bad for him, as it didn't take much to awaken old demons from his past.

Even though he might have been psychologically fragile, he was physically a tough old "ethnic" and demonstrated his mettle one stormy day on the golf course. On about the fifteenth hole he was literally knocked down by a bolt of lightning, but he finished all eighteen holes, because, he said, "Well, I had paid for eighteen." Again he came over after arriving home and chirped, "Hey, I need a beer. I'm tingling all over."

"John," I asked, "are you sure you're okay?"

"Of course, I'm fine. It wasn't a direct hit," he chortled. We had two, maybe three beers that afternoon.

One of John and Ann's favorite hobbies provided further evidence that he was a tough old bird. They would go up to Mount Lemon, ten thousand feet in elevation, and trek through heavily wooded areas, hunting mushrooms. They could literally smell the locations of the different varieties of the edible fungus! Several days after one of their excursions, John stopped over to report on the results of their search. He appeared a bit pale and shaky, and I inquired if he was feeling okay.

"Oh, sure," he grinned, "but Ann is in bed, out of commission."

"What happened?"

"Oh, maybe I got a bad toadstool in the last batch of mushrooms, and it knocked us down a little," he cackled.

"For chrissakes, John, those things could kill you."

"Oh, no," he offered, "We'll be good as new in a couple of days, ha ha." They did both recover, with no apparent residual effects.

John, of course, was always about half primed to engage in a spirited verbal battle. We had a good number of encounters, the outcomes mostly benign, as I had learned that there was a flashpoint in debates with him, beyond which point he could quickly become agitated and begin to lose control of himself. In the year or so before he passed away, he became much more sensitive to positions that opposed his views. We neighbors recognized his potential volatility and avoided controversial subjects, and we got along fine.

But the Jehovah's Witness folks didn't know John, and when they rang his doorbell, they had no warning that they were also probably ringing his chimes. About thirty minutes after they had arrived at John's place, the discussion had moved close to the sidewalk in his front yard. I think the Witnesses were attempting a slow tactical retreat. John was loudly berating three now completely cowed people as they endured his nonstop verbal barrage. Eventually they meekly hustled off, and I'd wager they made a note of his street address as a residence at which to avoid any further proselytizing. The entire scene was kind of a tragicomedy, and I felt a bit of compassion for both parties.

The last year that John lived on the block, he increasingly struggled to accurately interpret the intent or meaning of daily interactions. I had a magnetic-activated switch installed inside the back taillight assembly on my van to operate the wheelchair lift. When the dealer, a young Hispanic entrepreneur, delivered the van to my home, John noted the arrival of the van, and, as he often would, walked over and asked, "So, what cooks?"

"Mexican ingenuity," jokingly replied Ernie, who had installed the device. After Ernie demonstrated how it worked, John left, making no comment. Four or five days later he came over, visibly trembling, obviously very upset, and began a verbal tirade regarding that "Mexican ingenuity" comment.

He railed, "Who the hell was that guy? Doesn't he know that when his ancestors were spreading syphilis and gonorrhea across Europe, my people were busy building cathedrals, developing new inventions and advancing civilizations?"

I was dumbfounded and probably wasn't very effective in convincing him that the comment had been made in jest.

One Sunday morning not long after that incident, my wife and I were on our way to church, and we stopped to say hello to John and Merle (our next-door neighbor), who were chatting on the sidewalk. "Hey, we're off to church, boys. Shall I say a prayer for both of you?" I laughed when I made the query, but John never again would speak to me. Although I attempted on several occasions to hear from him what my comment had conveyed to him, he remained aloof and unapproachable.

John had a stroke, was moved to a nursing home, and shortly thereafter passed away in 2001 at the age of eighty-seven. I really miss John. He was, in retrospect, a great neighbor: nosy, provocative, bright, always ready for a good argument, and a highly proficient master of "Slavic slander." He was a connoisseur of fine cheese and was the only neighbor who would have a beer and eat Limburger cheese with me.

He had his troubles in life, as we all do, and fought many demons in his last days. In my view, he was a genuine old-school, blue-collar Chicago "ethnic." When I think about him these days, a saying that a friend of mine often used comes to mind; that is, "Ah, that fellow John was a real beauty!"

# A Professor

I once had a professor named Smith, David Wayne that is. He was just a small-town Hoosier lad, but he went on to school, got a PH.D, and in Arizona, became a legendary Higher Education whizz.

As Director of The Rehabilitation Center at Arizona University, he had boundless energy, vision, and programs galore. He was the unquestioned captain of the ship, and his standards were high, his goals were clear, if we started to slack, he'd crack the whip.

Now David, we all called him "Dr. Smith," was in truth, an independent, strong-willed cuss. The Dean and others tried to pilfer the Center's money, but Dave was too crafty, he outfoxed them all, with a fund he called "slush."

Each day he started off early and fast, and by noon he had become a blur. He tracked all his programs, budgets and students throughout the state, and nary a one was second rate.

With his doctoral students he built great teams, and I was fortunate to be a member of one. The ideas flowed forth, and his non-stop motion kept us all on the run.

Hard work and excellence were values he imparted to one and all; but if trouble arose, he would be there to support you, to cushion the impact, if you happened to fall.

Saturday in his office was a noteworthy time, he shed his tie, often wore saddle shoes, and every idea was okay to discuss. Innovative thinking and ideas charged the air, and as I think back to those days, they were remarkably sublime.

Many, as I, owe much of our career and later success to this matchless dynamic man. And today, there are few who posses his creative ilk, try to find one, I doubt if you can.

Now his eyes have dimmed and his hair is snow white, but his mind is still sharp and his thinking, as always, a cause for delight. Although he's reached the age of eighty-six, be alert my friends, he's not forgotten any of his old "tricks."

It's now forty years since first we met; many great memories, and yes it's true, we didn't always agree, but deep admiration and appreciation I hold for this man, David, who was a teacher and mentor to me.

# Robbie

Now here's Robbie and me, sitting under the Palo Verde, that we call Dale's tree. I did not hear him come beneath that tree, but when I glanced up he was sitting next to me.

"Well hello Mr. Robbie, how you be?" He didn't answer; just looked at me and asked, " How do you get in your house?" That's what he said to me.

Though he already knew the answer I replied, "Why I have a ramp to my door," said me. "Oh ya, I could put one at my house for you,"quipped he.

He's sitting on the porch swing, crunching hard candy, kicking his legs, his bright blue eyes peering up in the tree. "Aha", says me, "are you looking for Mr. hummingbird, is that who you hope to see?"

He didn't answer, gave me a quizzical stare and asked, "now why are you in that wheelchair?" It's a ritual dialogue, Robbie and me, the same questions, as "now why is your hand bent like that?" asks he.

"Is Mr. hummingbird here today for me to see?" "Well I'm not sure, lets keep looking in the tree, he may be perched on a limb for you and me to see."

It's Robbie sitting next to me, but his last name, I don't recall. I say, "so it's Robbie Watson sitting here with me." His head jerks around, those blue eyes flash, with disdain, and he answers with a scowl. "I'm Robbie Watkins, not Watson" he bristles at me. "Ah yes Watkins, I won't forget that" says me.

"Oh look, look," exclaimed he, "up in the tree, it's Mr. hummingbird and I think he's looking down at me." "Yes tis he, Mr. hummingbird" says me. "Well my little friend Robbie do you think he has a name, or do we need to give him one, you and me?"

"Yes, yes he must have a name. Who do you think he is," asks Robbie looking expectantly up at me? "Hmm," I pause, "let me see, could his name be Henry, Henry Hummingbird up in that tree?" "Yes," smiled Robbie, "maybe it is Henry Hummingbird sitting up there in the tree."

Then a frown crossed that cherubic, angelic face. He was thinking so loud those thoughts were falling on me. Quietly he murmured, "no, no, I think he's a girl, not a boy, that we see."

"A girl not a boy is that what you said to me?" He did not respond to me. "Well then if it's not Henry that we see, who do you think it could be?"

We sat in silence, Robbie and me, pondering who it was up in that tree. Softly I asked, "maybe then it's, it's Henrietta that we see." "Yes,

yes, it's Henrietta that we see, and maybe she's a mother and, and I know she's looking at me."

As if his little soul was salved, he gave a gentle sigh and again looked up at me. " I have to go home now, can I ride on your wheelchair, and will you take me?" He stood on the footrests and leaned hard against me, said goodbye to Henrietta and we left that tree.

Down the driveway into the street, no cars did we see. Robbie turned his head and looked at me with a pensive smile. Suddenly he shouted, "Hey dad, hey dad look at me!" His father didn't look to see Robbie and me, he was working on his motor home, busy as he could be. "Dad, dad look at me," his voice losing most of it's glee. Then he bolted from my chair, no goodbye said he.

As he hurried up the driveway I heard his plea, "Dad, dad can I have more candy?" "No Robbie you haven't had your dinner, maybe later then we'll see.""So long Robbie thanks for stopping over to see me." He disappeared into his house without looking back or saying goodbye to me.

So we had spoken awhile, Robbie and me, but he's an enigma and it seems there's a gulf between he and me, for into his soul I cannot see. There is a mind with great promise, a spirit that is strong and unbridled, and I wonder, who will he be.

# Brownie

I SAW BROWNIE TODAY. He was slumped on a bus stop bench in blazing 112 degree heat, with all his worldly possessions within easy reach. He was draped against one end of the bench and overstuffed, filthy, white, plastic grocery bags filled the rest of the space. There were more bags at his feet. At one time he carried only two or three bags, but now there are many more, testimony, I'd guess, to his increasing wealth in worldly goods. Many of the bags seem full of scraps and shreds of paper that he pulls out and appears to read. What additional treasures other bags hold I do not know.

Maybe for ten years or more, he has roamed the roadways, alleys, and dry washes of Tucson. For he is a street soldier, a solitary, disheveled, downtrodden fellow, trudging daily among the living souls of this town, but far removed from the humanity of us all.

He is brown; brown colored shirts, tan/brown slacks and brown sandals. His unruly tangled hair is a dusty brown color and his skin, dirt-encrusted with sweat, is brown and black. His feet, maybe unwashed for years, once brown, are now black with dust and grime.

Only once did I speak with him, on an Easter morning. He was among many other people seated outside a bagel shop in a local shopping center. A rather pompous, over-zealous, parking lot security guard had loudly and with much condescension ordered

Brownie to leave, claiming the coffee and bagel shop owners had lodged a complaint. I felt embarrassed for Brownie and disgusted with the guard, so I inquired of the shop owners and learned they had not complained. I confronted and chastised the guard, getting support from a number of other folks, and the guard then left him be. I asked Brownie why he thought the guard wanted him to leave. Emotionless, he replied,"Maybe he thinks I'm crazy." On differing occasions I would offer to buy food or drinks for him, but he always only stared blankly at me and would softly reply, "No, I'm OK." He used to attend a nearby Catholic Church and although there were offers of clothing, a place to shower and other necessities he almost always declined any assistance.

I don't know anyone who knows his name, including myself, or where he came from. One day he was just here. I have an awful feeling inside each time I encounter him. Is it guilt? Others remark, "poor devil, he's tragic." My wife says, "It hurts my heart whenever I see him."

I wonder if he has any family and if they search or worry about him? Did he drift away from them or did they desert him? Have I and all of us in this city abandoned him? We say that God loves each and every person. I wonder, is God walking with Brownie? He wouldn't forsake Brownie, would he? I don't know how to help Brownie, or is it that I'm really afraid to try?

# Children in Church

Sometimes I watch children in church, Mom and Dad too, praying silently the good name of the family the kid won't besmirch. Missing the sermon in peril of my soul, being much too curious to see what they might do.

Children were not made to sit in chairs or pews, it's interesting how many little ones are fascinated with shoes. There are exceptions, but most can't stay still, they fidget and squirm causing a stir, amazingly adept at testing their parents will.

What is the source of each creative antic? The family outwardly calm, but inside quite frantic. Is it the seed of Adam we see at work, a niche in the heart for Satan to lurk, or simply a child born untamed and free, given to nurture for you and me?

Church is a place where we might earnestly search for God, do we ruin the child if we spare the rod? So what shall I think of a child in undisciplined play? Disturbing the reverence and tranquility of some on this holy day. Would the WORD be more clear if the kids weren't around, should we banish them all with a scowl and a frown?

Then the service and hymns would be in order with nary a sound, but their silence would be deafening and joy couldn't abound. HE said, suffer the children to come unto me, and they must be with us for all to see.

One recent Sunday was difficult, as I was distracted a lot, by the shenanigans of a charming but precocious tot. She laid on the floor, drug out all her books, contorted her face and gave folks around her silly looks. I snickered and chuckled as she carried on. How sad I thought if she were gone. Unbridled innocence from the FATHER above, she as his SON came to teach us love.

# MacGregors Moved

Across the street the house is quiet, there's a lock on the door, the MacGregors are gone, they don't live there anymore. Rob and Chrissy, three little girls, and Chloe too, knowing they've left can make me feel blue.

Maybe we'll get fine new neighbors, some really nice folks, but damn I'll miss Rob's zany jokes. He took his family and went back East to start a new career, we didn't weep, but seeing them go, it would have been easy to shed a tear.

Sarah and Audrey were born when they lived across the street, when you ponder a new birth, isn't it really a wondrous feat? Katie, the oldest at three, we said was "cute as a bug;" a darling child we all liked to hug.

Chrissy and Rob, F-16 and A-10 pilots they were, capable and smart and full of "life" that's for sure. Really good neighbors are hard to find, and we came to love this family, they were a special kind.

Seeing the little ones come and go, always brought a bit of joy, Sarah learning to walk and Katie with a book or carrying a toy. Coming home they would open the house door, out raced Chloe, she would bark and run, watching her exuberance was really quite fun.

Often Rob would stop in for a beer or simply for he and Matt to have a talk; other nights he might go by, say only "howdy" as he took Chloe for a good long walk.

We had one last party with ice cream cake, which Katie and Sarah ate with glee. Marlys showed Katie the clay and metal animals in the yard and got too hot, so Katie said, "Marlys go sit under a tree;" Sarah scribbled all over the phone book, she said it was her name, we've decided to keep it and give to her one day when she's a lady of fame.

Life, as we know it, is often not what it seems, but one thing is sure, we should always chase our dreams. Changes bring challenges, new paths to find, being courageous and leaving memories behind.

They'll have more children, of that I'm sure, and Rob, as a doctor may discover a cure. Chrissy will prosper and the children will grow; as time goes by, I hope they remain a family we know.

Tis bittersweet now that they've gone away; and for me, and I think my family too, we'll miss every one a little each day. We feel a loss, but wish them well, and if we get too lonesome, we'll rekindle fond memories by ringing our reminiscence bell.

# IX

*Home in the Old Pueblo*

# Fine Leathered Friends

Some folks will tell you there are few animals in the desert, but in fact they are WRONG. There are birds and mammals of all different kinds, but nothing that's huge or extra LONG. So you won't encounter a python that's twenty feet long, or a Sasquatch as big as king KONG. But this is a short tale of reptiles, not deadly or scary snakes, but of three little lizards, including one who might sing you a SONG .

Now here in the desert there is an abundance of LIZARDS, Sometimes they lay and bake in the sun, I'll bet they're as leathery and tough as turkey GIZZARDS. Yes they love it here, as it's hot and dry, besides they wouldn't survive if we had lots of BLIZZARDS. "Don't worry, it ain't going to happen here, were way too far south," at least that's the gospel according to some of our local weather WIZZARDS.

Lizards, you say, all over the place, ah, don't be too quick, as they may not be what you THINK. A fact that some folks don't know, those one's with long tails are really a SKINK! I've never seen one in my house, not in a closet, behind the couch, or even under the SINK. Try to catch one, usually out in the yard, alas, all you'll get is a skitter of dirt and they're gone in a BLINK.

Each night we turn on an outside light, to attract bugs, moths and flies, and cute little friends we call GECKOS. They gorge on the insects, hang on the screen or upside down, with those amazing sticky TOES. You can see their tiny hearts (through a transparent body) from behind the light. They're a light tan color with a pattern of darker brown spots, ah mother nature's art DECO. Don't try to catch one, they're timid you see, just the faintest of touch will cause them to shed their tail, and away they GO.

Now, it's a gecko I meant who might sing you a song, well that's not quite true, it's more of a CHIRP. Some folks might say they can't make that sound; what you hear comes from stuffing themselves with all those bugs, and oh dear, it's really a BURP. One thing is clear, there is no doubt, they are really quite dainty as they gobble their meals, quickly and silently, not even a SLURP. So say what you will, I'll not argue the point, whether it's a chirp or a burp, the truth remains to be seen, but on one fact I think we all can agree, they are a cute little TWERP.

Now one of the species is really unique; there are no boys just girls you see, hard to believe, but it's true, they're really all the SAME. They have extra long tails, they're highly energetic and very fast; in the desert, you can find them almost any place, curious they are, and Whiptail is their NAME.

Parthenogenesis is their special trait; they're all females and don't need a male to mate or reproduce, no they don't have sex, for them it would be a waste of time, nothing but a silly GAME. Amazing, don't you agree, I think these gals surely belong in the lizard hall of FAME.

All three of these lizards, the Skink, the Whiptail and the Gecko belong to the classification order that someone named SQUAMATA. Wow, it's difficult to learn these scientific terms. I really don't want to, even though I probably OUGHTA. And what if I spend many weeks trying my best and still don't get it right, will my brain turn soft and lumpy like the cheese, RICOTTA? Whoever came up with this complicated scheme? Wouldn't it be nice, if they'd re-do the system into something more soothing, like a sublime SONATA?

Now I know this is is really quite a short tale, but it took me a good while to think it up; so read and study it slowly, that's all I ask, take your time, just don't RUSH. All these lizards are quite furtive, they like to hide, in grass and weeds, under rocks, in cracks; you may see them in dead cactus arms and under dense BRUSH.

I have loved all my dogs, they're really great pals; but what of a lizard, could we make one a pet? First I'd have to catch an elusive chap, then I wonder if he'd come willingly, or put up a FUSS? I'd make him a small house, a good place to hide, catch bugs and buy fruit, good things to eat, make him a sandbox to do his "duties" in a private spot. And if he decided to stay and be my friend, he would need, I think, a sophisticated name. Yes, something cosmopolitan sounding, how about GUS?[1,2]

Three bulls, one large, one medium, and one small, were standing in the pasture and had just heard a rumor that the farmer had just bought a new, even larger bull.

The largest of the three said, "Well, he ain't getting none of my cows."

The medium bull said, "He ain't getting any of my cows either."

The little bull said, "Well, if he ain't getting any of yours, then he sure as hell ain't getting any of mine."

Two days later, a semi pulled into the yard, and they unloaded the new bull. He was gigantic, and pissed from having been cooped up for the long journey. When the three bulls saw him, the biggest bull said, "He can have my cows."

The medium bull said, "He can have mine too."

The littlest bull, however, began to paw the ground, snort, bellow, and basically carry on. "What's with you?" the other two bulls asked.

"Well, I'm just making sure he knows I'm not a cow!"

# El Toro

I AM BY NATURE a person who believes in the intrinsic value of traditions. Rituals and ceremonies are important phenomena in every culture and society. For example, there are great national traditions in America: turkey at Thanksgiving, gift-giving at Christmas, marching bands during the halftime of football games, trick-or-treating at Halloween, hunting eggs at Easter, celebrities throwing out the first pitch in noteworthy baseball games, singing the national anthem before sports contests, the Indy 500 on Memorial Day, fireworks on the Fourth of July, and probably many more too numerous to mention.

While I would suggest that traditions, rituals, and ceremonies are deeply embedded in the fabric of most societies, I will confess that I have little expertise at distinguishing exactly what specific types of activities fall into each category. I'm fairly comfortable with my foregoing list of national traditions, but I'm reluctant to wade into the *ritual* versus *ceremony* versus *tradition* quagmire, for fear of being psychologically brutalized and humiliated by some punk college kid who's an expert in classification schemata. Now, having acknowledged my limitations on the matter, I feel able to continue with this rather brief tale.

To be 100 percent safe, I'm going to speak only to the matter of rituals, and in particular at the local community level. My home, Tucson, Arizona, affectionately known to all of us who love the high desert of the Southwest as "the old pueblo," is the setting for my remarks.

Here in Tucson there are some well-known community-wide rituals specific to this city. Though few in number, these rituals are deeply ingrained in the culture of the area. I'll list four: painting "A Mountain," predicting the "ice breakup," cruising Speedway, and the subject of this piece I've titled "El Toro."

Every fall the University of Arizona and its bitter rival, Arizona State University, clash on the gridiron. In preparation for the annual event, students and volunteers paint the A rock formation located atop, of course, "A Mountain." It's painted the school colors, red and blue, and surely failing to perform the ritual would lead to certain defeat. Well, maybe it's not a 100 percent guarantee of success, but I could foresee a calamity, like maybe a fifty-game losing streak!

Tucson can be quite hot in the summertime, but the temperature usually does not reach 100 degrees until late May or early June. Predicting not only the day, but also the exact time to the minute that "the ice breaks on the Santa Cruz" (first 100 degrees) has everyone's attention. The Santa Cruz River, which flowed year round with eight to ten feet of water as late as 1900, is now a bone-dry bed of rocks and sand. Of course if there is no water, there can be no ice; as to the matter of the temperature at which water will freeze or, for that matter, thaw, we Tucsonans simply choose to ignore the obvious.

A time-honored ritual among the testosterone- and estrogen-blooming crowd has been cruising Speedway Boulevard. On hot summer evenings, especially on Friday and Saturday nights, I guess the ritual is that you cruise a while, get the attention of some chicks or dudes, and then park your car in a spot facing Speedway and (do they now say this?) rap with each other. If you don't score or make any headway with the opposite sex, pull out on Speedway, and start all over. Throw in a good number of drag races and some loud car radio music, and the ritual has reached fruition.

Ah, speaking of Speedway provides a nice segue that will lead me to the real heart of the matter—well, actually not the heart! One brisk fall morning as I was heading west to work on Speedway Boulevard, I was suddenly taken aback—no, more like shocked, bewildered, and almost horrified, as I noted that one of the most significant symbols of ritual in Tucson was missing! "My god," I blurted out, "is nothing sacred anymore?"

You see, the object of my dismay was missing testicles—yes, gonads, *huevos*—they were gone! For in the parking lot, front and center of the Casa Molina Mexican restaurant, 6225 East Speedway Boulevard, stands a life-size concrete statue of a magnificent (I think he's Andalusian) fighting bull, fully engaged with a dashing, svelte matador complete with swirling cape. In my fantasy world I wonder who the matador could be; is it the great Juan Belmonte, or Manuel Benítez Pérez (El Cordobés)? The bull, painted midnight black and lunging at the cape of the matador, is an image of power, strength, and courage. Maybe the enraged beast is Islero, the bull that killed a childhood hero of mine, Manolete, arguably the greatest torero of all time. And you see, the bull, along with powerfully muscled legs and back, flaring nostrils and wicked, curving horns, also displays the most significant symbol of his power and being: his gonads! They are the vessel that ensures the transmission of the ferocious fighting spirit of the breed. They are the reason we call the animal a bull; but the testicles are gone, vanished, and without them the statue of the bull and the brave matador is meaningless. It's a rose with no fragrance, a song with no music, salt with no taste, and an eye that does not see.

Sad as it may be, equally tragic as the statuary castration is the apparent loss of one of Tucson's well-known, long-standing, and finer rituals: decorating those potent *huevos!* You see, while the beast is a coal-black color, rarely in all my years in Tucson have the jewels of that bovine been black. They've been many colors: purple, pink, blue, yellow, polka-dotted; red, white, and blue; one Christmas they sported tinsel and bells—jingle balls, I assume, in the spirit of the season. They have been pure white, flecked with sparkling glitter, and jailhouse black-and-white striped. Fuchsia, lavender, and lime green were a few of the more memorable efforts. One has to admit that much thought and creativity (not to mention stealth) have been demonstrated in this fine tradition of decorating the bull's maleness at the Casa Molina restaurant.

Yes, it's depressing; they're gone. Was it vandalism, a fundamentalist religious group of fanatics protecting "innocents," or maybe even PETA (People for the Ethical Treatment of Animals), sparing the dignity of the animal? Maybe they simply fell off from old age.

Well, traditions do pass, and new ones emerge to fill the void. For example, at the Kolb and Grant Road intersection, in the McDonald's parking lot, stands a massive (fifteen- to twenty-foot) concrete statue of a *Tyrannosaurus rex*. On Halloween he's draped with a giant white sheet and becomes "Spook-a-Rex." Antlers and a red nose adorn his head at Christmas, and he has large, floppy ears at Easter. Notwithstanding this possibly newly emerging tradition, I'll sorely miss those glorious gonads and the tradition one might refer to as "the basting of the balls."

I fretted and stewed a while about the loss of the Casa Molina bull tradition, but then I had a flash of inspiration. I decided to take the advice of one of my favorite crusty old curmudgeons, W. C. Fields, who once said, "There comes a time in every man's life when he must take the bull by the tail and face the situation." Rather than whine and lament the situation, I determined to start a fund drive to restore those *huevos*. A car wash was an idea, or a bake sale (how about "Baking for Balls"?), or a "gonad garage sale." Maybe Casa Molina would allow me to sort of pass a collection plate among their dining customers on a Saturday evening. Hmm, they might not go for that idea. No matter; now that I had an action plan, I began to feel better.

Rituals and traditions are important customs and practices in every culture. Their familiarity can bring comfort, a sense of continuity in our lives, and reassurance that all is right in the world. Anticipating and then being able to observe (in this case) the latest artistic endeavors applied to those large, truly magnificent *huevos* always elicited a serene feeling and an accompanying expression of appreciation: "Ah, yes!" But this is not the end of this brief story.

Hallelujah! In only a matter of days after having observed the missing anatomy of the bull, they magically reappeared! I was again driving west on Speedway and glanced to my right at what I thought was the disfigured bull. Wonder of wonders, he was again whole! There they were: his proud symbol of maleness. Initially I was completely baffled, and I pondered the puzzle on the rest of my journey to work. It was my morning coffee that cleared away the fog; they never were missing, but instead they had been painted dark black (I'd guess by Casa Molina folks), and they blended with the underside of the bull. From a the street they were easy to miss.

Now, some twenty years after I thought a great calamity had befallen our city, they are in fact still with us and, the tradition has persisted unabated.

Today, in July 2011, my son reported that those "jewels of the Southwest" are decorated with brilliant yellow and green rings. Aren't those the national colors of Brazil? I wonder if we have visitors from the land of the Amazon.[1,2]

# The Kumquat Tree

There is an Eden, an idyllic retreat, in the hot Southwest at Tucson town. A chance to visit this cool shady spot will bring a smile, and never a frown.

We locals know this fragrant garden as Mesquite Valley, it's a world-class nursery, and we think if you stop to look you might agree. Plants and trees, thousands and thousands, anything you want you will most likely find, they have such variety it may blow your mind.

Several years back, I was wandering there on a mild Spring day, when I spied a handsome little tree, dark green leaves, tiny olive-sized orange colored fruit, what in the world could it be?

I read the label that said it was a Kumquat tree, with fruit that's mighty tasty too. I looked around, saw no one, well why not, I'll just sample some, actually quite a few.

Alas, I was being observed by a chap named Rodney, a self-acclaimed Transylvania lad, who asked, "I say my larcenous friend, are you eating all the fruit, that's really kinda bad?"

Maybe of guilt I bought that tree, and tended it with loving care, but woe to me, despite abundant blooms, there was no fruit, it remained quite bare.

So I consulted that Transylvania bard, Sir Rodney, asking very politely, "now what could be wrong with that Kumquat tree in my yard?" With a smile, but somewhat sinister grin he replied, "now you ate most of the fruit from that tree, yes I remember it well, I admonished you then, and you've had no fruit for I cast a spell."

Humbly I beseeched him to lift that curse, even offering him some coin from my limited purse. He took no money, just turned his back, uttered some words and softly exclaimed, "I've lifted the spell," and from that day forward it has borne fruit exceedingly well.

But then in 2011 Tucson had a colossal freeze, 10 degrees or less really wrecked a whole lot of trees. The Kumquat fruit I knew was gone, I was really feeling blue, what in the world was a gardener to do?

"Why make jelly," said Cathy, the boss at Mesquite; now that's an idea, on toast with butter it sounds like quite a treat. But in five pounds of Kumquats there seemed a million seeds, extracting the pulp is sticky, messy work, after twenty plus hours we were almost berserk.

We got five pints of the tasty stuff, but doing the job one time was probably enough. Eating the fruit right from the tree is the only sane thing I can see. So now I have a plan; if there's ever to be another freeze that's hard, one from hell that could crack a bell, I'll revisit that Transylvania mystic and implore him, "Rodney, do your magic, recast that spell!

*A motorcycle policeman liked to hide himself behind large billboards and catch motorists who drove by, exceeding the speed limit. One sunny day, a worn old green pickup sped past the billboard hiding the policeman, who promptly gave chase and stopped the truck. To his surprise, the driver had a passenger in the other seat: a large hog. "My god, man," exclaimed the policeman, "besides breaking the speed limit, what possible explanation do you have for this pig riding in the seat with you?"*

*"Well, officer," the fellow replied, "I found him a ways back on the highway, and fearing he would be hit by a vehicle, I picked him up."*

*"Where are you taking him?"*

*"Gosh, I really don't know what to do with him."*

*A bit exasperated, the policeman said, "Well, take him to the zoo. I won't ticket you, but slow down, now, and be on your way."*

*Several days later the old green pickup sped past the same billboard behind which the same policeman was hiding. Again the officer raced after the truck and pulled over the fellow. Looking into the cab, he cried, "What is going on here? You were speeding again, and you have that hog with you once more! I told you to take that animal to the zoo."*

*With a big smile, the man replied, "Yes, Officer, I did take him to the zoo. We had such a good time that today I'm taking him to the fair!"*

# Traffic School

MOE HOLLAND LOOKED LIKE a cross between the old movie star tough guy Broderick Crawford and the chairman of the rehabilitation center at the University of Arizona, Dr. David Wayne Smith. Moe's opening line was, "My, my, you don't look happy this morning. Hey, I didn't do this to you."

The date was March 30, 1991, and I was crammed, with about fifty other disgruntled folks, into a relatively small meeting room on the second floor of the Double Tree Inn in Tucson, Arizona. I would be a guest of Mr. Holland for the day on account of traffic ticket #32105. Several days earlier (maybe even longer) I had been hurrying across campus to yet another meeting, and a young fellow—kind of a wiseass, I thought—wearing a campus cop badge said I didn't stop at a stop sign. "In fact, you accelerated through it," he stated, very sure of himself. Well, I knew I was hosed, as they say, and rather than pay the fine, I opted for Moe's Defensive Driving class.

It was 8:00 AM, and the group was a diverse bunch of lawbreakers, and immediately a young gal (a real airhead) started ragging about why she shouldn't be there. "I was driving the same speed as another guy, and he wasn't ticketed," she whined.

"Aha," said Moe, "you thought there was safety in numbers. *Wrong!*" End of discussion.

Sitting next to me was a sullen, skinny gal whose entire demeanor shouted, *You losers! I don't belong here either!* But she was silent, glaring straight ahead.

Session number one was on accident prevention; key concepts were (a) recognize, (b) evaluate, and (c) act. I stopped taking notes, but I know Moe waxed eloquent.

It was only 9:00 AM, an hour into school, and I'd describe the dynamics of the group as "down in the dumps." In the back sat a young black guy, slouched in his chair, wearing bib overalls, one shoulder strap undone, unmoving, almost catatonic.

Next we got a film, *The Defense Rests.* It features Maggie and a Jack Webb-type private eye, who are driving to the scene of another accident that Maggie had been in. She had apparently been carjacked by a guy who failed to put on his seatbelt, and they crashed. Maggie is fine, but the carjacker is in surgery. Moe asked the group what the message of the film was; I don't have any recollection of the right answer, as it seemed everyone spoke up at once, several arguments broke out, and Moe ended the mini uproar with, "Time for a break! You get thirteen and a half minutes." Why thirteen and a half, I have no clue.

I stayed in the room, as wheelchair access from the main floor was through the kitchen and a freight elevator, both of which really smelled rank. The break lasted from 9:50 to 10:07—seventeen minutes and not thirteen and a half as Moe had directed. Miss Personality next to me was still acting as if she had a "warped taint" (don't ask). She had not uttered a single word or even smiled. She was quite small, had a painted-on ceramic-looking face, and wore a black and white sweater and black leotards, along with a good amount of garish rings and other jewelry. It suddenly occurred to me that her attitude and persona could mean only one thing: I'd lay ten to one she was a Jewish American princess, a JAP, obsessed with her tiny body and immaculate grooming, and horrified to be trapped in the company of a bunch of lowlife criminals!

Moe bought me a cup of coffee during the break and wouldn't let me pay for it. It was really pretty thoughtful of him.

I noticed a rather strange-looking young woman who had an equally odd-looking doll on her lap. Thinking the doll was possibly a collectible, I decided to ask my JAP buddy if she knew anything about the doll. She actually responded! In a slow, monotone, lackluster voice, as if she were heavily medicated or depressed, she said. "I don't know, and why does an adult have a doll anyway?" That was the end of our conversation. Yikes, the gal was cradling the doll like a baby! She had a half-baked smile on her face and stared rather vacantly toward Moe. She was wearing a white T-shirt, Levis, and no makeup; she had very short dishwater blonde hair and large, protruding ears—my god, she looked like the doll.

It was 10:11 AM. Moe forged ahead with *Transportation Laws of Arizona, Title 28*. He stated that they really made interesting reading. Get real, Moe! Next, for discussion, he listed six conditions that are factors in collisions:

1) Lighting (see and be seen)
2) Road (shape, surface, and shoulder)
3) Weather (He said that *all* Arizona weather presents a hazard.)
4) Traffic conditions (amount, speed)
5) Parts of your vehicle (I listed nothing.)
6) Driver (He had six more factors in this category; again I didn't record them except to note that one, "physical impairment," he carefully avoided discussing.)

Moe's visual aids keep slipping off his tripod. He had a whiteboard that he wrote on with erasable markers (half the folks were high from the fumes); he placed little cars, wooden blocks, and printed materials on the board, but they didn't stay in place, instead migrating down. He didn't seem to get excited about the problems with his visual aids, but the troops were getting a little restless. Recognizing the increasing inattention of his audience, Moe tried a little humor; he asked, "What are the two kinds of roads in Arizona?" The answer, "Roads under construction, and roads that need to be under construction," got mostly groans. He tried to joke with the JAP, but she didn't crack a smile, and her eyelids didn't flutter; rather, they flicked in a sort of reptilian way!

Next Moe asked us, "At what speed does hydroplaning occur?" The responses ranged widely, and to each one he simply said no. "Now," he said, "let me tell you what my old physics professor told me. The professor said two different objects cannot occupy the same space at the same time. Therefore, if the street is wet, your car tires are not on the street." Moe said that one night in a hotel room, he began to think about that hypothesis and couldn't sleep, so he got up at 3:00 AM, headed to his car, and *listened* to the space between the tires and the pavement. He clearly heard the cries of little molecules as they screamed, "Help us! We're being crushed," thus proving the theory; that is, with no water between the tires and pavement, the tires are *on* the pavement, crushing those poor molecules. Wow, this class was rapidly deteriorating!

Undeterred, Moe had more humor for us; he said, "You know, if you lose the water pump belt, you can use pantyhose as a substitute to get you to a service station—however, you probably can't wear the pantyhose again!"

It was 10:45, and the Jewish American princess was checking her watch every fifteen minutes and constantly squirming in her seat; I was willing to bet her butt was so bony (as she wanted to remain tiny) that she really was uncomfortable. Whoa, another stretch break; the JAP lady was ready for this one, and away she went.

During the break a young gal who had worked for one of my staff members at the university came over. She said she recognized me, and immediately she began unburdening herself about being rejected by the graduate library school. Her name was Martha, and she really unloaded her frustrations with the library staff. She was very intense and quite plain in appearance; her voice sounded stressed, and she almost had no lips; she reminded me of a much older person with false teeth. What a day—it was enough putting up with Moe's cornball humor, but additionally I was seated next to a hostile broad, and now during the break I get a fifteen-plus-minute harangue from a strange young woman.

11:03 AM—back to action, and Moe was really on a roll. A little old lady fell asleep; everyone was giggling, and Moe had to wake her up. "You can't sleep in here," Moe said with authority. "If DPS walked in here and people were sleeping, I'd get fired!"

11:12. Aha, another movie; all the films were six to ten minutes in length and of poor quality. This time we saw *Trouble Ahead and Trouble Behind: The 2 and 4 Rule.* Moe was trying very hard to be enthusiastic, but the class was glum. We heard "great" lines in the movie, like "You can't stop a bowling ball on a dime, and a car isn't a bowling ball," the point being that weight times mass equals momentum. We also learned that if you are going fifty-five miles per hour, and the car ahead of you passes a tree at the same speed, if you reach the tree before you count "a thousand and one, a thousand and two," you're too close to the car ahead of you!

Part two of the movie followed. A Charlie Chaplin-looking fellow is walking and stops to pick a daisy on the sidewalk, and another

Chaplin type runs into him. The point is that you shouldn't stop your car unexpectedly. The group was getting numb; we were dying in there!

Movie over, Moe returned; it was 11:27. Moe told us that the number-one way to die in a car accident is being thrown out of the car. "However," he chuckles, "if your body don't hit nothing, you are going to be okay." No one laughed.

I was really struggling here, and I noted that the fellow sitting on the other side of our JAP friend was short and wearing shorts and tennis shoes; he had curly hair, thick glasses, and a close-cropped beard; I thought he looked like he was Hebrew! I know—maybe he was a psychiatrist, and the JAP was under his medical care; she was paying him to come to class with her. Jesus, I was losing it!

Moe gives us the "Four R's" to avoid head-on collisions:

1) Read the situation
2) Right-steer
3) Reduce speed
4) Ride to the right

Of course he had a bit of discussion for each R, which I have completely repressed. There was an older guy up front who answered every question Moe asked, and who continually asked his own questions. He was almost bald and had a fairly good-sized potbelly. He was wearing a white shirt with one button missing and the sleeves rolled up, and he had no upper teeth, He was really involved and apparently having a good time.

11:55, break for lunch. Back at 1:00 PM. I went downstairs (through the stink of the elevator and kitchen), had a sandwich and soda, and then I held my breath and headed back to the second floor.

At 1:10 we got another film: *No Second Chance: The Head-On*

*Crash.* We saw several pretty graphic head-on collisions but no bodies or mayhem to people. A whole bunch of folks laughed—not the reaction, I think, Moe wanted. Lousy film quality again; the narrator is a stuffy, self-righteous-sounding dude wearing a suit and tie, pontificating from the library of his home. I think everyone was laughing at him.

Hold on, here—the Jewish American princess spoke to me! She told me she was a therapist at Jewish Family Services. Her voice sounded like that of a person with severe depression or someone half bonkers on medication. She had an MSW (master's in social work). She told me, and the fellow on her other side, who was showing increasing interest in her, that her initials were JET, which she had on her license plate. She said very lethargically, "Maybe the police see that and decide to stop me. I don't know why—I never take chances." So everything I surmised about this gal was fairly right on.

Moe was telling a story to emphasize a point, and the older guy (potbelly, no teeth) was helping Moe tell the story by filling in where he thought Moe had left out important information. He was getting increasingly vocal, and he stated his views in a quite authoritative manner; I thought he saw himself as a "co-commentator" with Moe. I don't recall the specific discussion at hand, but the "commentator" had the last word, saying, "The yield sign is a California stop sign." Another question related to the current topic was, "If we approach an intersection and the light is yellow, can we enter the intersection?"

"Of course you can," said Moe's new "assistant."

It was 1:35, I was getting weary, the doll lady was clutching the doll tightly to her chest, JET was looking almost hostile (I think her male wannabe friend was beginning to leer at her), and the old pot-bellied guy had Moe in a one-on-one dialogue. The next thirty-five-plus minutes were a blur, and at 2:10 we got a stretch break.

It was 2:24, and Moe was racing for the finish line, throwing out all kinds of tidbits of information, maybe part of the required curriculum. To wit: to check for a recall on your car, phone 1-800-424-9393; in 1990, 99.7 percent of collisions in Arizona were preventable; you can be arrested for being under the influence of alcohol and also legally prescribed drugs; .05 blood alcohol content equals "driving under the influence"; and .10 blood alcohol content equals "driving while intoxicated." Moe's final attempt at humor was, "Black coffee to a drunk makes a wide-awake drunk."

The class ended at 2:50, and we filled out our evaluations. My response to "least liked" was simply "too long"; for "liked best" I said, "Moe—nice guy in a bad situation."

JET, the Jewish American princess (she did say her first name was Joyce), frantically rushed out the door without so much as a "so long" to Moe, me, or the little guy that she surely must have known was trying to hit on her. Maybe the poor gal, being Jewish, had reached a toxic level of "gentile overload," having been cooped up all day with a majority of likely non-Jewish white-trash types. Whatever her issues, I did sympathize with her on one matter: that is, never wanting to do another Defensive Driving class again!

# Death in the Sonoran

Softly, silently the feathers fell as gentle raindrops from the sky. White and light and dark and brown, falling down from high, and I wondered why.

A young Mesquite Tree arched overhead, and then "kek" "kek" "kek" something shrilly said.

Ah, there on a lower branch sat Accipiter Striatus, sharp-shinned is his common name and this raptor plays a deadly game.

In yellow talons holding fast, a white-winged dove who's life was suddenly past. A baleful stare from eyes bright red, that filled me with a moment of dread.

Awake at dawn from a tranquil sleep, the sweet morning breeze calls the bird to fly, then a flash of light a silent cry, death as a lightning bolt had come from the sky. For the hawk lives to hunt, so to eat, ripping apart the bloody meat.

Cruel little bastard crossed my mind the world would be better without your kind. Each day you kill an innocent bird, and none of your victims utters a word. Is there grief, is there pain, or is it simply what nature did ordain.

I watched for a spell as the hawk devoured his feast, and reflecting a bit it came to mind that it was the wisdom of nature that had created this beast. His destiny had made him a noble thing an unparalleled athlete on the wing.

Death comes to all, mammal, bird, and even man; but unlike most creatures, for no good reason, we humans will kill who we can. But that deadly messenger from the sky does what is just, he only takes a life when he must.

Some creatures die, some creatures live, always in life someone must give. And while there is death in this desert each day, it is part of the song of creation, God's own way.

In a small town in rural Midwestern America, an elderly gentleman stopped in at a local tavern for a nightcap. Unfortunately, he chose a seat at the bar next to a rather boisterous young man, an apparent self-proclaimed expert on a wide range of subjects. He was loud and argumentative, and he insisted on getting in the last word in every discussion. When the older man could no longer endure the unabated pontificating of the arrogant young fellow, he gently tapped him on the shoulder, saying, "Excuse me, sir, but you seem to be well versed on many topics."

"Well, as a matter of fact, I think I am," he boasted.

The older man asked, "Would you be interested in a wager testing my knowledge against yours, with the loser buying drinks for the house?"

The old gentleman hadn't said a word all evening, and the cocksure young man wasn't impressed. "Sure, what did you have in mind, old-timer?"

"It's quite simple," the old man replied rather coyly. "In turn, we each ask a question and then proceed to answer our own question."

"Well, that's rather silly, isn't it?" sneered the young fellow.

"Oh, no. It's more complex than you might expect. Are you game?"

"Okay, but this a waste of time."

The old man said, "I'll go first. My question is, how can a gopher dig a hole and leave no dirt on top of *the ground? My answer is, he starts at the bottom. Your turn."*

*The young man looked confused for a moment and then blurted out, "Hey, wait a minute, how did the gopher get down there in the first place?"*

*"Well, now," said the older gentleman, "that's your question. What's your answer?"*

# Dale's Tree

MY FATHER TOLD ME the above anecdote many years ago; he was a wonderful storyteller, and often there were simple moral lessons in his tales.

Dad's first name was Dale; at least that is what everyone, including his family, called him, even though his birth certificate read, "Leon Dale Kloepping." For some unknown reason his three siblings also used their middle names as if they were their first names. Aunt Lydia Corrine was always Corrine, Uncle Stephen Frederick was Fred, and Douglas Lamont was Uncle Lamont. Anyone who might have known the rationale for the practice is now long deceased.

I really liked and enjoyed my father, even though at times in later years we had some divergent political, economic, and social views. My parents began to winter in Arizona in the early 1980s, sharing a mobile home with my father's sister, Corrine. They purchased her share in 1984, bought a new mobile home, and became yearly snow-birds for the next twelve or thirteen years. Dad developed some significant medical problems, and they didn't return to Tucson after the spring of 1996.

Dad was born in 1910, and in the eighties, when he had entered his eighth decade, he was still a very durable, robust man. My wife, my son, and I spent many hours with them in their twelve-by-fifty-

257

foot mobile home in Far Horizons Mobile Home Village. Many evenings, if I stopped in without Marlys and Matt, Dad would ask, "How about a cup of coffee?" which I always accepted. Invariably, it seemed, our conversation would eventually lead to stories of my parents' childhood, their youth, and their early years of marriage. They had an unlimited fund of anecdotes about relatives, neighbors, and events of note that occurred in their community. Dad usually added a liberal dose of humor, jokes, and real-life incidents, many with extremely amusing outcomes. If Mom went to bed early, the anecdotes and stories got a bit more ribald.

I took notes on both Mom's and Dad's commentaries and archived the material under "family history." Some of Dad's stories, particularly concerning real people in the community, were hilarious and a bit off-color, including illegal activity he knew of (bootlegging) and romantic entanglements among respected citizens.

He had other talents in addition to his ability to weave a great story from the ordinary; he was a dairy farmer, but not just the average herdsman. In his profession of animal husbandry—and he was a professional—he developed an outstanding herd of registered Holstein cattle that were recognized throughout Northern Illinois for their high quality. In the early fifties he began a systematic program of artificial insemination for breeding his cows, and the result was a herd with excellent conformity to the standards of the breed, and more importantly, they were great milk producers.

Dad was accustomed to heavy labor, having been raised on a farm and then choosing dairy farming as his lifelong vocation. When he came to Tucson for the winter months, there was little in the way of everyday tasks that required much physical exertion; thus he was always more than willing to help me tackle any job around my home that could get his Midwestern work-ethic juices flowing. During his many winters here, he built a fence and a doghouse for us, dug holes and planted trees and large plants, hoed weeds, and painted. Those "work" days were always particularly pleasant and relaxed, with no deadlines, and punctuated with rest breaks for him to relate a story. Trimming bushes and especially trees seemed to have a special appeal for him; I wondered if it, in some small measure, rekindled memories of the many hours he'd spent in the timber on his home place as a young boy and youth. He was a hunter, an excellent shot with shotgun or rifle; he knew the names of all the trees, plants, animals, and birds where he roamed, in what must have been an idyllic place full of trees. When working with wood, trimming trees, a kind of tranquil calm came into his voice as he related stories of his younger years and carefree days of freedom years ago, often alone in the woods. His memories of and fondness for those times were powerful and poignant.

He was a master with a chainsaw (probably fortunately for my trees, I didn't own one) and equally adept at wielding clippers (he called them "loppers") in a machine-like, methodical attack on trees and bushes. One bright, balmy spring morning, probably in March, he had completed a precision shearing of the large olive tree in the front yard and was looking for additional vegetation to lay waste to. He spotted a three-foot Palo Verde tree, a volunteer, that was growing up through a juniper bush. In a flash he reached into the juniper bush and clipped off the tree at ground level. I happened to glance in his direction as he was retrieving the clippers from the bush, and I asked, "Hey, Dad, did you cut that little Palo Verde tree?"

"Why, yes, right at ground level. That should kill it or slow it down a day or two."

"Oh, crap. You know, I think Marlys wanted to save the darn thing."

"Well, for God's sake," he sputtered, looking chagrined, "don't tell her I lopped it off." He set the tree back into the juniper branches, and from a distance it appeared to be thriving and intact.

It couldn't have been five minutes later when Marlys opened the front and said, "Now, Kent and Dale, you leave that little Palo Verde tree alone. I want to leave it grow." Either he or I answered, "Yup, we know you want to save it."

Neither of us said anything about the dastardly deed, but one day several weeks later, Marlys remarked, "You know, that tree doesn't look good. Maybe it needs more water." She watered it religiously, daily, for probably a week, but each day it looked worse. One day she exclaimed, "I surely don't understand what's wrong with that tree!"

Matthew walked over to it and proceeded to lift the now bone-dry tree out of the junipers. "What?" she cried. "How did that happen? Who cut that off?"

I had to confess that it was an accident, as I had failed to warn Dad not to cut it off. She fumed a bit and then started to chuckle and said, "Look, Dale wanted to keep it secret and was going to leave town without me finding out, so let's leave it that way. Don't say anything, and let's see what happens."

The day soon arrived for my parents' departure back to Illinois, as, using an old Midwestern expression, they said, "Our feet are turning north." It was early morning, and they pulled up next to our mailbox in their fully loaded 1966 maroon Plymouth station wagon. They exited the car for hugs all around and a final good-bye. Dad was standing next to Marlys, and Mom was leaning against the mailbox. As Dad started to walk back to the car, Marlys asked, "Say, Dale, do you think that little Palo Verde tree"—which was four or five feet off to his right—"needs more water?"

He stopped in his tracks and stood expressionless. Mom visibly slumped, hung her head, and pitifully replied, "Oh, no. I had hoped we would get out of town before you discovered what had happened."

With that, Marlys erupted with laughter, and the rest of us followed suit, howling, tears running, and the hilarity lasting several minutes. Dad apologized, which Marlys graciously assured him wasn't necessary. They left on a high note, relieved that the secret was revealed, and we spent the rest of the day frequently spontaneously breaking out into laughter when recalling the folks' reactions when Marlys asked her question.

Later on that summer, a green sprout quite unexpectedly emerged from the depths of that juniper bush; it was the Palo Verde tree! Marlys made it abundantly clear to me and to Dad, when he returned the next winter, that we were to give her little tree a wide berth. Thereafter, I exercised extreme caution anytime I was doing any kind of yard work in close proximity to the tree.

The Palo Verde, which translates from Spanish as "green stick," continued to thrive under the watchful eyes of Marlys, and now, over twenty years later, it has grown to approximately twenty-five feet tall. It spreads a broad canopy of filtered shade over the mailbox, a portion of the driveway, the front flagstone patio, and the porch swing. The ground beneath it contains a bed of amaryllis, spectacular in the spring, nurtured in a microclimate provided by the spreading limbs.

As the tree grew rapidly, Dad once observed, "You see, it was the pruning I gave it, more than one time, that invigorated it!"

Sometimes when I go out front and look at the tree, I smile to myself, thinking of Dad and that fateful day. In his memory, the tree will always be Dale's Tree.

*Foreign ministers sometimes find themselves in very difficult situations. Take the case of the foreign minister of Uganda. President Idi Amin told him that he wanted to change the name of Uganda to Idi. The minister was asked to canvass world opinion and return in two weeks. He did not do so. He was summoned and asked to explain.*

*He said, "Mr. President, I have been informed that there is a country called Cyprus. Its citizens are called Cypriots. If we change the name of our country to Idi, our citizens would be called Idiots!"[1,2]*

# The Name Is

RECENTLY MY WIFE RECEIVED an "exclusive" offer to purchase the local newspaper, the *Arizona Daily Star*; as it is a left-wing rag, most folks call it the "Red Star." The cost was only ninety-nine cents for Saturday and Sunday delivery.

The address on the label was correct, but the named recipient was Marlys *Koralewski*! That's right, *Koralewski*! Now, as a last name, Kloepping can easily be misspelled, but *Koralewski*? How in the world could that organization (functioning at a more simian level than even I had thought) come up with that spelling?

I started thinking about the matter of folks butchering the name, particularly in pronunciation, and wondered if a change of my surname was an idea worth pursuing. I'm often a bit surprised, sometimes even impressed, by the variations that people come up with in pronouncing the name Kloepping. The correct pronunciation, English version (not Deutsch), is "Kluh-ping"—or is it "Kluping"? Crap, now that I write it phonetically, the two are so similar that it's difficult for me to decide. Neither version of Kloepping flows like Johnson, Jensen, or Jones, Baker, Barber, or Becker, but each is doable.

A relatively common faux pas that people make in saying the name is "Cop-ling," like we're the gendarmes. "Cup-ling" is also a favorite. More than once I've heard "Kloeppen-ger." They get the "klup" or "kluh" okay but insert "en" for "in" and add a "ger."

So what about a simpler moniker? Gee, I wonder what the relatives would think. There are instances when one can mount a substantial argument for a complete overhaul of a person's names, both given and the surname. Take the case of famous people, like movie stars. One of my early heartthrobs was that gorgeous gal with the husky voice and alluring eyes, Natalie Wood; what a tragic ending to a young life. Now, in her case, changing her birth name was probably a good move. How do you think Natalia Nikolaevna Zakharenko would have looked on the silver screen? Personally I like "Natalie Wood" better. On the male side of movie stars, how about that chiseled, dimple-chinned, studly fellow Kirk Douglas? He was originally saddled with *Issur Danielovitch*. Yikes!

Growing up, who didn't love that all-American cowboy Roy Rogers? I was a bit crestfallen when I first learned the he was really Leonard Slye! Wow, from Slye to Rogers—what a great marketing decision. Can you imagine? Roy Slye—gosh, that sounds a bit creepy, even sinister. And what about John Wayne, the quintessential embodiment of American manhood? I don't think Marion Morrison would have worked. If he had kept the name, I think he would have had to wear pink boots!

In recent years some well-known professional athletes have gotten into the name-changing business. One of the first that I recall was a basketball player named Lloyd B. Free. He changed his first name to "World," so now he's World B. Free. A more recent example is that of a pro football dude, seemingly always acting out, named Chad Johnson. His jersey number was 85, and he decided he wanted his surname to be "Ocho Cinco": in Spanish, "eight five." That means he is now Chad Eight Five. Also, though not official as of summer 2011, another toughie-type pro basketball player, who has been in more than one high-profile altercation during a game, Ron Artest, wishes to become "Metta World Peace"! I have no idea of the meaning or significance of "Metta World Peace" or his thinking, but I can assure the reader that I won't even bother to Google the term for any further edification on the matter.

Returning to the issue of the name Kloepping, my wife also now carries (she sometimes says she is "saddled with") that surname. Her maiden surname was Sternberg, German for "Star Hill," which I think is a pretty cool name; maybe I could become Kent Sternberg; sounds okay to me. For whatever reason, Marlys seems to have taken the brunt of some of the more creative demolitions of the name Kloepping. A child in the school where she worked as a speech pathologist had a habit of calling her "Mrs. Klo-pecking"; the child's mother also had "Klo-pecking" down pat. I assume she cured them of the problem. She also was known as Mrs. "Kloeppen-ger" by some of the good kids at the school.

Of all the problems people have with the name, I think one of the best all-time snafus was the result of Marlys joining a Weight Watchers group. It so happened that the group met at a local Jewish synagogue, Congregation Anshei Israel, and a large percentage of the ladies were of the Jewish faith. At the first meeting Marlys attended, an elderly, very Jewish lady met her at the door, being quite solicitous and helpful, insuring that Marlys's every need was met. Marlys said the lady seemed a bit nervous, doing a lot more talking than listening. She asked Marlys her name, which she made sure she repeated twice. "Oh, yes, I see," replied the helpful lady; upon entering the meeting room, which was filled to capacity, the cheerful, excitable host exclaimed, "Ladies, I'd like you to meet our newest member, Mabel Hufflinger!" That's a classic!

There have been many other verbal violations perpetrated on the name; to name a few, "Klee-ping," "Kleeps-ing," "Klutt-ing," "Korp-ling," and "Kalup-ing." If folks misspell the name, it follows that they will then mispronounce it. I am usually not put off when the spelling or pronunciation is fumbled, but I have an autographed baseball that I'm a bit chagrined about. I got to know this former major league baseball player, a Cub (I won't name him, as he's a terrific human being), and he signed his name to a ball, the inscription reading, "To my friend Kent Koepping." *Koepping?* What is that? How in the world can I claim to be fast friends with a big-time baseball player when he screws up the name?

Some folks pronounce the name as "Clipping," and a variation of the name is "Klipping." There was an old great-uncle, Charlie, who in fact did change his name to "Klipping." Another living relative told me he thought Charlie's motivation was to avoid creditors, or maybe to disown the Kloepping clan in general.

While I was penning this tale, I remembered a little boy from back in the year 1945 that was a fellow polio patient with me at the Kent Cottage in Rockford, Illinois. Kent Cottage, a former detention home for juvenile delinquents, had been turned into an early version of a rehabilitation center for children who had survived polio. I was seven years old, and another little guy, also seven or eight, was my new friend. He was, as my family used the expression, kind of a "sad soul," not the most popular kid in the institution, who spoke with a perpetual stuffy-sounding nose and was very shy; but we were buddies. One day when his parents came to visit, he proudly introduced me to them, saying, "Mom and Dad, this is my friend Tent Schruffing!" I didn't correct him at the time, nor later, and maybe even to this day, in his mind, he still recalls his friend Tent.

Outside of people having difficulty pronouncing the name Kloepping correctly, I don't think it's inherently a target for derision. Now, surnames such as Butcher, Butts, Bottoms, Beaver, Banger, Outhouse, Breast, Trickle, Swine, Swindle, Dick, Klutz, Fuchs, and Funckes are more likely to be targets for unkind or rowdy manipulations. There was a boy who lived in a community not far from my home back in the 1950s. His name was Richard Dick; he wasn't called "Dick Dick"; rather, his friends came up with "Double Dick." That's not bad, but I also know about a fellow named Richard Head, which needs no more discussion.

In retrospect, maybe I'll give this name change option some more thinking. If I were to change my surname, maybe I should also change my given name to really simplify what I'm known as. I could go with something like Chuck Church, Jim James, Willie Williams, John Johnson, Jeff Jeffcoat, or maybe Otto Olson. Ah, the whole thing seems like too much trouble. I'll bet it's a nightmare getting a new legal name on the myriad of documents that follow an individual today.

I have an idea; maybe from now on I'll only introduce myself to new people I meet as Kent. Thus one-time encounters will only have to remember one name, easy to pronounce: Kent. For more intimate or long-lasting relationships, these folks will have to learn the correct pronunciation. I'll even make it easy to learn; I'll carry a laminated flash card at all times that has the name Kloepping spelled out phonetically: "Kluh-ping"! If someone stumbles over the name, I'll immediately whip out the card and say, "Repeat after me—Kluh-ping." I'll make them say it three times to be sure!

*Throughout the fabric of every society are interwoven the fibers of celebrations that collectively serve to bind people together. It seems to me that even the smallest, subtlest changes—a word or a phrase—can alter or weaken these threads of our traditions and begin to fray the tapestry of our sense of unity as a nation. Such were my thoughts when I penned this 2011 Christmas season letter.*

# What Kind of Tree

To borrow a line from that iconic rock-n-roll superstar Elvis Presley, "Well bless my soul what's wrong with me," and also me, I always thought we called that thing a CHRISTMAS TREE? But now I hear that may not be, some folks think we should call it a "holiday tree."

Elvis went on to wail, "Well please don't ask me what's on my mind, I'm a little mixed up but I'm feelin' fine." Well me too, I'm mixed up and feelin fine, but holiday tree, who came up with that fatuous line?

But enough of Elvis, and it seems to me, if we celebrate Christmas, why isn't it a CHRISTMAS TREE? If it was a holiday tree, wouldn't the holiday we were celebrating be simply known as "holiday?" Nah, it's fairly clear to me, the holiday we are celebrating is Christmas and therefore it's a CHRISTMAS TREE.

Now most all children love this time of year when old St. Nick comes on, what, holiday eve? Oh no, I think not, he still always comes on Christmas Eve and leaves all the presents under the CHRISTMAS TREE.

There are folks who see Christmas as only a secular day, but historically it's a Christian holiday, that no simple change of name can take it's true meaning away. For those who fear the Christmas word and believe it divides us all, they miss the real message of Christmas, love, hope and brotherhood, for each a clarion call.

Like Elvis, who also intoned, "My tongue gets tied when I try to speak, my insides shake like a leaf on a tree," you might be feeling pressure from the "politically correct crowd." But take heart, remember you have a choice, just do your thing, use those traditional words, they'll set you free.

So my friends don't give in and timidly parrot "merry holiday," be of good courage, and have no fear, shout out that time-honored salutation, MERRY CHRISTMAS, for this year.

# X

*Attention, Mr. President*

*An atheist complained to a friend, "Christians have their special holidays, such as Christmas and Easter, and Jewish folks celebrate their holidays, such as Passover and Yom Kippur. Every religion has its holidays, but we atheists," he said, "have no recognized national holidays. It's unfair discrimination."*

*His friend replied, "Well ... why don't you celebrate April first?"*

# Cracker Day

We Americans, like people of many cultures throughout the world, have a fondness for celebrating national holidays and milestones in the life of our country. We also regularly recognize specific dates that we believe are significant. Many of these special days are deeply ingrained in our society and are celebrated by a majority, if not the entire populace; while other dates, less known, may receive little national attention and may only be observed at the local level or even in a single community.

New Year's Day, Christmas, Thanksgiving, the Fourth of July, Memorial Day, Labor Day, Halloween, Valentine's Day, Mother's Day, and Father's Day are all major national holidays; Easter, Hanukkah, Martin Luther King Day, Washington's Birthday, St. Patrick's Day, and maybe even Punxsutawney Phil's day (aka Groundhog Day) also enjoy national status. Other days as D-Day; Armistice Day; the first days of summer, fall, winter, and spring; Flag Day; Arbor Day; Earth Day; and Columbus Day may receive less attention, and their observance will vary greatly throughout the country.

But I digress from the main focus of this brief commentary; not only do we enjoy celebrating days we deem important; we seem to have a penchant for creating new ones to observe or honor. The array of special dates we have established will jiggle your innards. Consider this: Did you know that January 6 is National *Bean* Day? January 23 is Pie Day; April 18 is Animal Cracker Day (not saltine); May 13 is Hug Your Cat Day; February 11 is White T-Shirt Day; April 7 is Beer Day (celebrating the end of Prohibition); April 22 is Jelly Bean Day; and June 12 is Peanut Butter Cookie Day. In 1984 Ronald Reagan designated the third Sunday of July as Ice Cream Day. Oh, my, I almost failed to include Deviled Egg Day on November 2. This abbreviated listing is only to provide the reader with an idea of the diversity of what's out there. There are dozens and more designated days on the yearly calendar. While some of the days listed may seem worthy of acknowledgment, others could be viewed as frivolous. Notwithstanding the plethora of named days, I believe there is a significant and glaring omission in the list of important days that needs to be added and receive recognition. Within days of penning these words I intend to forward same to the United States Congress, requesting of that body or the prez (whoever does such things) that they officially designate a new day Saltine Cracker Day. I am quite optimistic (well, maybe cautiously optimistic) that after serious consideration of this proposal, they will recognize the versatility, utility, crunch-ability, taste-ability, store-ability, and enjoyability—that is to say, the efficacy of this truly delightful traditional American cuisine. I'm actually hopeful that the day in fact might be designated a national holiday! But if Congress or "Barry" thinks we already have enough national days, I can live with a simple Saltine Day. I already have a date in mind: September 7. It happens to be my wedding day, and I checked the Internet and discovered that the date is available.

Now I must get to the crux of this matter; that is, to substantiate the validity of this proposal and the inherent value of the saltine in our culture. Saltines, or soda crackers, originated as far back as the nineteenth century. Premium Saltines, originally called Premium

Soda Crackers, originated in 1876 in St. Joseph, Missouri.[1] Now, as Dick Nixon would say, I want to be perfectly clear that I'm speaking of the plain, white salted cracker, not the no-sodium, low-sodium, or low-calorie varieties (we might as well chew on cardboard or pressed sawdust). So such wannabes as Ritz, rice crackers, Triscuit, graham crackers, animal crackers, Kashi, Wheat Thins, or flavored types like garlic, cheddar, or sesame, are not included.

Let's consider the amazing versatility of this truly unparalleled wafer, the saltine. They are tasty right out of the package *anytime*—morning, afternoon, or evening. They are much healthier than potato chips, have less fat, are less expensive, and won't give you heartburn like overeating chips will do. Saltines are an absolute necessity as an accompaniment for any kind of soup. One can crumble the cracker into the bowl of soup or, for the more sophisticated types, sip a spoonful of soup and then nibble daintily on the saltine. I sort of prefer the "smash and dump" technique myself.

"Cheese and crackers"—what a melodious phrase! All varieties of cheese go well with saltines: cheddar, Swiss, Brie (also good with bread), brick, Muenster, Havarti, longhorn, jack, pepper jack, and the ever-popular Limburger. Yes, Limburger, an all-time culinary delight! Sadly, Limburger is now made at only one location in the United States. Apparently many Americans have never tasted this sublime cheese; maybe they have never even been exposed to its unmistakable aroma. It is truly an unforgettable experience.

You must have saltines to make that traditional outdoor treat, s'mores: marshmallows, chocolate, and of course saltines; they are gooey, messy, and an absolute delight around the campfire. Saltines with butter and jam are a quick, easy treat. In fact, saltines and just butter are really good. I'm told that peanut butter on saltines is gaining increasing favor and consumption across all classes of Americans as our economy continues to spiral downward. Forget the white bread, peanut butter, and jelly sandwich tradition; today it's saltines with peanut butter and jelly. Have you ever tried avocado on saltines? You'll like it!

When I was a young polio patient in the hospital, the late evening snack provided by our nurses was saltines crumbled into a glass of low-fat milk. It was delicious and nutritious, calorie-wise, and the carbs were soothing and led to blissful sleep.

Animals love saltines; every dog I ever had, as a kid and now as an adult, has enjoyed them. Almost everyone thinks of or utters the expression "Polly wanna cracker" when we see the bird, so ingrained in our psyche is the attraction of the cracker—saltine, I would submit!

Who doesn't use cracker crumbs? Saltine cracker crumbs, of course. All kinds of meats are battered, rolled in cracker crumbs, and fried or baked. Chicken, pork, beef, or fish with beer batter is almost an American staple. Again with a batter, zucchini, okra, eggplant, or red or green tomatoes, rolled in saltine cracker crumbs, are excellent. We use saltine crumbs in meatloaf, all kinds of casseroles, corn pie, (did you know?), chicken Kiev, and obscure dishes such as Amish cracker pudding, "bloomin' onions," and filet-o'-tofu sandwiches.

A cranberry dish is usually present on the Thanksgiving Day table. I've had them cooked, raw, and jellied, but I wonder how many folks have heard of or tasted a wonderful dish called *giftas*? I have no idea of the origin of the name or the country, but almost without exception, whenever my wife prepares the dish, it's met with oohs and ahs. It's a simple recipe. In a clear cut-glass bowl (as seeing the layered ingredients is neat), spoon in a layer of cooked cranberries; next add a layer of heavy whipped cream (no aerosol-can type) and then a layer of *saltine cracker crumbs*! Repeat the layering until the bowl is full, and folks, you have a treat that will titillate your taste buds. Again, who first put this combination together is a mystery, but clearly they recognized the superior quality of the saltine cracker.

Well, there you have it, my friends. In rereading what is essentially my proposal for the establishment of a national saltine cracker day, it seems abundantly clear to me (as they say in the vernacular) that the likelihood of succeeding is a slam dunk!

Well, now, wait a moment; as I expect this request to be in the president's hands early in 2012, that means "Barry" Obama would have to issue the proclamation. You don't suppose he'd quash the idea—you know, refuse to act, because it would be a "white cracker day"? He wouldn't do that, would he?[1]

*Sources*

# I. Illinois: Memories of Youth

## Mattie

1. Stewart O'Nan, "Songs for the Missing"
   http//www.goodreads.com/quotes/tag/restlessness

## Billy Goat Henry

1. Working Goats Goat Jokes
   http://workinggoats.com/?id=246

## A Day at Wrigley

1. Ernie Banks
   http://en.wikipedia.org/wiki/Ernie_Banks

## A Rite of Passage

1. Rite of Passage
   http://en.wikipedia.org/wiki/Rite_of_passage

2. Bizarre Rites of Passage
   http://listserve.com/2009/12/28/12/10-bizarre-rites-of-passage

3. Six Strangest Rites of Passage
   http://urbantitan.com/6-strangest-rites-of-passage/

*Friend*

1.  Bernard Meltzer Quotes
    http://www.braineyquote.com/quotes/authors/b/bernard-meltzer.html

## II. College and a Brief California Interlude

*Who Did You Say Was Driving That Car?*

1.  Short Blind Jokes
    http://addy85.hubpages.com/hub/Short-Jokes

*California Dog Days*

1.  Dog Jokes
    http://www.Best-funny-jokes.com/dog-jokes-222

2.  Gustav von Seyffertitz Filmography
    http://www.fandango.com/gustavvonseyffertitz/flimography/p73898

## IV. Fishing

*Deep-Sea Fishing, Episode Two*

1.  Funny Fishing Jokes
    http://www.free-funny-jokes.com/funnyfishing-jokes.html

## V. Foreign Affairs

*A Man Called Spice*

1.  Edith Sitwell, "Taken Care Of," 1965.
    http://www.quotationspage.com/quote7790.html

*Diplomacy*

1.  Professor Vejas Gabriel Liulevivius, PhD. *The Great Courses,* "War, Peace, and Power: Diplomatic History of Europe, 1500–2000," University of Pennsylvania (DVD).

## VI. Dogs and a Cat of Note

### Neighborhood Dogs

1. Best Dirty Jokes, Rude Dirty Jokes, Short Dirty Jokes
   http//www.lotsofjokes.com/dirty_jokes_30.asp

## VII. Positive Mental Health Activities

### Monday Morning Irregulars

1. "How the Marx Brothers Brought Norman Cousins Back to Life"
   http://www.joeyguse.com/2007/07/how-marx-brothers-brought-norman.html

2. Men Are from Mars, Women Are from Venus
   http://en.wikipedia.org/wiki/Men_Are_from_Mars,_Women_Are_from_Venus

### Quotable Quotes

All from BrainyQuote
http://www.brainyquote.com

## VIII. Tucson People

### Blue-Collar Czech

1. Edgar Allen Poe Quotes
   http://poestories.com/quotes.php
   (from "Eleonora")

## IX. Home in the Old Pueblo

### Fine Leathered Friends

1. Geckos
   http://www.auroville.org/environment/web_of_life/geckos.htm

2. New Mexico Whiptail
   http://en.wikipedia.org/wiki/New_Mexico_whiptail

## *El Toro*

1. Book Espana, "The 10 Best Bullfighters in the History of Bullfighting"
   http://www.Bookespana.com/bullfighting/10-best-bullfight-ers/

2. Manolete
   http://en.wikipedia.org/wiki/Manolete

## *The Name Is*

1. Funny Jokes, "Change the name of Uganda to Idi"
   http://www.funny.com

2. Movie Stars' Real Names
   http://www.digitaldreamdoor.com/pages/movie-pages/name_mov.php

# X. Attention, Mr. President

## *Cracker Day*

1. Saltine Cracker
   http://en.wikipedia.org/wiki/Saltine_cracker

CPSIA information can be obtained at www.ICGtesting.com
Printed in the USA
LVOW081345190712

290595LV00004BB/1/P